He has two strands to his life and both bring their share of concerns.

The National League basketball team loses its main sponsor and is forced to review its activities and possibly even cease to exist. At the same time, his working life changes dramatically as he is asked to take on a new role. With this alteration in his professional capacity, the door is thrown open to widen his scope of experience in the academic world. In turn, this leads to attendance at conferences where, as a single man, he meets a succession of women with whom he builds relationships. All the while this is against the backdrop of a college in crisis as management issues begin to dominate the scene.

Also by Jim Rumsey

Divided Families

A Sporting Rollercoaster

Allure of the Sea

BACKBOARDS AND BLACKBOARDS

Jim Rumsey

Copyright 2022 J. A. Rumsey

BACKBOARDS AND BLACKBOARDS

PART ONE

Dawn

CHAPTER ONE

Call me Seamus. It has already been a long day and we are still over a hundred miles from home. I have been driving the minibus with the team in it for nearly two hours when a cry comes from the rear to pull off the motorway. 'We need to have a slash,' is all I catch and so at the next exit I drive off on the slip road and bring the vehicle to a halt on the inside lane but also partly on the grass verge allowing other vehicles to get by. As it is early Sunday evening there are not many other vehicles around. The door immediately slides open and six of the team issue forth and begin to relieve themselves. I take the opportunity to say to Mick, who is sharing the driving with me, that he can take over the driving for a while.

As the players get back into the minibus a couple of them make another request. 'Look it's early and we need a break, but not in a motorway service station, please,' says one. The other adds, 'See if you can find a pub for a change.' It is rare for us to find ourselves on the road home so early in the evening. The National Basketball League in which we play stipulates that matches on a Sunday must finish at a time that allows the away team to get home by midnight, because some players have work to get to on Monday morning.

When we approach the next motorway exit, I notice what looks like a village on the top of a nearby hill. 'Take this exit,' I say to Mick. We go under the motorway and Mick takes the only exit that will not take us back onto the motorway going in the wrong direction. It is a dual-carriageway. 'I had to make a quick decision', Mick says in his own defence as we hurtle along the road that takes us away from our home direction. 'We can say goodbye to that village I just saw,' I respond. 'We'd better turn back as soon as we get a chance.'

The chance comes about four miles along the dual-carriageway. But, as we exit the road, we see ahead of us a cluster of buildings, one of which is a brightly-lit public house. Suddenly there are noises from the back of the minibus almost demanding that we pull into the car park. Most are unaware probably that we are so far from the motorway having been involved in card games or trying to sleep on the pillows some of them have brought.

Anyway, the players empty out of the minibus in quick time and disappear into the pub. After locking up, and clearing a bit of accumulated rubbish, I walk into a bar that is awash with people. It seems we had hit upon a home match in a women's darts league. Not only that, it is the first home game ever in a regional competition. The whole village must be here to support the team. The pub itself has a big main bar area and off it umpteen small rooms demonstrating that once it must have been a type of manor house. Our team soon become objects of interest. For a start they are taller than most of the locals, a couple are black and are the only black people in the pub. Our tallest player, Mike, is over seven feet and occasions a lot of comments, all of which he has heard many times before. I am slightly concerned that our appearance might detract from the sense of occasion for the ladies darts team, but I need not have worried since, after the initial fuss, the attention of the locals soon turns back to their team. The fact that our players can find a quieter room and concentrate on their drinking and the post-mortem of the recent defeat we have suffered in Sunderland helps take attention away from us.

I find a couple of the players in a small snug room which has several older men seated around a table and seemingly bemoaning the fact that their quiet Sunday evening drink has to take place with so many others around. 'Usually quiet as a grave here on Sunday,' one says to his companions, 'and you can find a place in the main bar to chew over various matters. Not tonight, though, it is a mad house in there. I hope they don't have many nights like this.'

I join the two players and we converse in hushed tones, anxious not to upset the locals even more. 'Quite a day for me,' I begin, 'this is not the first pub event I have been to today. After I dropped you at the Leisure Centre, I went to fill up the minibus for the return trip. We had driven nearly 300 miles in the fog with visibility about 100 yards at the most. I saw a pub near the filling station. It had a thatched roof and gave the appearance of being out in the countryside. Because of the fog it looked isolated and I thought I would just nip in and get a sandwich for lunch.'

I check that the locals are not being disturbed by my monologue and continue, 'Imagine my surprise when I went inside and found a pub just as crowded as this one. Even more surprising was the fact that about a dozen men were surrounding the full-size slate bed snooker table and were moving it to the side. This meant that the lights over where the table normally was positioned could be used by the female stripper who appeared out of nowhere. Sunday lunchtime, I thought, what is the world coming to? It was easy to get served because the bar area had been emptied for the customers to take in the show. I got my sandwich and sat at a table that offered no view of the proceedings through the three deep circle of spectators. The show did not last very long, ten minutes at the most, and I began to think about returning to the Leisure Centre. The same men lifted the snooker table back to its place and the drinkers who had been noisy throughout the show dispersed to various parts of the bar. I was then witness to another event when the stripper and her minder came and sat at the next table and I saw money change hands, presumably for the performance. When I got outside, the fog had lifted a bit and I saw that the pub was on the edge of a large housing estate which explained the number of drinkers there. I drove back to the

Leisure Centre to find out that you all had to wait outside after I dropped you because of a bomb alert.'

'Yes, that wait, especially after the long trip here, did not help our chances in any way,' comments Russ, from the other side of the table. He is one of our English players approaching the end of his career but an invaluable asset to the team. 'We were outside in the cold and fog for over half an hour, and now we learn that you were enjoying a strip show in a warm pub.'

'Well, I had my disappointment too,' I continue 'I was expecting to meet a relative of mine who lives in Wallsend, where I was born. She was going to come and watch the match and it would have given me an opportunity to catch up on the family who live up there. As you were warming up, I heard my name on the public address system being requested to go to the entry desk. When I got there it was to be told that my relative had telephoned to say she would not be coming because of the foggy driving conditions. I thought as we had just driven over 300 miles in the same conditions, she might have made an effort to cover about 30 from where she lived, especially as the fog was lifting by then.'

One of the regulars who had gone to refill the glasses of his mate and himself comes back and bemoans that the drinks had cost him more than he wanted to pay. 'Bloody raffle tickets that I was forced to buy to support the Ladies Darts team when I got the drinks. Seems the raffle will take place in the interval of the match. Better make sure we can hear the numbers. They told me to expect the draw in about half an hour. Some big bugger is going to do the draw. I suppose that is to avoid any trouble from those whose numbers don't get drawn.'

At the mention of big I guess that Mike has been inveigled to pull out the tickets. I also realise that our stay in the pub will be much longer than I have planned for. I had mentioned 30 minutes as the players had got out of the minibus, but at that time I thought we might be going in to a normal pub, not the busy one in which we seem to have ended up. My weak pint of shandy that I had ordered, bearing in mind I would have another spell of driving, would have to last even longer.

Finally, we are able to round everyone up, after the draw, and get back to the minibus. Only then does my co-driver Mick announce that he has consumed four pints of lager, using as an excuse that he had got caught up in the excitement of the evening. I get behind the wheel and prepare myself for the next two or three hours of driving, punctuated, I anticipate, by regular requests for 'pit stops'.

The only saving grace I could say to myself is that as we pass by on the M1 an area full of radio masts, I will not be assailed by Mick's description of his life as a radio operator at sea and how messages were reduced to a 'ping' as they were picked up by these self-same aerials. I can almost recite word for word his memories of those times, having heard them so many times.

Eventually, later than I had anticipated, I pull in to the Leisure Centre car park where everyone, but me, has left their cars. It is a silent group that gets out of the vehicle, although one of the younger ones does actually express his thanks to me for the driving I have done. Once everyone is out, I proceed to the premises of the company from whom we have hired the minibus. I take the bag that is full of the playing kit and put it in the boot of my own car. I check on the inside of the bus, collect up some rubbish, mainly crisp and peanut wrappers which I put in a nearby bin and finally post the keys of the minibus through a letter box which is used for out-of-hours vehicle returns.

Just one more event makes the trip memorable. As I drive home along the motorway there is a full moon. I see also that there is a plane in the sky. Of the many times I have seen this combination and hoped that the plane would cross the moon, this was the first time it actually occurred. It lifts my spirits no end.

CHAPTER TWO

On my way to work at the college, I drop off the playing kit, as I usually do, at a local launderette.

Luckily, my college hours are flexible and I have made sure that Monday is a late start for me. I am not sure how long this situation will be able to last. My life of late has begun to be different from what it had been before.

Twelve years ago I had been a teacher in a Comprehensive school and that would have meant a completely different situation from now. No matter what time I returned from a trip such I had just made, I would have to have been at the school by 8.30am. I had applied for a post at the local college thinking that I needed a change from the routine into which I had fallen. Surprisingly, despite having no experience of teaching in higher education, I got the job. At the time I wondered if my experience in basketball might have been a deciding factor. The college had a full-size sports hall but no profile in the local community for indoor sport. Only a couple of years before the same sports section had appointed an ex-England international rugby player to help with gaining a presence in the outdoor sporting scene.

I had set about raising a basketball squad. It was helpful that the college had a Craft course which attracted students from Greece, in the main who were coming to avoid National Service in their country. Also with trouble in Iran there were several Iranians at the college. These two groups of students who had played basketball since infancy coupled with some talented home students, had soon begun to make an impression in the local league. Initially, I had also played but now had retired from competitive matches, although I have continued with the college soccer team.

For many years I have been the secretary of the local basketball association. This role has suddenly become much

9

wider through a combination of circumstances. A local property developer had a passion for the game and also saw a business opportunity. He reasoned, so he told me, that in just about every other country in the world, basketball was a major sport. Being a man of purpose and conviction he had immediately devised a course of action. I was hardly likely to question his reasoning.

Some years before, thanks to a Government initiative at the time, a Sports Hall had been built for the local – and wider - community. John, our developer, had a plan. 'We can supply the centre with seating and use it for basketball matches.' He had announced that at a meeting which he had called. The attendees were local basketball people including schools and adults. 'I need people like yourselves to help promote and support a local team in the National League.' I remember at the time that there had been a collective gasp. We had been summoned and were hoping that perhaps we were getting sponsorship for local competitions. None of us realised what John had in mind. Apparently a lot of work had already been done regarding the playing of the home matches. John had met with both the local authority and the sports centre manager and agreed a course of action, which he now unveiled to those present at the meeting. Even more news unfolded as he said he had been in conversations with the English Basketball Association who had agreed, in principle, to his owning a local franchise for a national league team. 'The franchise is important,' John had said. 'I've got to know that I will be in control of the game in this region, so that I can sell sponsorship with no fear of others offering competition.'

That meeting had changed the outlook of the game in the area. A further move came as quite a surprise to me when John approached me later to ask if I would be interested in becoming a director of the newly-formed basketball franchise. 'I need local people who have been involved in the game with a proven track record,' he had said. If I had felt any hesitation it quickly evaporated when he added, 'I can give you £10,000 to run the local league. Not only that, you can have an office in my work building for all your administration. You can even use the services of any of the secretaries you need. Give yourself an hourly salary and work whatever hours you need. Use the money to organise courses, advertise games and so on.' I explained about the job I already had, with its flexible hours, and that I thought I could work something out. Eventually I had signed some forms for Companies House and had begun to appear in John's office from time to time.

All that was some time ago but the arrangements still held. I was able to use the imported players, usually Americans, to staff various youth camps and held other sessions for local player development. The local leagues gained by having professional looking copy for the fixture and results list and a regular column in the local newspapers kept everyone informed of the basketball being played in the area.

After a couple of years, John's ambition in the sporting area had grown and, taking advantage of a current craze for fitness, he had set up a Health Centre in the town. Without asking he had registered the directors of the basketball club as owners of the Health Club. The other three and I had all gone along with this development, having been assured that we were there in name only and would not be taking any risk. Nearly all my dealings with money had been done through the office and I was very happy with that arrangement. I had never seen any audited accounts for anything but was assured that the books were in order. I knew, by my standards, that a lot of money was involved. We were allowed two overseas players for the national league team. They usually came from America and their fares, salary and accommodation had to be paid for. John had also taken advantage of a loophole in the rules whereby players who had access to an English passport, through family connections, could also be included in the squad. I remember that in the first season we had five players on court who all had lived most of their life in America and spoke with strong accents. Although the game was being well-supported by the local population, there was no way, I thought, that expenses could be covered by the gate receipts. I should have been more suspicious, I guess, when once having sight of a cheque that was being paid to one of the players, I noticed it was from an account of a Nursing Midwives company. Still, I thought, John is an accountant and it is his business after all.

Soon sponsorship was coming in from some local companies anxious to join in the growth of the game locally. This also allayed my fears about where all the money was coming from to defray expenses. Channel Four TV then got involved and showed games on a Monday evening. They were a great attraction for local supporters. Special TV lights had already been installed by an arrangement with the local authority. These were augmented by the TV company itself for matches which also supplied a marked carpet as a playing surface. Our seating capacity, and hence Fire Regulation number, was about 800 spectators. By various means such as using the balconies for standing supporters, one night we had receipts from over 1000 spectators. We had increased our income also by the selling of courtside advertising boards. I say all this, because when everything came out in the wash, I felt justified in saying that I thought we were paying our way.

My involvement with the national league men's team gradually grew over the years. It started on home match nights when, as was traditional in game presentation, an announcer was needed to introduce the teams and make comments throughout the game, usually to help the crowd understand the reason for any on court decision made by the referees. There were, I found out, strict guidelines about what I might or might not say. For instance, I should not talk whilst an opposition player was taking a free throw. For that he stood on a line 15 feet from the basket and tried to score without any interference from the defending team. The home crowd usually made as much noise as possible by stamping their feet to put the player off his concentration. I remember a game at Coventry when the announcer did not speak whilst the shot was being taken, but just before he exhorted the crowd to 'make a noise'.

John encouraged me to make our home games known as widely known as possible. I was soon in contact with the local papers and eventually with a couple of local radio stations with news about the team and its upcoming match. I was to make people aware of the Hampshire Hoops basketball team. The name had been chosen to widen the catchment area and encourage more people to identify with the team. There was no other team in the county and the franchise gave us an opportunity to be the sole providers of national league games over a large area with a high number of people in it.

I became more and more involved in the club's activities, not only on match days but also at training and gradually for away games, as well. I had spent a lifetime avoiding meetings if possible. I would rather do something than sit and discuss things. I was aware that professionally it was a feature of my life that probably held me back. My experience in school teaching had formed my approach. I remember long staff meetings when teachers who had difficulty exercising control of their pupils, and who to my mind were in the wrong job, would make overtures that certain pupils should not be allowed to play sport for the school teams if they had misbehaved. Originally I had tried to defend such pupils saying that we could use playing for the school as a tool for getting better behaviour. Most times I had been shouted down by a few of the staff who saw a chance of controlling boisterous boys. Eventually, I realised that the members of staff who complained were, for the most part, just wanting to express their frustration at their own incompetence, as I saw it. So, I changed tact. I agreed with everything they said but still chose the boys to play in the school team. None of the staff ever followed up by reminding me of the staff discussion. They had made their point in the meeting and that seemed to be enough for them. I decided then and there that meetings were usually a sounding board for people who wanted to make a point, but that action spoke much louder than words.

Despite my aversion to meetings, there were times when in the basketball world I was encouraged to attend, especially occasions when sponsors were to be present. I guessed John wanted to help them feel that they were getting something for their money, although the returns so far seemed pretty poor to me. I was asked to personalise the reports as much as possible and stress how much we were involving ourselves in the local youth scene with training sessions and camps, usually in the school holidays. After the meetings we would adjourn to a local restaurant. Often it was an Indian place, which was not good news for me. There the alcohol flowed and business stories abounded. I could only listen to the others since I felt none of them would get too excited about tales from higher education. I spent time trying to work out why any of them would be interested in bankrolling a team in a sport that despite worldwide popularity had such a small presence on the British sporting scene. Only later was I to become aware of motives that I had not even considered in my naïve approach to the situation.

CHAPTER THREE

I am now 44 years old and probably holding a job that will, with careful cultivation and not upsetting too many apple carts, keep me occupied until retirement. In truth, the job is not too onerous, allowing me, as it does, time to spend with my favourite pastime. Most people, I guess, have hobbies that fully involve them and for me that is running a basketball team. I gain a lot of satisfaction from the time I spend organising both the local scene and the national league team. The latter is bringing me into contact with, what I consider, serious businessmen – and it is all men – up and down the country running teams in the National League. I often accompany John to these meetings, usually held in a hotel in the middle of the country. Sometimes representatives from the national association are present and it is interesting to see how the minds of those involved in the pursuit of profit are at odds with the officials who hold the Sports Council purse strings and caution against too entrepreneurial an approach to the public.

One item that had recently demonstrated the difference is the huge amount of money, to my mind, donated by an international company to the English Basketball Association. The businessmen are all for using the money to advance the National League whilst the national amateur association wants to put the money forward for a scheme that will allow for the erection of basketball goals all over the country in parks and playgrounds. The talks are heated at times but the National League owners soon realise that they were going to be outgunned on this issue. For me the discussion will continue all the way back home in the car. John realises I wear two hats on this issue with my interest in the local scene. Eventually he comes round to thinking it is no good putting up opposition and devises a strategy that makes it look as if it is not a national decision solely but it has been backed by Hampshire Hoops for the benefit of the local community. I am supposed to make this clear to everyone at all opportunities.

As well as that task I have to firm up the organisation for the week to week running of the club. Early on, John asks me to furnish him with a list of people who are helping the club and in what capacity that is. When I get round to it, I realise that we are relying on the help of a lot of unpaid people. John's secretary, Marie, acts as the secretary and a business colleague, Trevor is the nominated Chairman. I have the role of direct link to the actual playing team as well as the liaison to local basketball. Other roles stated, all volunteers, are Team Coach, Team Manager, Court Manager, Sales, Physiotherapist, Statistician, Table Officials, Electrics, Programme Sales, Raffle Organiser, Cheerleaders, Door Officials, Bench Helper. At the moment I am sort of Team Manager without the actual title.

I ruminate over all I have done as I make my way to college on the day after the Sunderland trip. Later in the day I am due to go to John's office to work on local basketball issues. As I approach the building in which the office is located, over a parade of shops which includes a hairdressers salon, I notice a small gathering of people, including a couple of the secretaries, outside the entrance where the stairs begin for the first floor office. 'What's up?' I enquire. 'The door is locked,' replies Marie. 'No one knows where John is. We have tried telephoning him but there is no answer. He is not at home. We know that because we have been there to find out. The house looks closed up. There is no car on the drive and his wife is also not there.'

My immediate concern is that at the end of the week there is a home game in the National League. If John does not surface anywhere, there could be major problems. Marie, apart from her role as secretary to John, effectively handles the day to day finances of the club, including paying the referees on the match night. That is the only immediate expense I can foresee since most other outgoings are on a monthly basis. This will mean that any situation has to be resolved within the next few weeks. As a precautionary measure I immediately get in touch with the most recent main sponsor, a company that had only come on board in the last few months, but also had a known profile on the sporting scene. I ask for a meeting. We are only halfway through the season and to default now would be calamitous, I think.

It seems that once again I had come late to the situation. My close involvement with the team coach and players and making sure arrangements are made for all aspects of running the club has left me unprepared for what has been happening on the financial side. When I arrive at the factory site of the newest sponsor I am directed to the office of the General Manager who introduces himself as Dave. 'We looked into the finances of the club before we made a commitment,' he says. 'It is small beer compared with our dealings with a local professional football deal we have. The turnover for your club is less than £10,000. But you play your games in our local area and we felt it sensible to fund some of your activities. We did not count on the main person going AWOL. I can only guess it is one of the property deals that has gone wrong, or, in a more sinister development he may have been using the basketball club to launder some money. It would be fairly straightforward to cook the books with a business that seems so under the radar. 'Mind you,' Dave adds, 'I'm not saying that any laundering was going on, only that it is a possibility. If we find out he has gone to the Cayman Islands or somewhere like that, there is a strong possibility that some skulduggery has taken place.' I think back to my earlier thoughts and wonder if this is an example of the innocence of my accepting why anyone would want to invest in basketball.

I have to think fast. 'Is there any way we can retrieve the situation?' I ask. 'We need to get everyone together,' replies

Dave, 'and see how much commitment we can get from the other sponsors. I still have the paperwork from our earlier discussions so I know what we all will have to commit to if we want to see the season out. You may have to make some serious changes, and here I am thinking of the overseas players. Can you compete without them?' This is a difficult question. We have a good number of talented local lads but the engine room of the team is the two Americans. Against that, the height for the team, so important in rebounding the ball if a shot is unsuccessful, is Mike who is English and lives locally. However, I realise that one asset is not enough to compete successfully in the National League. We still have about ten matches to play and it could prove embarrassing without the Americans. I say as much to Dave and, at his suggestion, we agree not to overstate the importance of the foreign players. 'We can make a big point about developing local talent,' he says. I know that the coach always has had that as a target and will happily go along with that policy. I am not sure whether or not he is ready to accept the inevitable defeats that will be incurred with this policy being put in place immediately.

Dave says he will telephone the other sponsors, four in all, and arrange a meeting for tomorrow evening. In the meantime, I am to proceed as if all things were normal. However, things are not normal and I go to see Mick, the coach, immediately. He is quite philosophical about the whole situation. As I had thought, his first reaction is that it will be a chance to blood the local players. Some of the overseas players have been prima donnas, Mick explains. 'The English lads are willing to learn and grateful for the opportunity to play for the team. My coaching win-loss record will take a hit, that's for sure, but I'm not worried about that,' Mick continues. 'I'd like to attend the meeting of the sponsors and put my case.'

Next day, in the evening, we are all assembled in Dave's office. Mick explains the playing situation and everyone seems to be at one with Mick as he lays out his plans. Dave soon gets to the point of the meeting. 'Can we afford to sponsor what will probably be, no disrespect Mick, a losing team in the National League? Will people still want to come and watch and will anyone else be willing to put money in to a failing concern? In fact, do we want to continue to support the club in these circumstances? These are questions we must resolve now.' The discussion goes to and fro but there is a consensus. Mick's enthusiasm on the playing front seems to have worked and everyone present is satisfied that the playing arrangements, providing the actual putting on of the matches, is done in a professional manner.

Whilst the situation financially is dire, the club can, if it plays its cards right, still be a force, albeit a weak one, amongst the top teams in the country. We have experienced English players who are reaching the end of their careers and a cohort of young, talented players also, one of whom has played for the England Under 22 team. The older English players know that their careers are coming to an end and each of them has made inroads into jobs that sustain them financially. Their basketball money is an addition to their living wage and it will take perhaps a lot of persuading to tell them that there will be no money in future, but still expect them to commit to regular training sessions and some long, mainly uncomfortable, away trips in the National League. Knowing the players concerned as I do, I feel sure we can sell them the package at least until the end of the season. The overseas players will have to be let go and this might impact on the experienced English players who realise that they will be put to the test to make up for the lack of the Americans.

All this is explained to the team at the Thursday training session. Mick makes a good case for continuing to play at the highest level, despite losing our American players. They, he says, have already been appraised of the situation and have decided to leave immediately, after contacting their agents. The rest of the squad seem up for the challenge, although I am a bit concerned about the longer term. 'What will be the situation in a few weeks' time,' I question Mick when we were alone, 'do you think they will still be up for it after a series of defeats?' 'Don't think that way,' is Mick's retort.

A few days later comes another hammer blow. Marie gets in touch with me about a letter the club has received from the local authority. In the past we have been granted favourable financial terms for the hire of the Sports Centre for matches and training. True, the club had bought the seating that enabled the Sports Centre to accommodate not only the basketball matches but also other events. In one sense it was a tit for tat arrangement. Probably it had been able to continue because of John's friendship with Lillian, who was the chair of the Recreation and Leisure Committee. No one knew what the exact relationship was although over the years rumours had abounded. However, John had disappeared with his wife so perhaps Lillian had decided to eke revenge on his erstwhile empire. Now, in the letter Marie is telling me about, the local authority is telling us that the favourable terms are at an end and a commercial rate will be applied.

Straightaway I contact Dave to put him in the picture. 'We'll see about that,' is his immediate retort. 'Our firm is one of their biggest sources of industrial income for the local authority, so they can cut us a little slack, I reckon. I will ask them to delay the changes to the end of the season, at least. That will give us a bit of breathing space. We can renegotiate then.' This gives me a modicum of comfort in what I know are going to be awkward times.

Looking at our playing schedule I see that we have still to go to several away venues. We have to travel to Manchester, Derby, Leicester and London. Because there are only eight teams in the National League we meet each team three times. I see to my horror that there are actually two extra away trips to Manchester and Derby. This means six long trips in all, each costing the hire of a minibus and the fuel. Income from the gate receipts at the remaining seven home matches will help add to the sponsorship money but it will mean there will be no extras for player expenses. Despite Mick's assurances I am still apprehensive about our ability to see the season out.

I send out a letter to all the local clubs explaining that the previous sponsorship of our leagues has suddenly been withdrawn, but I will hope to maintain a service for them by using the accrued funds of the Area Association. Over the past week I have rather let the local scene lapse and make a determined effort to bring everything up-to-date. Many of the local players are also supporters of the Hampshire Hoops, taking advantage of seeing the game of basketball played at its highest level in the country. I feel those supporters need to know what was happening, although I realise that for many playing local basketball is a pastime only and they do not feel any allegiance to the National League club.

Each match stretches the team to the limit of its ability. There are close games and there are matches when Hampshire Hoops is just not in contention. The few wins we had at the beginning of the season and the low ability of one of the other clubs that is going through a torrid time also means that, come March the team finishes in seventh position out of eight. I consider that a triumph for the club because we are not at the foot of the table but, more importantly, we have seen the season out. Our crowd figures manage to keep up as the followers recognised the parlous state of the club and the valiant efforts of the coach, players and support staff to keep the show on the road. We are extremely fortunate that Marie has developed a soft spot for the basketball players and officials and says she is willing to continue as secretary using her home address for any correspondence.

Now the summer begins and we have to go searching for sponsorship way in excess of what we currently have. To keep the team in the national Carlsberg League will cost £35,000 alone. To put that in perspective, the previous season's turnover had been about £10,000 according to the accounts presented to Companies House. Dave and his company have promised to stay by us if at all possible, but are not willing alone to match the kind of money that is required for the National League. The other sponsors, although willing to help, are never going to give us enough to compete on par with other clubs.

After several meetings a contingency plan is drawn up. I explain to the local press what our future may look like. 'We have entered a team in the Fourth Division as soon as we realised the financial problems we were facing. We are anxious to keep the name Hampshire Hoops going at some level. This will mean the end of top class basketball locally for at least four years. In that time we will try to work our way back up to the highest division in the National League. Division Four is regional with probably seven or eight teams. We will take the opportunity to blood local players who will be able to compete with the best.'

Just one week after making this statement the club withdraws its application for the Carlsberg League and prepares itself for a new beginning.

Knowing that this will mean a summer of unprecedented activity to try a keep the show on the road, I tender my resignation as secretary of the local basketball association. I have been doing the job for twenty years and I know that there are several people I am probably holding back who are keen to give their services. This proves to be the case and at the Annual General Meeting there actually has to be a vote to elect a successor. This makes me feel that I have not left the association in the lurch by retiring in the way I have. I have explained my actions and it seems that most of those assembled have no problem with my decision. I only hope I have made the correct choice.

CHAPTER FOUR

Of late, my life has become dominated by matters concerning basketball. But I also have other ideas that relate to my job. I feel that professionally I need a challenge. Over the past few months I have been mulling over the fact that Sports Centre staff could perhaps have some kind of career structure. Sports Centres are a growth industry and rely on an increasing cohort of staff members who are being drawn in from all parts of the general public with diverse backgrounds and training. One conduit is for ex-military personnel, but other than that the backgrounds of those now forming the workforce is varied.

The college has courses that include management and supervisory skills. I approach the Head of the Management Division. 'Is there a course that could be adapted to include people who work in the leisure industry?' I ask, 'not top management, who would come through a different pathway, but those coming in to work in leisure for the first time. I am thinking mainly of Sports Centre workers, but it may be applicable to a wider intake.' His reply is very positive. 'We have just the thing,' he says, 'The National Examining Board of Supervisory Studies is the course you need. It was set up to serve just the people you are talking about. However, it is very biased toward the general needs of industry and you would need to tweak it, by having a part of the course devoted to the Leisure Industry.' 'Sure,' I reply, 'there is a lot of literature coming out these days. Much of it is about outdoor leisure, parks and recreation that sort of thing. I am sure the theories they are looking at, for example, people's free time, the need for exercise, time management studies could all be adapted to the kind of thing I am considering.' 'Why don't you go away and come back with a module that we can incorporate into our main course which we can then advertise?' I am asked.

Now I have two new challenges, basketball and writing a course module. The third challenge comes right out of the blue.

At the college I share a staffroom with my three physical education colleagues and three members of the General Studies Department. Of the latter three, one, whose name is Gerry, teaches a course for Teaching in Further Education. It is a part-time course, one day a week which caters for anyone wishing to teach those who are above full-time education age. In early September, Gerry was taken ill and it is now disclosed that he will probably not be returning. I am called to the Director's office.

'You know the serious illness that has occurred with Gerry,' the Director begins, 'we are in a parlous situation. The two courses he runs are fully subscribed and should begin in two weeks' time. I've looked at your record. Apart from your initial teacher training, you completed an Open University course mainly in Education and you also did a Master's at Bristol University on a part-time basis, which we sponsored as part of your staff development, that resulted in you getting a Master of Education degree. I have spoken with your Head of Department and he is agreeable to release you to take on these courses if you are willing.'

Just as I had not too long ago with the basketball situation, I have to think quickly. It is obvious that a decision is needed and I am not going to be told to go away and think about it. I also have to consider what effect it might have on my ability to help with the Hampshire Hoops. I now consider it lucky that I had made the decision to relinquish the secretarial role of the local basketball association. One key factor in my thinking is remembering how Gerry had been so often out of the office. He said that it was part of the courses he ran to have to go and observe the course members actually doing some teaching, wherever that was. Our college does not provide any teaching opportunities for the course members, they have to make their own arrangements before being accepted on the course. I realise that this could still give me the flexibility I feel I might need, rather than being tied to an office desk or lecture room.

'Of course,' the Director continues, 'there are big changes coming for us. As you know we are trying for Polytechnic status. If that comes about, your role could increase as we will have to consider new methods of course delivery and you will be in a strong position to head up any such initiative. Promotion would be part of that, with a new pay scale I am sure.' That does it. My decision is conveyed to the Director straight away. I then go to search for a course syllabus for what I am about to teach. Luckily for me, the course is very prescribed and it will only need a minimum of effort on my part to translate the written course syllabus into an active course. Only one slight issue raises its head. I remember the Director had said two courses and I have in front of me Gerry's file for the intake of one course of sixteen students.

On enquiring to the Head of Social Services, the department I am now working in, which includes my previous Physical Education section, he is able to answer my query. 'We provide a service to the local hospital where they want to train their personnel to teach. The course is run at the hospital one day a week.' 'But I know nothing about hospital procedures,' I object. 'Nor did Gerry,' came the reply. 'For some reason the hospital is satisfied that a general course in teaching is what they require and as it brings in money, we are only too pleased to supply it.'

I make a telephone call to the hospital and finally track down the woman I should be talking to. 'I'm afraid Gerry is ill and cannot teach the course for you this year. However, I am taking Gerry's place and wondered if it would be possible to come and see you regarding the delivery of the course. I realise it is only two weeks away before the first session and I would like to go over some details with you, not least to find out who is actually undertaking the course. As I understand it, you select the students.' Barbara confirms that this is the case. 'Why don't you come tomorrow at 10.00am. The Academic Block is situated on A Level and is clearly signposted. Once here you will easily find my office. You can park in the car park and I will give you a ticket to avoid having to pay.'

The rest of the day I spend mugging up on the course I am about to deliver and going through Gerry's files that are kept in his filing cabinet which, fortunately, is unlocked. One thing I discover is that the course has an External Examiner who signs off the results at the end of the year. His name is Charles and he works at Reading College of Technology. I try to get in touch with him but it seems he is unavailable until the term begins. No help there, I think. I cannot find any details of a network of lecturers that might exist for the course and began to realise that I am on my own for the time being.

The next day I arrive on time to see Barbara. I am impressed by the layout of the Academic Block which contains several large teaching areas and a host of smaller rooms, presumably used for tutorials and such like. I am informed that there is a large lecture theatre nearby used for visiting speakers. It is my decision not to let Barbara know that I have never taught this course before. I make what I hope are the correct noises about being in Gerry's office and giving the impression that I am fully involved in teaching our own course at the college and that Gerry had taken sole responsibility for the hospital course. Barbara gives me a list of nursing staff about to attend together with their areas of responsibility. Most work on specialist wards, including Intensive Care. I wonder to myself what kind of teaching I will have to observe in that case. 'Please feel free to ask any questions you want,' Barbara says, 'it will probably be different from your other course which, Gerry tells me, usually includes hairdressers and people like that.' 'I guess it will be,' I reply, thinking what an understatement that is. There are just a few other items to arrange, including a hospital car park pass and the names of several people who might be able to help should the necessity arise. My parting remark is, 'Why have this course? Hasn't nursing got its own course for teaching?' 'No,' Barbara replies, 'but there are moves afoot at the national level. Perhaps you would be willing to contribute when we have local meetings?' This was not the reply I expected and I beat a hasty retreat, mumbling something like, 'Of course, of course.'

I get back to lunch in the college refectory and I am approached by the Head of the Management Division. 'Still thinking about the course option we might include for your leisure people?' he enquires. 'We could run a late advert for anyone interested, but you would need to have the course content vetted by our staff.' 'Sorry,' I reply, 'you may have heard that I have had to take on two courses because of staff illness. I promise I will look into the possibility of getting a module of some sort together, but I think it will have to be for next year's intake.' He seems to understand my predicament although I wonder if he is fully aware of what the Director has in mind for me and the college as a whole.

Over the recent years I have become more aware of the changes that are taking place in higher education thanks to the comments made frequently by Trevor, who is head of the Physical Education section. He had been present at the inauguration of the college and is nearing retirement. He often harks back at the times when everyone knew one another and was involved in the way things were decided. He knew that as the college grew bigger that situation could not continue but he still held on to the notion that we are all in the same boat and should have a say in developments. 'The turning point for us,' he says to anyone who is listening in our office whilst proclaiming, as usual, 'was when we came out of the control of the Hampshire County Council a couple of years ago. It meant there was no safety valve to any ambitious Principal who would want to do anything. Our new Director was appointed at that time and it is clear he came with an agenda of developing our college on commercial lines. His first action was to reorganise the college into a small number of Divisions to bring this about. To add to that he created a small group of people, himself, the Chairman and Vice Chairman of Governors who now make all the key decisions. To show his intent, it was he who even decided he would be called a Director rather than Principal.'

From recent staff bulletins and meetings I know the drive is on to achieve Polytechnic status. The Director has even mentioned it to me in our recent meeting. To achieve that we will need to vastly increase our student intake, put on far more courses and expand in every way possible. According to Trevor, the Director had virtually become a Dictator. All the Heads of the Divisions had been ordered to increase the number of courses run and up their student intake. This means, because of the nature of higher education, submitting any developments through internal and then external verification procedures. All of this is taking its toll on the existing full-time staff, both teaching and administrative, although new appointments are being made to help facilitate the process.

It seems to me that by default I have now become involved in this process. My erstwhile existence of teaching in the Physical Education section, which provides a service for any course that wishes to include a leisure part in their content, is coming to an end. It looks as if I might have to be part of the academic development of the college on our journey to Polytechnic status whether I like it or not. This will inevitably lead me to attend endless meetings, a thing I had rejected when considering my future whilst teaching in school. We had just over 4,000 full time equivalent students when we left Hampshire's local authority oversight and already we have over 1,000 more and the target, we are told, is 10,000 in three years' time. This will involve building student accommodation as well as increasing the size of the college campus. I think of the Chinese proverb, 'We live in exciting times.'

Now it is the middle of September and we have coming up our first match in the Regional Basketball League. It is a home game, but we can no longer afford the hire of the whole hall and will have to play in half the hall with a curtain, solid from the ground up to eight feet and then with a mesh to the ceiling. For seating we can only use a small fraction of the apparatus. It is capable of holding 200 spectators who will be seated at each end of the court. There is just room alongside the court for the team benches and the table where the scorer and timekeeper sit. At the end of the table a small public address system is set up. This is where I will operate.

The coach has trained the team well over the summer and all the local players are looking forward to the match. I am apprehensive still about what kind of following we will get, bearing in mind we are now no longer playing at the top level. Also, sponsorship is necessary still to defray expenses and sponsors will not want to be associated with a losing team, albeit comprised of local talent, all playing for no expenses.

Therefore, I am pleased and relieved to see a good following at the game almost filling the available seating area and providing an atmosphere at least. Our tallest player from the previous regime has announced his retirement over the summer but has made himself available to act as Assistant Coach. This gives us a coach called Mick and an assistant coach named Mike. They made quite an incongruous couple when they stand at courtside, one being so much taller than the other.

We have decided to try and keep the presentation of the game in line with what the crowd had become accustomed to. So five minutes before the start of the game the two teams leave the court to allow me to introduce the players, who run on to the court when named. First I introduce the players from the visiting team, Swindon Sonics. They are not used to doing the procedure themselves, but they know the traditional way of starting the event. When I start to call the home players onto the court, I am taken aback by the noisy reception. Obviously we have returning to us the hard core supporters of earlier days and it gives the whole occasion an uplift. Ken, the most experienced player from the previous season, has returned to play for no wages. He lives locally and is setting up his own business but still wants the challenge of playing competitive basketball. He orchestrates the play of the team and with help from the younger players sees us through to a convincing victory. A new player, a student who had joined the college and played for my team last season, has also made his debut after I had recommended him to Mick.

In the bar afterwards everyone is in a good mood and begin to talk about the fact that the club has entered two cup competitions that will give us a chance to play against teams in the National League. I am more relieved to see that Dave has attended the game, although I know he is not an aficionado of basketball. He has brought two of his children with him and I guess that might have been a reason for his attendance. 'The kids really enjoyed it,' said Dave. 'I guess they liked the frequent scoring which gave them an opportunity to cheer. I can see why families would welcome a chance to watch a game. It is indoors and warm with plenty of action.' I am pleased to hear this, hoping that he will spread the word amongst his business friends. I have never had occasion to join organisations like the Chamber of Commerce but guess that Dave will have connections in that area.

All too soon the weekend ends and my thoughts have to turn to the oncoming term at college which will begin in a week's time. Having given it some consideration I have realised the logistical problem that will need to be overcome.

The courses will require me to have twelve teaching hours or class contact as it is described. However, there also has to be teaching observation to be undertaken. The course delivery requires each student to be observed for twelve hours of their thirty hours teaching that they must undertake over the period of the course. For me this means that I will have to go over my allotted eighteen hours of teaching time per week if I am to fulfil the requirements. I will need to cover three hundred and eighty four hours of observation over the thirty six weeks. In round terms this is ten hours a week which added to my mandatory class contact of twelve hours will mean at least four hours overtime a week. I wonder how Gerry had managed with previous courses. I could only guess that he had not fulfilled the complete requirements for teaching observation. I mentioned the situation to Don who is the Union Representative for the teaching staff.

'You will have to get another member of staff to help you,' is his advice. 'Go to Edgar and demand assistance. Our Director is hell bent on getting us Polytechnic status and should back you on this. We must be seen to be running courses as per the book.'

I follow his suggestion, but not before trawling through our existing staff to see if any has a teaching qualification which I do by asking the Personnel section to look into it for me. They come up with several people. More, in fact, than I am prepared for. My experience is that the teaching staff at the college is comprised of people who have done well in their professional field and then come into teaching. One name, in particular, is of interest to me. Graeme was just the kind of person I feel I can work with. We have socialised occasionally and got on well. I approach him for his reaction to helping with the course. 'I know of it,' he says, 'but I don't know too much about what it entails.' 'I have the syllabus here,' I reply, 'look it over and let me know if you are interested in helping. I will need about four or five hours of your teaching time, so you will probably have to drop something you are currently involved in.' 'That could be fairly easy,' he adds, 'they are phasing out some of the General Studies I teach because they want to concentrate on the core subject to give more time for the students to study that. We are now results driven as the Director keeps telling us. The Quality Council is only interested in colleges that produce good results, to quote him.'

My interview with Edgar is quite short. He knows of my predicament. 'Gerry used to come with the same request, but I had to tell him we had no spare staff with any hours free and no money to employ anyone else. I think he adapted his approach accordingly. My guess is that the teaching observation hours were limited. How he squared that with the external examiner I do not know, but it all seemed to work. I know you are a new broom and so will want to do things as they are supposed to be done. I have spoken with Graeme's head of section and he is able to release Graeme for the number of hours we request.'

This is a load off my shoulders, but it means I will have to bring Graeme up-to-speed with my intentions for the two courses that we will be teaching. He, like me, has never taught a course about teaching but he has the advantage that he has worked, albeit briefly, in a Technical College and can relate to most of the issues covered in the syllabus. We get together on the Friday morning before the course is to begin on the following Monday. By the end of the day, we have divided the delivery of the course up into sections that we are most comfortable with and can now only await the attendance of our first cohort which we agree we will both be present for.

CHAPTER FIVE

Before the beginning of the course at the college, there is the small matter of a trip to Oxford to play our second game in the Regional League. I drive the minibus with the players optimistic about the first away result. After some of our previous long treks to the north of England, the short distance to Oxford soon passes. The match is to prove a disaster for the team. A sloppy first half performance, as later reported in the local newspaper, sees us trailing at half time and despite a better second half we can only get within four points of the opposition at the end of the game. Mick's lesson to the players in the changing room after the game is clear, 'In previous seasons you youngsters could rely on our Americans or experienced English players racking up the points. They are no longer here. The scoring is up to you and our first half showed that we have a long way to go.' The time going back home in the minibus seems to pass far more slowly.

Monday finally arrives and I get to the college early in readiness for greeting my first ever group of students in a classroom setting. The actual room is on the first floor of a corner of the building which overlooks a busy crossroads controlled by traffic lights. There is no double glazing and the noise, if a window is open, is uncomfortable. Unfortunately, it looks like being a warm late September day and we will have to have some kind of ventilation. The room itself is adequate enough for the sixteen students expected and the first thing I do is arrange the seating in the form of a rectangle so that everyone can face one another. For some reason there is a filing cabinet in the room, but it is in a corner and therefore does not get in the way. Graeme arrives shortly after I have finished doing that. The students have been sent information about the starting time and the room number. I say to Graeme, 'We need to leave the room now and let them arrive. We will come in after fifteen minutes.'

When we return there are sixteen course members in the room. Some are sitting, some standing. We introduce ourselves and start by asking what they had first thought when they arrived. One immediately speaks up and says, 'I thought someone might be here to greet us. It seems bad form to leave us in limbo like this.' 'Lesson One in teaching,' I reply, 'there are lots of reasons why you should be punctual. We deliberately let you stew for a while so that you can remember this important lesson.' I have taken a calculated gamble with this ploy because now we have to overcome any feeling of resentment that may have built up.

I have been present in the past at several occasions where ice-breaking activities have taken place. I have also read up about ice-breaking activities in general. The one I choose for this group is to pair them off with someone they do not know, give them five minutes each to interview the other, and then introduce that person to the group. After the introduction, the person who has been introduced can add to what has been said or make sure that what they want to emphasise about themselves has been done. As a result of that exercise, at the end of the morning session everyone knows the background of the others. In all there are five hairdressers (Ann, Kerry, Joanne, Val, Kathy), two older women (Kay, Margaret) who seem to teach in care homes, one Navy man (Jack), two caterers (Ian, Julian), two plumbers (Alan, Ken) one physiotherapist (Gill) and two typing school workers (Carmen, Janet). Each of them has a teaching role and some are fairly new to teaching whilst others have quite a lot of experience of teaching. All of them are seemingly anxious to gain a teaching qualification. I find out that the hairdressers are so well represented because the salons are taking on a teaching role and relying less on intakes from students of the local Technical colleges.

The day progresses well, I think, as I explain the details of the course and what will be expected of them. I tell them about the various assignments that will need to be undertaken and the visits we will have to make to wherever their teaching takes place. I feel that the atmosphere in the room is friendly, if apprehensive. There is a wide variety of backgrounds and teaching experience in the group which I hope I can use to my advantage.

That evening I review how the day has gone. I wonder if the next day, when I am to teach at the hospital, will go anything like today has gone. Should I, for instance, use the same ice-breaker when all of them work at the hospital? Since it has gone so well today, I decide to go with the same format, except I will be there on time to greet the students. Graeme is not going to be so involved with the hospital course bearing in mind the limited number of hours he has available to help me.

At the end of the next day, I know the placements of the nurses with whom I will be dealing. Two come from Intensive Care, six are Ward nurses with various responsibilities, four are from the Maternity Wing, one is a Physiotherapist, two are from the Oncology Ward and the remaining one comes from the Orthopaedic Ward. There is altogether a different feel to the group than the day before, which I put down to the fact that they all come from a similar working background and do not have the variety of experience that I had been faced with the previous day. That said the day, I feel, has also gone well. Certainly the teaching conditions are far improved on the college. The classroom is more pleasant with a lot of natural light and no external noise. It even has a carpet which softens any sound when movement is involved, as when I arrange the desk formation as I had used the day before. I make a point of seeing Barbara before I leave and ask her to give me any feedback she might get about how the day has been received by the group.

At basketball training that evening, I am heartened when Mick tells me that Eddie is to rejoin the squad. He had been one of the English players who had contributed so much to the success of the team over the previous seasons. It had looked as if we had lost his services when we told him we could no longer pay him. Perhaps he had tried some other clubs and found there was nothing going elsewhere. In any case, like Ken, he has decided he wants to continue playing even if it means no income. It is reassuring to see that at practice he seems to have lost none of his keenness as he gets fully involved in all the training.

Our next match involves a trip to Bristol on Saturday. Once again, the trip is short, less than two hours. The team is anxious to get back to winning ways and with Eddie playing like a dervish and scoring 35 points the win is easily achieved and it is a happy group of players that makes its way back home. On the way home Mick mentions that our next opponents are another team from Oxford. 'They have already beaten the other Oxford team who we lost to last week. This will be a test for us, but now we seem to have Eddie in the fold, I am hoping for better things.'

The next morning, I have a surprise when the telephone rings and the caller is my sister. 'It's your birthday, tomorrow,' she begins, 'and I have forgotten to buy you a card.' I am not sure how to react. It sounds as if she is blaming me for her forgetfulness or for having a birthday when she has not got me a card. 'I'm past thinking about birthday cards,' I reply. 'I am just glad to hear your voice and, hopefully, know all is well.' 'Yes, everything is fine, especially with the children who have settled in well in the new term at their school.' I tell her about my change of role at the college and she is interested in what I am doing and asks me a lot of questions. Eventually, she ends the call with an invitation to go and visit her family as soon as possible. 'I will keep your present here, so you will have to come and get it,' she adds.

Sharon, my younger sister, was actually christened Siobhan. She got so fed up with people not being able to pronounce it or spell it that, as soon as she was able she changed her name by deed poll to Sharon. 'I've never even been to Ireland,' she used to say, 'so I don't see why I should be saddled with an Irish name. Quite headstrong is our Sharon. We both had Irish names originally because our father was Irish. He had come over from Belfast to find work in the shipyards on the River Tyne. He met, but did not marry, our mother. A few years after Sharon was born, the relationship foundered, so much so that we were placed in foster care. Unfortunately, we were not placed with the same family. Even more of a rift occurred when my family decided to move south in search of work, ironically also in a dockyard. We had kept in touch over the years once we were old enough to have explained to us what had happened. It was one of the relatives of my mother who in last season's basketball fixture had not been able to drive down to Sunderland from Wallsend because of the fog. Sharon now lived with a husband and two children near Kings Lynn. No National League basketball team played in that area so there had been little chance to meet on that basis, but I had made the occasional visit to see her and her family.

The week passes quickly as I find myself taking the classes and attending training, as usual. I arrange to meet with Dave to keep him in touch with developments on the basketball front. He suggests his local pub as a venue. I know the pub concerned and I also know it is a hot bed of political activity for the Labour Party. When I mention this to him as we meet he says, 'I know that, but it also has a bar billiard table. Most of the regulars are so involved in political activity business and planning the Revolution that usually the bar billiard table is free for me to use.' At the time we arrive, there are two people playing billiards, so we put our money on the edge of the table which means that we have booked the table for the next game. When playing it soon becomes apparent that Dave is a far more experienced player than I am. However, I do get a chance to tell him about our next basketball match and keep him informed of what is happening at the club, especially the return of Eddie who has strengthened the team. 'I am still talking to people about getting involved,' Dave says, and I am pleased to hear it. I tell him that this week's opponents have beaten the team we lost to a couple of weeks before. 'It will be a good test then of how this Eddie has made the team better,' Dave replies.

Eddie, together with Jon, rattle in 57 points between them in a one way match against the Oxford opponents. In fact, their 57 points is six more than the Oxford team can score in the whole game as Hampshire Hoops pass the 100 point mark again.

In the next few weeks at college I begin to see the size of my task and that, perhaps I am expecting too much of my students. The first written assignment concerns some of the theory of teaching. The scripts we receive are, in the main, rather mundane. Usually it is a rehash of what we have talked about in our first few sessions, but it is the language and grammar, particularly grammar, that is disappointing. I meet with Graeme to discuss the issue. He has come to the same conclusion. 'We have to remember these students have not had to go through any selection process to get on the course. For our own course it is has been good enough for them only to be able to supply their own teaching situation. The hospital nurses are a different case. Most of their scripts are coherent and demonstrate the gulf between our college group and them,' says Graeme trying to come to terms with the work he has seen so far. I have only shown him a few of the scripts from the nursing course but he has already reached that conclusion. 'Perhaps we should try to contact the external assessor again, to check on the level of written responses we should be getting,' I suggest. 'I can't think our group can be so different from others,' Graeme responds. I make a note to do just that.

However, wearing my basketball hat takes priority during the week. Our next match is against the current unbeaten league leaders, Camberley. After much persuasion, Mike is to play for the team. With Ken and Eddie also in the team, Hampshire Hoops have far more experienced players than the opponents. This is seen from the outset of the game. All three may be approaching the end of their playing careers, but they demonstrate that there is still life in the old dog yet, as coach Mick puts it. At one point, Hampshire lead by 30 points making a mockery of Camberley's top of the league position. Once again, Eddie heads the scoring closely followed by Jon, the club's England Under 22 player. Mike is only used for six minutes at the beginning of the game when Camberley find it almost impossible to pierce the Hampshire defence and lose their momentum. The Hampshire Hoops team starts the game with five players who had recently played in the top league in England. I make this observation to the coach. 'With Eddie, Ken, Mike, Jon and Joe we ought to be able to walk this league,' he responds.

My attempt to contact the external assessor, in order to get him more involved and look for feedback for Graeme and myself, meets with a muted response. 'I am snowed under at the moment,' he tells me over the telephone line. 'Let me get back to you when things quieten down a bit. Just one word of advice, don't expect too high a level of academic type essays, remember most of these students you have are in practical jobs. They don't have to write too much usually and when they do it can be difficult for them. Cut them a little slack on their efforts. I will remember your concerns when we meet.' I report the conversation to Graeme and we agree to spend more time helping everyone frame their responses to the written assignments. The term 'spoon feeding' is uppermost in my mind, but I dismiss it having taken notice of what I had just been told by Charles, the external assessor.

At basketball training Mick tells me that he is disappointed to only have used Mike in such a limited fashion for the last game. 'We have a cup game coming up against Chiltern who are in Division Three of the National League and I want to give Mike more court time ahead of that match. We have Herne Bay as our next opponents and Mike has expressed a wish to be further involved on the playing front. We must encourage that. He might be a bit slower now getting up and down court but his height is invaluable.'

The very next morning, Marie contacts me. She has just received a telephone call from the Herne Bay secretary saying that they will be unable to honour this coming weekend's fixture claiming injuries to their players make it impossible to raise a team. The Regional League is small in the number of teams and we are already without a game for the two following weekends prior to our National Cup match against Chiltern, so the situation is serious. I talk to Mick and we agree to use our contacts to try and find some opponents to keep our team in a competitive mode. At short notice we visit an Army base on a Thursday evening and win the game comfortably. The Royal Corps of Transport provide our next opponents, replacing Herne Bay, for a home fixture. We are far too strong for them, even without Eddie and Ken who are rested, and it is a very one way game, but it does give Mike a lot of court time. Finally we go to Oxford to play a University team. The players travel by car to help defray expenses. The game is harder and we are put to a stern test before winning by a margin of nine points, but for once failing to get a total of three figures. Our next game will be the biggest of the season so far. Entering the National Cup had been almost an afterthought. However, money has been found for the entry fee and, at the time, we have no idea that this one action is to prove the turning point of the club's future.

CHAPTER SIX

I have just suffered another defeat at bar billiards at the hands of Dave. We then sit down in the corner of a crowded bar where I can hear occasional snatches of conversation from others about various political events. Dave then says to me, 'Good news, at last. I have persuaded one of the sponsors to put up the money for hiring the whole hall for the National Cup game. I used the old argument of speculate to accumulate, and he could see the sense of that what with more spectators and more press coverage. Plus, I told him, his company will be seen in a good light locally for trying to bring back the successful recent times.' I am delighted to hear the news. 'What about the booking of the hall?' I ask, 'others are using it now whilst we play our games in one half.' 'I thought about that and contacted the Sports Centre myself using our company's leverage with the council. They had no hesitation in acceding to my request. However, whilst on the subject of my company, I have decided to set up a separate company for the basketball club, under the umbrella of my company where I am General Manager.'

I take a moment or two to absorb this information as my mind goes back to that eventful meeting all those years ago, when John had told us about his plans for basketball. Once again I am being asked to be a Director of a company, this time it is called Starbright. Dave dips into his briefcase, which I had noted he brought with him, and fishes out some sheets of paper. 'Have a look at these,' he says. The four main sponsors, he tells me, are listed as Directors along with me. The Company Secretary's name I am not familiar with. 'He is the parent company secretary,' Dave says, 'he has agreed to act for the club as his son is keen on the game and even attended some of the camps you ran last year. Also he works in the Planning Department of the local authority and you never know what doors that might open.'

Looking through the document I see that the Principal Activity of the company is 'the promotion and running of Hampshire Hoops Basket Ball Club.' The Directors are allotted 100 shares each. Whilst I know and have socialised with Dave, I am not so familiar with the other names. They are obviously connected with the firms that have been supplying the funds through Dave, as he informs me. He tells me they are all players in the local council scene too. 'Probably best if you stick to the basketball and let me deal with the others,' he says. I have to express some reservations on that score. 'Look what happened last time,' I begin, 'John set up the company, even expanded it with the opening of a Health Club. Then he disappeared. That is how we find ourselves in this position.' 'I know the history,' Dave continues, 'and it is not going to be repeated. John was into some things he should not have been and, I believe, he was using the basketball club and Health Club to try and legitimise some money operations from abroad. That is the word I hear on the business grapevine. He was successful, too, up to a point. Some deal went awry, we think, and he had to flee the country. No one seems to know where he went to. There have been rumours, Majorca was one last year, but other places have been mentioned also.'

Early the following morning I contact Marie with the news that we are going to have the whole hall for the next game. 'I know that,' she says, 'Dave telephoned me yesterday with the news and told me to expect far more spectators on the night and I should have enough tickets ready for that.' I take a moment to absorb that news and decide that Dave, for the moment at least, is a far more hands-on sponsor than John had seemed to be. I leave a message on Mick's answerphone to give him the news also.

I look at my diary for the rest of the week and see that I am due to watch three people teach at a variety of locations.

Just after lunch, I go to a hairdresser's salon where there is a small room on the first floor which has been converted into a classroom. I am aware of the move by hairdressers to open their own training locations instead of relying on products from the local Technical Colleges. The classroom is adequate for the purpose of teaching the ten assembled youngsters. I find out all about the Bob Cut but more importantly I am impressed by my student's approach to her teaching session which is well planned and involves the girls, no boys to be seen, in appropriate ways both theoretical and practical. I spend a little while debriefing her before returning to the college. Also, I try not to be surprised that the woman I have just watched was so good. All the people on the college's own course are obviously keen on the notion of teaching and are willing to put into practice things that Graeme and I are telling them.

Mick is ecstatic about the upcoming home game. 'It will be just like old times,' he says, 'except that now we are having to fight our way back into recognition. This is a game we must win.' 'Hold on,' I counsel, 'don't put too much pressure on the players. Yes, we need to get back on the national scene, but remember that we are rebuilding a team. Luckily for the actual event, we can call on a full complement of helpers to make the evening go smoothly. Everyone I have spoken to is up for helping out just like the last time we played in the whole hall. As far as I know, this is a one-off but it will end our current run of ignominy in half the hall. Let's hope that by pulling together we can show everyone what we are still capable of. And, yes, a win would be very desirable,' I conclude.

On Thursday, as I am sitting in the shared office, the talk is about the current situation in the college. There is growing disquiet about the way management seems to be acting. Trevor, as usual, has his theory. 'This drive for Polytechnic status will cause unrest everywhere. Already people are being moved around to help create new teaching spaces.

They say it is only temporary but I bet it will not be. Two good classrooms have been commandeered for spacious offices for Administration. The staff were promised new classrooms to compensate. A member of staff tells me that one of the rooms has an open drain running through it, no heating and smells of welding fumes. This just proves that former workshops cannot be used as classrooms. Where is all the money to come from to fund all the building developments? Do you know,' he continues to anyone who is listening, 'that we are building student accommodation in various places near the college? What is more, I hear we are buying the building next door to expand that way, too. Where is the money coming from?' While nearing retirement, Trevor, still has the college's interest at heart and also has known the Union Representatives for many years. It is obviously these who are keeping him up-to-date.

There is also weekly newsletter that is sent to all. This claims to be apolitical and serving as a conduit to keep staff appraised of events. However, sometimes it strays into commenting on developments. This week's edition contains a short item about a Branch Meeting of the Union at which a motion was passed by the 93 members stating that the Branch 'has no confidence on the ability of management at the college to satisfactorily conduct industrial relationships'.

I am also taken by a second issue reported on in the newsletter. There has been a debate about the use of the Senior Common Room that has been going on for two years. Certain members of the Administrative staff believe that they should have access to the Room. In this week's edition there is a rebuttal of sorts from one of the academic staff who uses as his argument that it is a place to discuss academic issues. He goes on to say 'non-academics are not usually interested in estimating how many fairies can dance on the head of a pin'. I think he is joking but things of late have become very edgy.

The next day I am summoned by the Director's secretary to his office. He gets straight to the point. 'I want to try and get everybody on board for our drive to become a Polytechnic. It is the only way forward. I know I will have trouble with the old hands who seem to resist any notion of change. However, any new appointee must be clear on our goals. To that end, I want you to be in charge of the proposed Induction for new members of the teaching staff. I propose that we will run it at the beginning of September for anyone who is joining or has joined the college in the previous year. Some, of course, will have been here perhaps for two or three terms already, but I am sure you will be able to use them for the very recent newcomers and the completely new. What do you say?'

I know I have little choice, and, indeed, I am quite interested in the role which would give me a chance to meet people from across the college. Over the years I have made contact with a lot of staff through the leisure and recreation work I have been involved in. The staff three-a-side football sessions one day a week has helped me develop relationships with male teaching staff, who form the majority, all over the college. 'I am quite happy to take on that role,' I reply. The Director continues, 'Good. It is important also that I get a chance to address the newcomers. I want them to see how serious I am to pursuing my goal for the college.'

When I get back to my office I take a little time to try and make sense of what is happening around me. It is easy, I realise, to get so involved in delivering any course that there is a chance to miss out on wider developments. For that, I guess, I should be grateful for those members of staff who do speak out. The obvious mouthpieces are the Union Representatives who point out items in the weekly newsletter sometimes draw attention to small changes that are taking place that may eventually have much larger repercussions.

One huge issue that I foresee in the expansion of the college is the admission of females. The college was founded in the 1960s as a College of Technology. At that time for the Privy Council to approve a name for an educational establishment, there had to be a reference to its geographical location. Rumour has it that when a name for the college was being proposed one of the serious suggestions was Stanley (the neighbourhood where the college is situated) Hampshire Institute of Technology. This was almost carried through to the final naming stage until some perceptive person noted the acronym of such a name. So the Stanley and Institute were dropped and replaced by College. Be that as it may, the college was very male dominated and courses were also aimed at what were historically male preserves, building, craft, printing, plumbing and so on. It followed that the facilities for toilets and the like were built to accommodate the mainly male population. Oddly, there was one course that seemed out-of-place. It was for students who wanted to become Personal Assistants. It was a popular course and easily enrolled two cohorts of thirty female students every year. Facilities had to be available for them and the female members of the administrative staff that were employed. Having said that, the new facilities are proving woefully inadequate for the increasing number of students that we are enrolling. Building work is going on all around the college and some of that is addressing the issue of making the college more female friendly.

The whole situation with the increase in the number of female students makes me even more aware of my paucity of involvement on that score. I went to a boys' grammar school, followed by an all-male college of education. Since then I have attended another male physical education course in Leeds. At least there were girls and female members of staff at the schools I taught in but since coming to the college I have come back into an almost male preserve. But it will not only be me who has to adapt to the projected influx of females. There are a lot of dyed-in-the-wool staff members who have never had many dealings with the female of the species in a teaching situation. At least now I am involved with two courses that are dominated by women, if only on a part-time basis.

On Saturday I awake and immediately feel some of the excitement I used to have when we had a home match in the National League. Only this time, it will be a cup game against a National League Division Three side. No matter, I think, we are going to play in the whole arena with the TV lights, just like old times. I have contacted all those who help set-up the arena. The seating is put out by the leisure centre staff, but there are a lot of other jobs that have to be performed before we can let the public in. I still have the job of taking the kit to the game, having already checked with our opponents to see that there will be no colour clash. We have access to the hall and changing rooms from 6.00pm for a game that begins at 8.00pm. The ticket desk and the p.a. system have to be installed. The courtside advertising boards have to be put out. It is good to see that everyone seems to remember what to do after this long break away from using the whole arena. The opponents, Chiltern Fastbreak, arrive in good time and are shown to their changing room. Some change quickly and come on to the court to practise shooting. We, too, have several of the squad out on the court. The large scoreboard is high on the wall at one end of the court. Convention dictates that the visitors play towards the scoreboard in the second half. The referees are shown to their small changing room and apologies are made that there is no shower in the room. They are advised they can use the showers in the public swimming pool area which is nearby. I am encouraged to see a queue beginning to form over an hour before the game.

Eventually I take my place at the end of the scorer's table and check the public address system. The acoustics in any sports hall, I have found, are usually pretty dreadful and ours is no exception. The players have cleared the court, and with 20 minutes to go before the game is scheduled to start, the TV lights are turned on. They take a couple of minutes to warm up to their full potential. Then I announce the arrival of the teams on court. My next action with six minutes to go before the commencement of the game is to introduce each of the players. The away team players run out on court as they are introduced. The home crowd gives lukewarm applause to each player. Then I introduce the home team and the noise becomes deafening for each introduction.

We need to put up a good performance against Chiltern who are doing well so far this season in Division Three. Mick puts on his strongest five players to start the game. All five have played at a higher level. For Mike it is his first playing experience in front of his home crowd and he has already been given a special cheer from the crowd. Jon, Eddie and Ken are joined by Toby who has been playing well all season, if slightly in the shadow of the main scorers. It soon becomes apparent that our starting five is stronger that the visitors. Mike is winning nearly all the rebounds and posing numerous problems to Chiltern. At half time we have a commanding lead of 18 points. Early in the second half Hampshire pile on the pressure and eventually win the game by over 40 points. This would appear a National Cup upset with a National league team being so convincingly beaten by a team outside the National League. We know that our next opponents are Leicester Riders from the First Division. The last time we played them in the National Cup was in the National Cup Final in 1984, Mick informs me. 'We played to a packed house at the Royal Albert Hall. We won then making us the first team to win the trophy three times in a row. That was when we were the best team in the country. It will be interesting when we go to Leicester after Christmas to see how we do now.'

Mick's use of the word Christmas makes me aware that I will soon have a couple of weeks away from the college and also there are no basketball matches in the offing. Perhaps I should honour my pledge to go and see Sharon and her family in Kings Lynn.

Before that, I have suggested to the Monday course that perhaps we might have a get-together prior to the Christmas break. I ask for suggestions for a venue when the group agree to the idea. It is then that the two caterers, Ian and Julian, come into their own. 'Leave it with us,' they say. The final session of the term comes and we are told that a venue has been established. It is to be a local casino. Apparently, one of the chefs used to work there before branching out into teaching at a local college. 'We won't have to become members,' we are told, 'and the casino has agreed to lay on some refreshments.' The group members are looking forward to the night out.

I arrive at the casino and am impressed by the layout of the interior with its gaming tables and slot machines plus a bar and a small dancing area as well as an intimate eating area. We are all having a good time when I notice one of the previous sponsors of the basketball club having a break from the gaming table and getting himself a drink at the bar. I go up to him and introduce myself. Soon we are talking about basketball. 'It came as quite a sudden blow when John disappeared from the scene,' I say. 'It was quite a blow to a lot of people,' he replies. 'I have known him for a long time and knew that occasionally he would fly close to the wind, but I never expected such a calamitous ending. As you know, we had already got out of the basketball sponsorship before he left. He had sold us the idea saying that the game was about to take off nationally and we would benefit from our involvement. It never happened and after a couple of years we withdrew our backing. Then, one day, he was gone.' 'Any idea where,' I query. 'No,' he replies, 'I had heard that he may be in the Caribbean somewhere.' 'And I had heard he that may be in Majorca,' I counter. We both agree that the two rumours are probably way off the mark. Further conversation is not possible as he wants to return to the tables and one of my group comes over to ask me what I want to drink.

The evening is a great success and I feel that the group is bonding well. It also reinforces my feeling that it is good not to get involved in such places as I watch various people, including a disproportionate number of foreign looking characters, place huge sums of money at the various card and roulette tables. Thankfully I notice that none of my group is so inclined.

We now have a couple of weeks to reflect on the course. Graeme seems to have had a good time also and I wonder how many other courses finish their first term in a casino.

CHAPTER SEVEN

I had enjoyed the Christmas break spending a few days in Kings Lynn. The only downside to that was fielding my sister's questions about any love life that I might have. My reply of, 'No, there is no one in my life at the moment,' did not stop the steady flow of interrogation about who might fit the bill. 'What about the people you work with?' I was asked. This led me to catalogue some of the female staff members in the Administration. I picked those who were already married in the main and for others I made up characteristics which explained why they were single.

Now back in my flat, I telephone Mick to find out the state of the basketball team. 'We have not done as much training as I would like, considering the importance of our next game. A lot of places were closed for the Christmas break and some of the players have visited family away from here,' Mick says. I sense some frustration in his voice. He is divorced himself and probably did not have too many obligations over the holiday. I feel it may be unreasonable on his part to expect the players to give up everything because of the next match. However, even I am not ready for his next bombshell. 'We won't have Ken for the next game. He will be on holiday, he tells me. It was planned and paid for even before the season began. He hadn't foreseen our progress in the National Cup. He is upset, but that doesn't help us.'

I feel for Mick but in my heart of hearts I know that our chances of victory at Leicester are virtually non-existent but it will be important to put up a good show. Unlike rugby or football where upsets do occur, basketball only has five players on court as opposed to the fifteen and eleven at the other sports. In addition, Leicester will have at least two American players who usually prove better than any local player.

The game is the weekend before the college term begins. We travel to Leicester in a minibus minus not only Ken, the club captain, but also Jon, one of our leading scorers, who has succumbed to some sort of illness that kept him from any training session in the last week. It feels good to be back in the major league atmosphere engendered by the large crowd, the music, the cheerleaders and the sense of occasion. Our players do not seem overawed and play as well as can be expected, surprising our hosts who, I guess, had expected an easy ride. With just three minutes of the game remaining we are just ten points behind Leicester who realise that there is a potential for a major cup upset. We have fought back from being thirty points behind at one stage. Leicester bring back into the game the two American players and the chance of an upset is gone. Afterwards I am approached by the Leicester owner, who I had got to know when we were in the top league. 'We need you back,' he says, 'what are the chances?' I can only mumble a few platitudes about sponsorship but try to give the impression that our goal is to be regular visitors at some time in the future.

Returning to the college I am delighted to see that everyone arrives for the first session of the second term of our teaching course. This session is about assessment and the group are interested in the various forms of assessment that exist and for what purpose that assessment can be used. Everyone has an input into how they have been assessed in education in their life. Most think that assessment means showing how much you have remembered of what you have been taught. I have to make them aware of the purpose of assessment and that there are many forms that it can take. 'For instance,' I say, 'there are two main reasons for undertaking the assessment of students' work. One is called formative assessment which you will need to teach the student, the other is summative assessment which you will use to report on the student and how much he or she has learned.' I then open up the discussion hoping that I am making clear that assessment is not just what most of them have experienced so far. I decide to leave the subject of any reliability and validity of the assessment method chosen to another time. At the end of the day a couple of the hairdressers, the physiotherapist, one of the plumbers and Jack from the Royal Navy stay behind to continue talking about the subject of assessment and I feel gratified that they are taking such an interest.

In the evening, I receive a telephone call from one of my friends. 'I am thinking of getting together a group of us to play basketball over the summer. There is an outdoor court locally that we can book on a regular basis. Are you interested? So far I have positive responses from seven of the former team you played in after we left school.' I jump at the chance. I have tried to keep fit over the years and regularly go for runs locally and join in activities in the Sports Hall such as three-a-side football and basketball training for the college team. 'Count me in,' I say, 'and let me know the details. Most nights are OK for me, such is the pathetic social life I lead.' Brian laughs and replies, 'I am sure it is not so desperate as you describe.' Oh yes it is, I silently say to myself as we end the conversation.

It seems like fate, therefore, when Pete, my former colleague in the Physical Education section, asks me if I am interested in a night out with a couple of the girls, as he describes them, from Administration. One of the women, Meryl, is an Australian who has been working over here for a year or so and is about to return home. 'Jacqui is her best friend and suggested that perhaps we could go for a meal and a few drinks.' I have had, over the last few months, far more dealings with Meryl because of the student enrolment on my courses. Previously any student I dealt with was part of someone else's course and I had no reason to have any dealings with Meryl. I think she is attractive and a good example of what I imagine the outdoor Australian women are like. She has managed to keep a healthy skin colour which sets off her blonde hair. 'Friday week, then,' Pete questions, 'is that alright with you?'

The week ends with another cup game for Hampshire Hoops. This time it is in the Founders Cup which is for teams outside of the National League. Now that we have been ousted from the National Cup this is the only remaining cup competition we are involved in. Our visitors are Plympton, who, like us play in a Regional League. Again we are playing in the full hall and I sense the visitors are a bit overawed by the standard of the presentation and the good size following of the spectators. Ken is back from holiday but Jon is still ill. It is the referees that take centre stage in the game constantly blowing their whistles and not letting the game flow at all. Soon, before half time, we have lost two players who have fouled out of the game by committing, in the eyes of the referees, five personal fouls. Plympton have also lost one but up until that moment he had been their most influential player. Without him the visitors seemed to lose heart and we run out easy victors.

At half-time I announce to the crowd that we are making an application to rejoin the National League next season. This had been agreed, Dave tells me earlier in the evening, between the directors at a meeting I had been unable to attend because I had been coaching the college team which had been playing a fixture in the local league. The news is greeted with much applause and I am immediately starting to think of the ramifications for me. Division Three, which, if we are accepted, is the Division we will play in, will not have the profile of Division One and I hope that it will not involve me in the way the last season in the top Division had. I make a mental note to talk to Dave further about this matter. Mick is, of course, overjoyed.

'Don't forget tomorrow,' Pete reminds me on Thursday, 'we've got a Pizza place lined up which is near Jacqui's flat. After that we can go back to her place, she has said.'

We meet up for the meal. I realise that although Meryl has been at the college for a year and I have had more dealings with her in the last few months, I do not know any personal details about her. 'Why did you come here?' I ask. Meryl is a bit coy in her reply. 'Personal reasons,' she replies, in a way that suggests I should not pursue the subject. Only when she goes to the Ladies does Jacqui quickly fill me in on the details. 'It was the breakup of a long time affair. Apparently her partner wanted to start a family, but she was not ready although she was 30 years old at the time.' I can find out no more because, as with the way of women, Jacqui leaves to join Meryl in the Ladies.

When they return, Meryl tells us more about her life in Australia. Jacqui probably has heard it all before, but Pete and I are all ears. 'I come from Townsville,' she begins, 'which is on Bruce Highway, the main road running north – south in Queensland. Boats go to the Great Barrier Reef from there, which makes it a popular tourist destination. I used to work on those boats and also on the small ferry that takes people to Magnetic Island. That is a good place to go to also. You can catch a bus from the ferry terminal to Acadia, by way of Rock Bay and Nelly Bay. There is also a coral path you can walk along at low tide. People go to use the beach there also. The ferry goes to Acadia as well so you do not have to return to the original terminal.' Meryl also mentions the town itself with its mall and bandstand. 'I bet you are looking forward to returning there and getting away from the miserable weather and dark nights here,' I venture.

After the meal, we go back to Jacqui's flat which is nearby. I have brought a bottle of wine, as has Pete. Jacqui already has her own supply of wine, as well. I give Meryl a set of coasters with local scenes a reminder, I say, of her time here. She seems quite taken by the gesture. We drink wine and we all are very relaxed. Suddenly, Pete and Jacqui get up and it becomes apparent to me that the evening may be more about Pete and Jacqui than Meryl and myself. They disappear into

Jacqui's bedroom. Meryl does not seem surprised or perturbed about the developments. She stands up and reaches for my hand. I am now being taken along the short corridor to where there is another bedroom. Meryl says, 'They shouldn't be the only ones to have fun.' We kiss and it is all I had hoped it would be. Soon we are in the bed. I am still trying to puzzle out how this situation has developed. I give up and allow myself to enjoy the intimacy of two bodies pressed close together. 'I'm on the pill,' Meryl whispers. The invitation is too good to resist. I can barely remember the last time I was in this situation. There have been times but none of them have led to more permanent relationships. In this case, Meryl is about to travel to the other side of the world, so I guess I can just let myself go, which I then do.

Saturday morning dawns and we are still in the bedroom. I can hear noises coming from the rest of the flat. This turns out to be Jacqui preparing a cooked breakfast. Pete is no longer here. I surmise he has returned to his wife sometime in the night. I am still not clear as to who may have been the instigator of last night's celebrations, but in a way I am glad that Meryl has now left the college employ and there will be no awkward meetings at work. I am not so sure about Jacqui. I guess that she, too, will not want to talk about last night.

In the evening I find myself back at the next home basketball match. Our opponents are Bristol Renegades who are just above us in the league, but have played three more matches than we have. It has been nearly two months since we played a league game. I am delighted to see that Jon is back after his illness, but a bit apprehensive when I am told by Mick that Mike, Toby and Eddie are all carrying injuries. I see that Mike and Toby are on the team bench, but thankfully are not needed as we manage to run up yet another three figure score in an easy win.

My next week includes five teaching observations varying from catering to plumbing plus three hospital procedures.

Each one is interesting for me both from the content of the sessions plus the way the teaching is delivered. I have to visit the General Office at the end of the week. The physiotherapist on my college course has telephoned in to say she has a cold with 'flu-like symptoms. That explains her absence on Monday and in that session I had given everyone several handouts. I need her address to send a copy of each handout to her. Jacqui is not at her desk when I go in, but Andrea, who is Meryl's replacement is. She has the enrolment information I need which gives Gill's address. I am not sure if I am imagining it, but the general hubbub of the office seems to stop on my appearance. Has Jacqui said something, I wonder? Perhaps it is just my suspicion but I am glad to get out of their office as quickly as possible.

The next day there is a basketball trip to Oxford Coyotes, a team we had beaten easily in our home fixture. Because of injury our three most experienced players will be missing. Mike, Ken and Eddie are all sidelined, although Mike is able to make the trip as Assistant Coach. At first their experience is missed as we are unable to dictate the pace of the match and the Oxford team start off in high gear. Gradually, however, we come into the game and then take it over completely in the second half to win by over 30 points. Mick is relieved having had doubts about the ability of his young English team against more experienced opponents. I am pleased to see that the student I had brought to the club from the college is the game's highest scorer.

I have my first taste of student rebellion in the following week. It is one of the nurses and she states, 'I have to explain the procedures to my colleagues and the only way to do it is to tell them.' I know she is reacting to my earlier session when I explained that telling is not teaching. 'There is no point in asking them for an opinion or suggesting that they might work in small groups to discuss what ought to be done or could be done,' she continues. I realise that she is one of the older school who thinks that the course is probably a waste of her time. I can only counter with the question, 'Has the procedure always been the same?' 'Oh, no,' she replies, falling into my trap, 'when I first started it was quite different.' 'How, then,' I continue, 'did the changes come about? By your reckoning you should be teaching the procedure that existed then. The nurses need to know why the procedure is as it is now and need to examine the process. That's where the teaching comes in and also, in the fullness of time, why changes take place.' I am not sure she is convinced, probably feeling more secure as the provider of knowledge than in questioning it.

More teaching observation visits follow. I have explained to the students that the conditions of the course require twelve hours of teaching to be observed of the thirty that must be done over the length of the course. However, we do not have the staff able to do that, so we will guarantee to visit them at least three times and ask them if they can get a colleague to perhaps observe them also. We do require, however, lesson plans for the twelve sessions that should be observed to be in their portfolios along with any handouts and course assignments that they have to do. I can sense no objection to the reduction of teaching observation which, I know, some can get quite worked up about.

It is about now that I really begin my involvement with matters that will come to a head in a couple of years' time and lead to huge changes in the way the college is administered. I am summoned to the Director's office. As usual, he wastes no time getting down to the matter in hand. No questions about how the courses are running, for instance. 'You have agreed to oversee the Induction Course for new members of staff in September,' he begins. He does not seem interested in the content of that course or any of the details. 'I will need a session on the course to explain my vision of our future,' he continues. Then, almost as an afterthought, but I suspect as something already carefully thought through by him, he adds, 'I have spoken with the

Principal of a local Technical College about the delivery of the course you are teaching. He has agreed that the course could be run by his staff at his college. The qualification is Teaching in Further Education, so it seems logical that it should be taught in a Technical College.' 'What about the hospital?' I query. 'Can I leave that to you to sort out? You can explain why we think it better to move the course. However, I want to talk to you about developments here.'

I begin to feel uncomfortable. Running this new course, for me, has involved me in a lot of work. Basically, I have been keeping one step ahead of the course members. The syllabus is fairly closely prescribed in the City and Guilds literature. What I have to do is make the dry words on the syllabus content meaningful to the course members. It has meant for me a lot of preparation which has to be worked around all the other activities in which I am involved. I turn my attention back to the Director.

'We need higher level courses if we are to be successful in our bid to become a Polytechnic. I want you to look into the possibility of our conducting a course for those staff members who join us who have no experience of teaching, but are extremely well qualified in their chosen field. It will have to be at Post-Graduate level since the staff will need to know we are not expecting them to undertake a course like the one you are teaching now. I want you to assemble a team to help you in this task. If you find any difficulties about Section Leaders not releasing people to help you, you are to come to me.'

I leave the room and my head is spinning. Now, I have to deliver two courses that will soon be consigned to the scrapheap, from the college's point of view, and design a course to run at Post-Graduate level. Luckily, I think, the basketball is running smoothly and then I remember we have applied to enter the National League next season.

The away game at Swindon Bullets at the weekend is an easy win but it does not have my full attention as I wrestle with college matters.

CHAPTER EIGHT

My first task following the meeting with the Director, I consider, is to find out the content of Postgraduate Certificate in Education courses. This takes me into the world of established Department of Education courses. In my research to discover what already exists I come across an organisation called The Standing Conference on Educational Development. After delving deeper, I see that this is just the thing for me. There are details about a Post-graduate Course for Teaching in Higher Education. This is appropriate for me, I think.

I involve Graeme in my research. He is able to talk about his experience of such a course. 'I even still have my course notes,' he declares. 'I will bring them in so that you can see what I was involved in.'

A visit to Edgar is called for, I think. I bring him up-to-speed with the Director's latest thinking. 'First I've heard of it,' he announces, 'but then, things are being decided that most of us Heads know little about. Rumour has it that big changes are about to be announced. What is happening to you must be part of the larger picture. Until now we have had twelve fairly autonomous Divisions and a number of Sections within them. I hear on the grapevine that there is going to be another level of management imposed. We will have to wait and see what is in store.'

I decide to go to the hospital to speak to Barbara. She had not been present on the Tuesday when I had gone to the hospital that week. 'It seems we will soon be losing the current course I teach. It will be taken over by the Technical College.' Barbara does not seem fazed by the news. 'Perhaps it is fortunate timing,' she says. 'You have already expressed some views about the suitability of the course for the nurses. It just so happens the English Nursing Board is coming up with a course of its own and has asked us for our comments on the proposed content. I am in the process of getting a group together to discuss the matter. Would you be interested in joining us?' Because of some of my earlier comments to Barbara about the course, it would seem churlish to decline the invitation. 'I'll let you know the details,' Barbara concludes.

College matters are put to one side at the weekend when the basketball team has an important match in the Founders Cup. It is an away game against Sutton, who play in the London League. We need to be at full strength and luckily Mike and Eddie have declared themselves fit. Only Jon, it seems will be missing, I am told at the final practice. 'He is working in Guernsey for his firm and they have to stay over the weekend', Mick tells me. The morning of the game he telephones me to say, 'Jon will be playing. His firm has agreed to fly him back for the game. I guess Dave may have had something to do with that, but I don't know.'

The team are quiet on the journey to the Sutton court. The opponents prove to be an awkward, bustling team but we manage to keep our composure and a three point score by Toby on the half-time buzzer gives us a ten point advantage. This is followed by a further burst of twenty points at the beginning of the second half almost without reply. Coach Mick even has the luxury of giving all ten players time on the court and each of them rewards him by scoring at least one basket in our twenty four point win.

I am therefore in a good mood when I return to college on Monday. Perhaps I should not let sporting results affect me in that way, I think, but I definitely have an inner glow when the team has done well over the weekend. I look at the fixture list and see we have no game in the coming weekend and resolve to give all my attention to the college matters.

Having made that decision I am perhaps in a better position than I would have been otherwise to absorb the contents of the pieces of paper that come to me through the internal post. Rumours have been rife for some time about changes that are being planned for the structure of the college management. In our apolitical weekly staff newsletter there has been the odd question about what is being planned for the college's future. Everyone is already aware of the drive for Polytechnic status and knows that changes will probably ensue from that goal. As I study the proposed new structure even I, never the most politically astute of people, realise that it is almost the setting up of an oligarchy to rule the college. The existing twelve Divisions are to be subsumed into three Schools. I can foresee a situation where the Director plus an Administrative Head plus what are to be called the Deans of School will form a cabal which will make all the important management decisions. I wonder how the existing Heads of Division, should they not become a Dean, will react to the changes.

I am not alone in my thinking and soon all conversation in staffrooms and the refectory revolve around the changes. It seems the structure is a fait accompli having been agreed by the Governors. Advertisements for the posts of the Deans have already been drafted. Needless to say our apolitical staff newsletter suddenly changes its policy to include comments, mostly negative, about the future structure of the college. This prompts the Director to issue his own newsletter, from the Directorate, where he states that he wants to counter the misinformation that is currently going around the college. He headlines his bulletin 'The Truth'. It is only a matter of days before a clandestine rival newsletter is circulating. This does not go to everyone through the official channels, but is obtainable on demand from some to the Union representatives. Interestingly it is titled 'The Lies' and pulls no punches in its comments. However, no names are used, instead anagrams and nom-de-plumes abound. Usually it is clear who is being referred to.

Two weeks have quickly passed whilst all this is going on. I still take the Monday and Tuesday classes and complete quite a few teaching observation visits. My attendance at basketball training helps pass a couple of evenings and I continue to manage to meet Dave in the pub for a game of bar billiards and a chat. He is pleased with the team's progress and says he has several people and firms interested for when we get back in the National League. I remind him that we have applied but, as yet, have heard nothing back from the National League management.

'This is the crunch game,' Mick says to me as I arrive at the home court, 'we are playing Oxford Park and they are the only team to have beaten us in the league this season. We must win and by more points than we lost to them earlier in the season. It was only four points difference, but we don't want a close game this time. If we finish level on points in the league it will be the results of our two games that will be taken into account. Currently we have both lost one game. We are at full strength tonight so let's go for it.'

Mick must have laid it all out to the team in the Changing Room because they came out firing on all cylinders. Having only managed 17 first half points in the away game, we lead by 20 points at half time having already surpassed our total for the whole game at Oxford. There is no letting up in the second half and Hampshire Hoops win by 38 points, far exceeding the five points necessary. My only concern is will the crowd be satisfied with such a disparity in ability between us and our opponents?

Marie sidles up to me in the bar after the game. 'I have had a letter from Companies House about John,' she says. 'They want to know if I have any information about his finances, especially concerning the basketball.' All I can do is point her the way to Dave, who is sitting with some friends at one of the tables. 'I would suggest you do not mention anything about the cheques that were being paid out. There is no reason for you to know that the account often was a Nursing Midwives company. That was just for the basketball but he may have been using it for other business as well.' 'He signed things and I just posted them,' Marie says, 'I never thought to question anything.'

I hope that Dave has been able to assuage Marie's concern, but I do not have a chance to talk to her before leaving, with the wet kit, as usual.

Monday and Tuesday are taken up with my college courses both of which are running smoothly with me just able to keep ahead of the syllabus content by having a couple of late nights at home. One new piece of information I pick up at the hospital is that I can avoid going through the crowded part of the building to get to the canteen at lunchtime. I am made aware of an alternative route that takes me past the mortuary. I now appreciate the deference of the porters who I notice have a different style of pushing the trolleys with curtains down the sides if they are approaching the mortuary or going away from it.

There is one nurse who I have not been able to observe teach. She maintains that she works nights permanently and any session she runs usually takes place at midnight. I arrange to see her one night after basketball training. She works at a hospital in the town centre, one with which I am quite familiar having visited it over the years after accidents. I can remember three occasions. One when I was about ten and helping the milkman deliver his pints. I fell over, broke a bottle which gashed my hand. Later, in my teens, I had discovered a way of carrying my jacket on a warm day by hanging it over the handlebars of my bike. It caught between the wheel and the front fork and I pitched over the handlebars to land on my chin, requiring more stitches. Finally, a football gashed knee had required a tetanus injection. Now, at half past eleven at night, I approach the entrance I have always used. The door is locked tight. I begin to slowly circle the building to find an entrance. I become aware that I am driving slowly around the hospital, but on the other side of the road I know is the edge of the 'red light' district. I pray that no overzealous policeman is about to challenge me.

I cannot think he will easily be convinced by my explanation that I am looking for a way to get into the hospital to observe a lesson being given by one of the staff at midnight. I eventually find the way in and all is well.

At the college I go to see Edgar. 'What do you think of the changes?' I ask him. 'The Director is desperate to achieve Polytechnic status,' he replies, 'and for that I cannot blame him. If we do not move with the times, we will get left behind.' 'But, what about your position,' I query, 'you will have yet another tier of management to grapple with.' 'Well,' Edgar continues, 'we are all pretty punch drunk at the moment with change after change. Just in our Division we have had to develop a Business Administration degree course in pretty short time and get it validated by the authority. It has taken a lot of manpower and time to get it through the national validation process. It would be so much easier if we could validate our own courses, so I can see what the Director is driving at when he has this Polytechnic goal.' Edgar then goes on to explain what he thinks will happen. 'Already we are in talks with a college in Ireland about it teaching our course for our qualification and I think there are others in the pipeline too.' Another subject he brings up is the possibility of having a module for the National Examining Board of Supervisory Studies. 'The Head of the Business School is still keen to get into the Leisure market,' Edgar says, 'see if you can do something to help him.'

His comments about validating our own courses makes perfect sense to me. We are increasing our own student numbers and making provision for them by building accommodation and new teaching rooms. Another way I can see of increasing numbers is to franchise the courses. Then they can be taught elsewhere without us having to increase our facilities. One problem will obviously be to ensure the quality of the delivery of the courses. The Director is anxious for me to get a teaching course up and running and I can see how this will fit into his overall plan.

This week's Times Higher Education Supplement carries advertisements for the proposed Deans positions. Careful scrutiny of the wording gives some indication of the type of management skills being sought. A cynic in the Refectory tells me, 'The only quality not mentioned is that of being subservient to the Director's every whim.' The Lies edition rewords the advertisement along similar lines to my cynical colleague. 'Willing to be downtrodden and overruled is a key quality required' it says in part.

I am relieved when the working week ends and I can concentrate on our next basketball match. The college team has had a good win in the local league in the week and I take this as a good omen. In particular a couple of the Greek players have combined well to form a formidable force on court. I only hope that Hampshire Hoops can play as well in our Founders Cup semi-final against Hounslow. I know that they are an experienced side and last year appeared in the Founders Cup final.

It is gratifying to see that despite my earlier reservations about the crowd not wanting to see one-way games, we have the largest number of spectators so far for this particular match. All the helpers are in fine form as they get the court and the surroundings ready for the game. There is a small hiccough about the Visitors Changing Room being ready in time. A couple of women are being awkward about getting out of the Changing Room, which is used for the visiting team. The centre's staff is sent in to hurry them up. We are told it is a couple of local Travellers who use the showers by entering the Changing Room without having used the sports centre at all for any activity. The group of Travellers had arrived and camped on a local playing field earlier in the week. However, the fuss is soon over with before our opponents arrive.

A close game is anticipated and indeed, in the first half, fortunes sway this way and that. We look a bit disorganised in defence and coupled with frustration at some of the refereeing decisions with just four minutes of the first half remaining we are only leading by four points. At this point, Mick introduces Eric into the game. He opens with a couple of long distance scores and as the Hounslow team has to move out to defend against his shooting, the other Hampshire players are freer to drive through and score from close range. Mick's action means that by half-time we are nineteen points ahead and the spectators are in full voice. In the end we win by fifty two points and strangely I do not have the feeling I had previously about one way games as a very contented crowd makes its way out of the arena. Eddie has contributed 46 of the 134 points scored and is in a fine mood in the bar afterwards. He approaches me and says, 'I am glad I changed my mind about playing. At first I thought that with no payment for playing I was not interested, but I can honestly say I have never enjoyed playing so much. The youngsters help. There are no prima donnas in the team like we used to have with some of the Americans and I really like the atmosphere.'

The next day Eddie is missing when we go to play Swindon Rakers. 'I told Eddie to rest,' says Mick. 'I am sure we can take care of Swindon without him.' I sit on the bench doing the odd jobs that are required like supplying towels and water to the players coming off court and watch as we virtually annihilate the hapless Swindon team allowing them to only score 35 points whilst we again pass the three figure mark with a now fit Jon scoring 25 of those points. I am glad it is not a home game because I think the crowd may feel let down by the opponent's lack of fight.

Back in the college on Monday I am immediately immersed in the debate about the future of the college. Once again it is Trevor who is holding forth. 'It is Thatcherism that is dictating what is happening here,' he rails, 'we are seeking to be entrepreneurial and diversifying to increase our sources of income. One way to do that is to increase our number of full cost international students. In most cases that would mean bringing more students here, but it looks like, if I am to believe what I hear, we are going to take our courses to the international students. I can see a lot of problems with that.' I wonder if Trevor has had a similar conversation to the one I had with Edgar a few days earlier.

CHAPTER NINE

Despite all that is happening at the college, it comes as a surprise to me when it is announced that our application to award degrees of our own has been rejected and we are to remain on the existing arrangement of a National Council control. We already have a few degrees that we are offering to both full and part-time students. These we will be able to franchise, presumably, subject to having some sort of quality control. However, we will need to increase our portfolio of courses considerably if we are to attract more students. I guess the Director is anxious to do just that and is constantly exhorting staff to be more ambitious in the courses they offer.

I am called in again to the Director. I begin to feel that he must suddenly come up with ideas that must be put into practice immediately without any period of gestation. 'I want to give teaching a higher, more co-ordinated profile,' he begins 'I want you to head up a, let's call it, a Unit. It will include yourself and the Media Resources team plus, perhaps, another member of staff. You will be charged with supporting the teaching and coming up with ideas to help students with their learning as well. I will make the post part of the Administration and give you a pay rise commensurate with your position. What do you think?' I immediately baulk at the idea of joining the Administration part of the college. 'If the post is to do with teaching, then I must remain in the Academic sector,' I say. 'There will, I feel, be resentment by the lecturing staff if they consider that they are being guided from an Administrative position. I know the support staff feel they are considered inferior but this has nothing to do with that. This is purely an academic matter, lecturers helping lecturers. In fact, if you want to put the Post Graduate Course in Teaching in place, I would need to be on the lecturing staff to deliver it, otherwise it will just look like a staff training course.' The Director shows no sign of how my remarks are being received. 'Let me think about it,' he says.

Later in the day, I am in the Staff Refectory when I am joined by Edgar who has come for a coffee. 'A bit of a blow not getting our own way to validate courses,' he begins, 'this just makes the process more convoluted. Luckily we have the Business Administration degree course on the stocks already for the next couple of years before it needs to be reviewed. Our section does not have much to do with that course, however, just supplying some of the social work aspects. We are still trying to get a Social Studies degree course together. We already deal with Social Workers with our short courses and we have co-opted some of the managers to help us flesh out a degree course. Other section heads are under pressure to come up with degree courses and I know some of them are baulking at the idea. They consider the service we provide to business and industry is best served by the way we do it currently. I don't think they like the idea of a lot of young people suddenly descending on the college.' I know that there are some of the staff who are looking forward to the challenge of teaching degree level students. 'Look at the Maths section,' I say, 'they have made lots of plans to get a degree off the ground. I guess we can see a rift arising between the old brigade and the newer members of staff.' 'The Director has had a lot to do with that,' continues Edgar, 'he has made it clear that new appointments must be done with an eye to increasing degree teaching. It is definitely a hands-on approach by him.'

It seems the Director must have been stung by the rejection of our application to be given our own degree awarding powers. It is almost as if he expected the rebuttal and already had a Plan B to put into immediate operation. The next edition of The Truth contains details of the major reorganisation of the college structure that we had been informed about earlier. Only now the Director uses those details to demonstrate how importantly the changes are needed, citing the recent rejection of degree awarding powers as the reason. He also takes the opportunity to announce a new appointment to be in charge of the Administration Service which is now to be called the Registry. The actual position of the new role was not as yet named.

Trevor is immediately in full flow when I return to the office after one of my teaching sessions. 'We've had all this before,' he says, 'when we amalgamated with the local Art College which took place at the same time as the Director was appointed. We had our own Acting Principal then. Our Principal had retired a year before and the local authority had appointed an Acting Principal from within the college. The Art Principal then retired but in between we were taken out of local authority control. The governors appointed our current Director to head both establishments. Once the new Director had decided on his own title, the Acting Principal did not want the title of Assistant Director and insisted on keeping the Acting Principal title. He only lasted a year before being eased out.

I know only a little of these goings on. Referring to the new unnamed post, 'It seems logical to call the role that of Registrar,' I comment.   'I doubt if logic will enter into it with this Director,' Trevor concludes.

I get a 'phone call in the evening from Brian. 'We are all ready to go in the summer with our team. I had originally thought of hiring an outdoor court, but now I see that there is an unofficial summer competition running at one of the outdoor courts. I have said we will enter that and if we think it worthwhile we can consider entering the local league next season.' 'I'll have to think about that,' I reply, 'I will still be coaching the college team and there may be a clash of interest.' Brian then adds another detail. 'We may struggle to raise a team from time to time and I was thinking how your access to hundreds of students might be able to help us out.' I laugh and tell him I will consider it, but let's get the summer out of the way first and see how that goes. I must admit that I am looking forward to playing with my friends again.

Basketball is again on my mind when the weekend comes. It is a home game against Camberley and a win will put us within reach of the league title because it now looks as if our opponents are our main rivals. Mick tells me that Mike is unavailable having, of all things, caught chicken pox. So he will not be at the game. Marie who has been on the door issuing tickets for the game informs me, just before the start, that we have the largest attendance of the season. Once again it is the introduction of Eric with his long range accurate shooting that helps us to a 19 point half time lead. The crowd are aware of the importance of a win and when the game ends there is a huge cheer. The supporters know we have won the league. Everyone in the bar is talking in a loud voice and the atmosphere is electric. Gone are the doldrums of last season when we exited the National League. We have managed to keep a professional approach to the presentation of the matches thanks to the return to the whole arena for the games.

The final league game of the season has to be played the following Wednesday evening. Ironically it is a midweek game, despite there being so few league fixtures overall. This game will confirm our title and mean that we will be going to Melton Mowbray to play in a weekend competition against the winners of the other seven Regional Leagues in Division Four. Swindon Rakers are never in the game which is played in front of a smaller crowd than the game of the previous weekend. In fact Eddie, who had not played in the away game against Swindon, is on fire and scores 51 points of his own, threatening the club record of point scoring in a game. The Swindon coach is devastated at his team's poor performance and chooses to comment to Mick,

'You shouldn't be in this league.' His own team has not won a game in the entire season. This is his second large defeat in a few weeks against us. Obviously he feels that his team have been demoralised by having to play against such strong opponents. Mick, on the other hand, is delighted that his mainly young, local players have come on so well in the season. They are about to be put to the ultimate test with the National Play-Offs and, prior to that, the home and away Founders Cup Final which will be against Liverpool.

There is now more information forthcoming about new appointments at the college. Someone is joining us from a local authority role to become the Head of Finance. Once this is announced, the academic staff conjecture that the Administration of the college is to be conducted by Heads of various functions like Personnel, Building Services, Marketing and so on. It looks as if the General Office staff is going to be split up into smaller units. My experience of the General Office has always been one where the, mainly female, staff members formed a happy cohort and I wonder what they will think of working in much smaller groups. Jacqui, for one, tells me that she believes it is not a good move. 'We all get on so well, it seems a shame to separate us,' she moans.

The recently designated Schools will be run autonomously, it seems. Quite a few changes will be necessary to make them function efficiently. Already some staff are jostling for the newly created roles in the Schools. On the other hand, the academic Union officials are scrutinising any move the Director makes with a view to questioning the motives. 'He is hiding behind the necessity to achieve Polytechnic status,' Don says to me, 'but I smell a rat. Divide and rule I think is the name of his game. It may even be an opportunity for him to get rid of some of the established staff who have not been convinced by his push for financial gain.'

Having cultivated a resistance to the vicissitudes of others, I cannot bring myself to get involved in the politics. The Director has already given me a role, although he still has not come back to me about my request to stay on the academic staff. I think it best not to mention my negotiations with the Director. Don has enough on his plate without my situation. I will only involve the Union if the Director persists in trying to get me to join the Administrative staff.

In any case, I have to devote some of my energy to the forthcoming basketball Founders Cup final. I hire the minibus and, for once, the trip will be like the old days in the National League. Liverpool is well outside the area we have been playing in the Regional League. We played against them some eleven seasons ago when they formed an alliance with Warrington but since then our only meeting was the following season when we beat them in the National Trophy final.

Our current team only has two members from that squad, Ken and Eddie. I drive the minibus, sharing the duty with Mick. I remind Mick of the time he let me down with his drinking at the darts match in some village or other's pub. 'We will stick to the motorway services,' he says. 'In any case it will be late when we return, so there will be no chance of any alcoholic drink.' On arrival at the Liverpool court the team leave the minibus to go into the court. I am getting the team kit bag out of the minibus when some urchin approaches. 'I wouldn't leave the bus unguarded,' he says, 'you won't have any hub caps when you come out.' I wonder if he wants some money to guard the minibus, but I dismiss the idea and take the kit into the hall.

Since their breakaway from Warrington, the Liverpool club has sought to do the kind of thing that Hampshire Hoops is undertaking. Like us, they now play outside the National league, hence our meeting in the Founders Cup final. Their playing arena is basic and there are few spectators, in part because there is little room for anyone wanting to watch.

There is little ceremony before the start of the game and the whole event from a presentation point of view, bearing in mind it is a national final, is underwhelming.

For the match, we are fortunate that Mike has overcome his chicken pox to return and that we are at full strength. We miss several early lay-ups and I am concerned that nerves might have taken over. However, three quick baskets by Jon take us to a twelve point lead and force the Liverpool coach to call a time-out. The home team is always playing catch-up as the Hampshire Hoops squad show they are in no mood to be denied this first leg victory. The highlight of the second half is a thirty foot defence splitting pass by Toby to Jon who then puts the ball above the basket for Mike to dunk. We win by twenty three points which we will take as a lead back for the home game. I have the usual administrative dilemma, will people want to turn out to watch what, I hope, will be a non-event? However, I do not express this view to Mick who is in the changing room with a jubilant team. We call in at Leicester Forest East Services on our journey home.

We are approaching the Easter break on the courses I teach when I introduce the notion of micro lessons which will be caught on video. Those involved will be able to take their video home for the week. 'We reuse the videos,' I explain to the group, 'so there is no chance that you will receive a blackmail threat in years to come.' The joke is well received by both groups, although I know that the thought of being filmed is not well received. I tell them that the lesson must last about fifteen minutes and include all the facets of teaching that we have learned, including the objectives of the lesson, the content and some form of assessment. 'You can choose any topic you like,' I tell the groups, 'it can be something you usually teach or something completely different, like a hobby or skill.'

At college, Henrietta, one of the General Studies staff with whom I still share an office, tells me of her next event she has organised. 'I don't see your name amongst the staff list who are coming to the Cheese and Wine Party in the Staff Common Room tomorrow night,' she says. I try to bluster my way out of the situation. 'I can never commit to evening events in the basketball season because we so often have matches, sometimes rearranged.' 'Have you got one tomorrow?' she persists. I have to admit there is not a game and also it is not a training night for the Hoops. 'Then, you can come,' she concludes. Henrietta I know, spends all her waking life organising events for the college, whether it is lunchtime concerts, trips to the theatre, directing student plays and a host of other things. I admire her tenacity when I know she is working against the current culture of staff feeling which, to describe it mildly, is not pro-college. The changes being wrought are having a deleterious effect on a lot of the staff members and most usually say when being invited to any staff event that they have other things to do. I buy a ticket from Henrietta but think that I will keep my options open should something else come up.

So it is that I find myself in the Staff Common Room with a group of other staff some of whom who have brought their husbands and wives. As usual, it is a male dominated occasion because of people like myself who are male and form the large majority of the staff. I am introduced to Pete's wife. 'Oh, you are the one he goes drinking with all the time,' she soon mentions. I protest, 'My basketball life does not leave me much time to do that.' Pete takes me aside. 'Just play along with her,' he pleads, 'I must admit to using your name sometimes when I have to go out or come back late from college.' This, I guess, is one of the prices you pay for being a bachelor. People feel free to use your name, guessing that you probably have no social life of your own. I have to admit to myself that he is safe to do so because, apart from basketball activities I do not have a social life. I don't think I can count the evenings I spent going out to observe someone teaching to be a social activity. I return to Pete's wife. 'I'm sorry if I keep him from you too often,' I say, 'but, as you know, I have no family duties. I will make sure he has your permission next time I suggest a drink.' I will talk to Pete later about what he gets up to.

I am surprised to see Graeme at the event. He had not mentioned it to me at any time when we were together in the previous weeks. 'Have you brought along your wife?' I query. 'No, she doesn't like these sort of occasions,' he replies. 'In any case she lives quite a way from here. I have a small studio flat and just go back at weekends. With the longer holidays we get, it works out alright.' We chat for a few minutes and then he says, 'Well, I guess I had better mix.' He moves off and is soon is conversation with Sally, who lectures in his section. I can't help but notice that every time I see him he is still at Sally's side. So much for mixing, I think.

Before leaving I seek out Henrietta and thank her for organising the event. I tell her it has given me the chance to talk to colleagues I rarely see. I notice no one from the Administration Services is present. The Party has obviously been restricted to academic staff and I can see a wedge being driven further into the fissure between the academic and support staff. I decide not to mention this to Henrietta.

CHAPTER TEN

The next big event in my life is the return Founders Cup Final match against Liverpool. My reservation about people not wanting to come to a game where we already hold a commanding lead seems to be without foundation. Over 600 spectators turn up. In a way, I am pleased for the opposition because it cannot be many times that they play in front of such a large crowd in a large arena. The game is not a classic as we barely move into top gear to win by a further twenty seven points. The second half becomes scrappy and more physical with Mike, of all players, being fouled out with ten minutes remaining. A happy feature for the coach is that nine out of the ten players get on the scoresheet in the game.   On the night top scorer Jon is named Man of the Match. He is also Runner Up in the Player of the Year Award which had been voted for by fans at the previous home game. The crowd's favourite is Eddie. Now we have the Play Off Championship to look forward to in a couple of weeks' time.

This will take place over a weekend and will mean staying in a hotel overnight. My concern is centred around funds. I ask Marie if we have anything in the kitty to help cover the hotel expenses. She promises to give me the information the next day. Dave is sure that we will be able to cover the costs.

Back on the teaching course, the micro lessons sessions are going well. Jack, from the Royal Navy, gives a session on naval flag recognition. He does not attempt to pass on too much information and finishes with a quick question and answer test administered verbally. Carmen from the typing school uses her time to explain the keyboard and tests the group with a keypad where some of the letters are missing. Alan, a plumber, teaches how to wire a plug. He gives out four plugs for group work and his test is to identify where the earth, neutral and live wires go. All of them illustrate their teaching with the use of acetates on the overhead projector.

Whilst I am encouraged by the sessions, I have a setback when I go to see Kay for a teaching session in a Care Home setting. I realise the problems with trying to teach something to older people, and this is my first experience of visiting a Care Home. I pass a group of people sitting in armchairs who do not look very well at all. Several are fast asleep despite it only being two o'clock in the afternoon. I am encouraged to see that Kay's group looks more alert. There are eight in the group and they are sitting in a circle. Kay does not bother to introduce me and I take my place at the side of the room. The feature that disturbs me is that Kay, in her haste to explain the different types of crochet ignores some of the basic tenets we have been discussing on the course. She fails to ask about the experience of the group with crocheting. Even worse, I consider, she explains about another type of crocheting and illustrates her point with an example. This is good, I think, but she then goes on to mention other types which she also has examples of. In no time at all four samples are being passed round the group whilst she is still talking about crocheting and illustrating features of the next specimen. So she is dividing the attention of the group and paying no heed to the necessity of keeping the process simple. I decide not to debrief her after the session, which those taking part in said they had thoroughly enjoyed. It would seem a shame to criticise her in what, for her, had probably been a tense situation with me sitting in the room.

Another observation this week is one of the Intensive Care nurses. She is going to teach a small group of nurses how to turn a patient on a bed. We start off in a small room where she explains the theory. She stresses that the nurses should talk to the patient in a normal voice as they undertake the procedure. 'Although they may appear unresponsive, it may be that they are taking everything in,' she says. We then move to the Intensive Care ward for the student nurses to actually turn someone on a bed. I think that this is probably the ultimate in assessment. The atmosphere in the ward is one of quiet reverence and the nurses begin the process. Everything is going well when suddenly we are assailed by very loud talking. Two women have entered to visit a man several beds away. They have not been the recipient of the good advice taught by my student and proceed to talk in a very loud voice to the comatose man they are visiting. My nurse detaches herself from the group and goes to have a word with them and they soon quieten down. In the debrief I mention the incident and she says, 'It is not uncommon for that to happen. Visitors think they have to shout to make themselves heard. They were probably told not to speak too loudly but it is such a temptation when you are getting no response.'

My college basketball team completes the season with a win and we finish third in the league. Yannis, an ever present player for the team, is voted as next season's captain. He tells me his parents are coming over soon from Greece to see his college. I ask him to let me know when they are here so I can recount to them about the part he has played in the basketball team. 'I think my father is not only coming to see me,' he explains, 'there is some business interest he wants to discuss with the college.'

With all the activity I have undertaken in the last two weeks, I suddenly realise that it is the weekend of the Championship Play Offs in a few days. Dave has been good to his word and six rooms have been booked at a hotel on the outskirts of Leicester. There had been no accommodation in Melton Mowbray, probably because we had been slow off the mark to book anywhere. I will be sharing with Mick and the players will pair off. I go to the last practice session to be greeted with bad news. 'Jon will be unable to play because of a viral illness and Eddie has a twisted ankle,' Mick gloomily relates to me.

Two days later we are on our way in cars to Melton Mowbray. With eight teams involved there is much activity at the Sports arena where the games will take place. The eight finalists have been grouped in two pools of four. The games are of shorter duration than normal games, bearing in mind each team will play three times on the Saturday. Our first opponents are a team from Nottingham. To make matters worse, we are told that they had won the title in the previous season. Eddie has made the trip and is anxious to play, but Mick decides to rest him as much as possible on the first day. Nottingham, surprisingly, prove no match for us. In addition, a couple of players seem to lose control and we are awarded a succession of free throws for technical fouls. Eric, as usual, scores each one.

In the second game, against City of Leeds, Marc, who has been nearly an ever present in the team for the season, plays out of his skin in defence to deny the opponents many easy scoring opportunities. It is another comfortable win and Eddie has been spared trying out his ankle. It is early evening when we play our last game. This is against Flaxman, who had won the Central London League. These prove our hardest opponents restricting us to just a two point half time lead. Mick decides it is time to let Eddie onto the court and hope his ankle will stand up to the strain. Ten quick points just after half time with Toby scoring eight of them put us in a commanding position which we do not relinquish.

Mick and I then go to a local launderette which has been pointed out to us whilst the players head off to the hotel. We join them later on and persuade the players that they need an early night bearing in mind a semi-final in the morning followed, we hope, by a final in the afternoon. What has seemed a most successful day is followed in the morning by what so nearly can be described as a disaster.

We have planned to leave the hotel at half past nine. I walk out to my car at nine o'clock to fetch a paper where I have completed some of the crossword. I immediately notice a smashed quarter light window. The car has been broken into and the kit, which we had washed the night before, is gone. It is the only item in the car and had been left on the back seat, not out of sight in the boot. I rush back in with the news. We realise that the thieves will probably be disappointed with the contents of the bag and so set out to search the local area, which has a lot of woodland. We find items scattered around and eventually have all the vests but only nine pairs of shorts. The bag, too, is missing. All of this delays us leaving the hotel and we arrive at the arena with minutes to spare.

Our opponents are Liverpool, who we have so recently played against. Jon has arrived to give us support having been driven up by a friend. He had telephoned the hotel the night before to talk to some of the players, so knew we had a morning game. The game is a close one. At one point in the second half the scores are tied. Mike is proving a tower of strength on court with his rebounding ability and he even scores some vital points. The pressure gets to Ken who shortly before the end is charged with a technical foul for disputing a referee's call. This gives Liverpool possession of the ball with little time left and trailing by just two points. However, they miss their shot, Mike rebounds and hurls the ball upcourt to Eddie who makes the game safe with a basket. We are in the Final and our opponents will be Warley who have comfortably disposed of all their opponents.

Eddie is complaining of a sore ankle and Mick uses him sparingly in the first half of the final. We struggle to stay in touch with Warley and are five points down at half time. It is a defence dominated game, aided by nervousness in shooting by both sides. Eventually we gain the upper hand by denying our opponents any scoring for seven minutes whilst we score at regular intervals. In the end it is a nine point win for us with Toby being declared Man of the Match. We have lifted our third trophy for the season and now just await the news that we will be elected to join the National League.

This confirmation comes a couple of weeks later, and Dave immediately calls a meeting. He has asked Mick along also to tell us the player situation for next season. Once, that would have been a conversation about replacing one or more of the Americans. But now that is no longer the case. 'The college player is leaving but all the others will still be around,' he begins, 'I have my eye on an experienced player who is leaving his present club, according to rumour. There is also an American who is based over here for another year. He would be expensive to register but at least we wouldn't have to pay to his travel and accommodation costs. I would have to be sure about his playing, though. At the moment I only have someone's recommendation.' Dave then turns to affairs of sponsorship and the day to day running of the club. I pledge my continued support.

Once I was footloose and fancy free, and that was just over a year ago. Now the noose seems to be tightening. As well as the promise I have just given at the meeting, I have to attend to matters at the college that look as if they will mean a complete change of lifestyle.

I have spent some time looking into what I think the content of the module for the Supervisory Studies for Leisure should include. The staff at the centre where we play our games have been a good sounding board and coupled with my knowledge of recent research findings about leisure time management, I think I have devised a workable module which I submit in the first case to Edgar so that he can look it over. He later telephones me to say that the Head of Management would like to include the module and would I be willing to teach it for two hours a week?

It is with trepidation that once again I approach the Director's office having received a message to come and see him. 'I have given some thought to your idea of staying as a lecturing service and see that it makes sense,' he begins. 'More than that, I want you now to put yourself about a bit. Visit other universities and Polytechnics to find out best practice for training lecturing staff and supporting students. Once your courses are finished, you will have more time to gain information. I will give you a budget for your new section with the Media Resources and suggest that you employ a secretary. I have just made a new appointment in the Administration. He will need a secretary also, but not full-time. I have already suggested to him that he might share with you. I will locate you both in your offices next to one another so a shared secretary should work. How is the Post Graduate course coming on?' I tell him about the Standing Conference on Educational Development. 'Excellent,' he comments, 'make sure you join the movement and keep tabs on the latest thinking.' Finally he gives me a further detail, 'Your Unit will be unique in that it will sit outside the three Schools and any Administrative section. You will be directly responsible to me until we have the Post Graduate Course up and running. Then we will have to think about which of the Schools we can put you in.'

Once again my head is reeling as I leave the Director's office. This move could leave me outside any of the protection offered by the lecturing Union and I will have no link to the Administration should things go wrong. Also I have now to appoint a secretary, well, a half secretary. I had better get in touch with the new appointee the Director had mentioned.

A couple of days later I manage to track down the new member of staff. He apologises for being so elusive. 'I have just moved down from London and am staying in a small hotel,' he says. 'I have been getting my things down from where I was and trying to find room to accommodate them.

I am also looking for somewhere to live. At the moment I have stuff all over the place.' 'I think I can help you with a cabinet to store things,' I explain. 'I teach in a classroom in the corner of the building and since last September there has been a large filing cabinet in the corner. The name on the cabinet drawers is someone who died over a year ago whilst working here. I have looked in the unlocked cabinet and it is full of his files in one drawer but the other three are mainly empty. I will ask Danny, the maintenance man, to move it to your new office.'

George-Henry, for that is how he introduces himself, is grateful. We discuss our requirement for a joint-secretary. 'My job entails a lot of memos and letters, so typing and shorthand are paramount skills,' he says. I find I cannot be so specific saying, 'He or she will have to run a booking system for Media Resources equipment and eventually, because I have been charged with getting a Post Graduate course up and running, I, too, will be looking for typing skills. Now you know my requirements are you able to get a job specification together and take it to Personnel?' I ask. George-Henry agrees to do just that. 'I will let you have sight of it before I take it to Personnel,' he promises.

Graeme and I begin to put the pressure on our course members to get their portfolios containing their assignments and course handouts together. Most of the teaching observations have now been concluded and, save for my crochet experience, have been generally satisfactory. One of the last micro lessons by Joanne, one of the hairdressers, is about the braking distances at various speeds for cars. She has made ingenious use of the overhead projector and the class has been full of praise for her efforts. They say that anyone about to take their driving test would benefit from this lesson.

Bob, the member of the college staff who had been on the course, takes an opportunity to talk to me after one of the sessions. 'I've really enjoyed the course,' he begins, 'not just for meeting such a cross section of people, either. I think some of the other staff I know ought to have something similar. One group of students on a Chemical Engineering course has just complained. Apparently, they timed the lecturer's presence in the laboratory for the hour's session at just twelve minutes. The rest of the time he was in the small room off the laboratory. They felt that they needed more guidance and oversight doing their various projects.'

I explain to Bob what the Director has in mind for the future and how this present course will be handed over to the Technical College. 'Good luck to you,' is all he can say.

CHAPTER ELEVEN

I make contact with the External Examiner over the telephone. 'Just send me your Pass Lists and I will countersign them,' he says. 'Surely, you want to come and see the groups?' I say. 'Normally, yes,' comes the reply. 'However, I am retiring this year and there is a lot of clearing up for me to do at this end. My contract expires at the end of the month. I could see if anyone else could visit,' he adds. 'But you are the nominated External Assessor with City and Guilds,' I reply, 'surely they would not take the word of someone else?' 'That is why I say that you should just submit the lists to me,' he repeats. I can see I am getting nowhere with this debate and end the telephone call. I feel for the students on the course. Some, I am sure, will want interest to be shown in how they have done. I will have to think of a strategy to assure them that their work will be reviewed by an external source.

Despite all that is happening in my life, or perhaps because of all that is happening, my thoughts turn to the forthcoming vacation. One feature of my job that I had not planned for is the length of the summer vacations in higher education. I know the theories put forward about research time and attendance at Conferences to keep up-to-date with developments in chosen subject areas. However, in the first years for me, there have been no pressures of that sort. I must admit it came as a surprise at the end of my first year when the students started leaving at the beginning of June. I had no exams to mark or Exam Boards to attend. In effect, there was nothing to do. That same situation has lasted until this year when now I am involved in marking and Exam Boards. It seems, however, that my foray into Exam Boards will be to send a list of recommendations by letter to the external assessor. In a way, I feel let down having no one to show any interest in how my courses have done. Set against that, the Director has now taken that course out of my hands and given it to another college so perhaps I don't need any feedback about the course at all.

I can see my life changing as more responsibility is being put on me by the Director. This summer, I guess, will be spent visiting other colleges, seeing if there is any Conference that will be of value and preparing the syllabus for the Post Graduate Certificate in Teaching in Higher Education. Before that, I determine, I will have one last period of holiday to get away from everything. One last chance to be foot loose and fancy free, I think. I begin to look at the options and come up with the notion of driving Route 66 in America.

My love affair with the United States had begun some fifteen years ago. I had trained as a teacher of physical education and taught, by then, in two different secondary schools. There had been no family ties for me to consider when looking for a job. My foster parents had both died. I had a steady girlfriend back then. We had met in the town where I was at college. It looked, at one stage, as if we might get together but suddenly she cut me out of her life and took up with someone else. I was distraught, to say the least, having no inkling about what was about to happen. In the same week, whilst in the staffroom I was looking through the Times Educational Supplement when I came across an advert for the Teacher Exchange Programme with the USA. Probably because of what had just happened I went to the Headmaster and asked him if he would be agreeable to me applying for the scheme. He was quite happy to do that and so I wrote, that night, to the British Council, who administered the scheme, for an application form.

Fate is a fickle thing. Normally the applicant is a family member and expecting to be matched with a lone male for physical education was a long shot. Quite often the exchange includes homes and cars. Whilst I have both, albeit only a flat rather than a home, it lessens my chances even more, I think, because no way could a family live in my accommodation.

We had a visit at the school over the next month from someone who was coming to inspect an aspect of the school. All the staff members were on edge and made efforts to show their courses at their best. A lot of preparation went into various parts of the school programme and even the caretakers put in more effort to keep the school spick and span. When the day came, a lady arrived and spent the time with me. The visit had been part of the vetting process for my application. Needless to say, once the rest of the staff realised the efforts they had put in were for nothing, I was not very popular.

Eventually, to my surprise, I was matched with a teacher from Valley Stream, New York. Looking on the map, I saw that Valley Stream was right next to Queens, a borough of New York City, and close to Kennedy Airport.

That year had changed my life but one result was that I frequently went back to the States. At the end of the year I was there I had travelled extensively. That trip plus a lot of other visits meant that I was familiar with many places. However, I had never driven Route 66 and, as it looked like my future holidays would be much shorter, I decide that his will be a suitable swan song.

A visit to a local travel agent and I have booked a three week trip starting in Chicago and driving to Los Angeles. This trip will take care of most of June, so I begin my research to find out about organisations which might be able to help me with the role the Director has assigned. I come across an organisation called The First Year Experience and make a note to follow this up in the future. In the meantime I must get as much information about the Standing Conference on Educational Development as possible.

With the basketball season concluded I have more time on my hands. Brian gets in touch again about the team he is putting together for this unofficial outdoor summer league. 'I hope my knees are up to it,' I tell him. 'Matches on concrete courts are much harder on the joints than the sprung wooden floors.' I have to tell him, also, that I will not be available until the end of June. 'You will miss the first two games, then,' he says, 'but we have four more after that in July.'

I want to see the Director again, but his secretary tells me that he has gone off to Malaysia to discuss a franchise with some colleges over there. 'He won't be back for three weeks,' she says. My business will have to wait until July.

There is just one more teaching observation visit to make. It is at a local cottage hospital and it is to see the physiotherapist that is on the college course. She has arranged a small group to be taught some massage techniques. I drive to the venue and park my car. The student concerned comes over to me whilst I am getting out of my car. She seems distressed. 'It has taken me a lot of arranging to make today possible,' she says. 'The hospital have been very good and allowed me to use their facilities and I have spent a lot of time persuading local physiotherapists to attend. I have just been told by the hospital switchboard operator that the person I was going to use as a body for the session has rung up to say he cannot come. I will have to cancel.' Her distress was palpable. I have an idea. 'What if I take his place,' I say. So it is that I spend the next hour being pounded by a group of people I do not know. From my point of view, I can now offer feedback from a complete perspective.

Graeme and I tie up all the loose ends at the conclusion of our courses. He has been mainly concerned with the college course but has helped out on the occasional teaching observations of the nurses. Like me, most of the time he does not know the procedures that are being taught by the nurses but as long as the correct approach to the lesson is taken, we have to be quite content. Graeme observes, 'What is being taught could kill the patient, but as long as the lesson plan is submitted and the teaching is done to good practice, we will be satisfied.' I have to agree.

We never do meet the external assessor from Reading but all the paperwork is in order. We gloss over the fact that the students' work that they have provided has been assessed by no one other than Graeme and myself. I am pleased that we will have nothing more to do with this programme. I have enjoyed teaching it, but have felt quite isolated from the process because of the lack of contact with the external examiner. I wonder how many other courses are concluded in such a laissez faire style.

Barbara calls me for one more meeting of the English Nursing Board who are devising their own teaching course. I have enjoyed giving input to their meetings. Barbara takes me aside after the meeting. 'There is going to be a lot of work that could come your way,' she says. 'Education is a hot topic right now and there will be a lot of courses that might be of interest to the college. You have social studies and community courses already. We will not have the expertise to cover a lot of the way things are going at the moment with community involvement. We could franchise a lot of the work to you,' she concludes. 'I will certainly mention it to the Director,' I say, 'when he returns from his visit to the Far East.'

There are the usual collections for members of staff who are retiring or leaving. The atmosphere in the college has not lightened. Most of those leaving openly admit that they are glad to be going. The older hands, in particular, are scathing in some of their comment about the college and its approach to the growing numbers of students and the emphasis being placed on finance in our bid to become a Polytechnic. The students have mainly gone now, but Yannis from the basketball team comes to my office. 'My parents will be here tomorrow,' he says. 'Well, if he wants to see the Director he will be unlucky,' I reply bearing in mind an earlier conversation. 'He knows that,' Yannis comments, 'but he has arranged to talk to someone, I gather,' he says.

I have two days before my holiday in America begins. Yannis appears again at my office the following morning, accompanied by his parents. I take them down to the Staff Refectory. There is a corner with comfortable seating which we make for. My first impression of the parents of Yannis is that they are probably quite well off. Certainly the mother is festooned with jewels and looks quite out of place in our humble Refectory. His father is well-dressed and looks to have an expensive suit and shoes. In contrast, I feel quite plainly clothed. We speak about the basketball team and I am told how much Yannis has enjoyed playing and that it is often a topic of conversation when he is at home with tales of various matches. After a while, his father turns the conversation to more business like matters. 'I believe you are beginning to operate in other countries,' he says. 'Are you involved in that?' he queries. 'Not at the moment,' I reply, 'although the Director has intimated that I might be required to check on the quality of teaching at some point or other.'

'I have arranged to see a lecturer from Yannis's course,' the father continues, 'I will have a proposition to put to the college and I want to see the reaction from the authority. If it is favourable, I will return in the summer. Yannis still has one year left on his course.' By chance one of the staff who teaches on the Craft courses arrives for a coffee. Soon he is in deep conversation with the father and I make my excuses and leave.

I have left my preparation for my Route 66 trip rather late. I go into a bookstore and find just the thing I need. Lonely Planet has issued a book about Route 66 which seems to contain all the information I want. It refers in the introduction to the Mother Road of John Steinbeck's *Grapes of Wrath*, a book I had read years before and a film I had also seen. I begin immediately to look forward to the opportunity of seeing the route for myself. I am gratified to read that one should plan for two weeks to do the trip and early June is a good time. Chicago, the starting point, here I come.

CHAPTER TWELVE

I arrive at Chicago's O'Hare International Airport in the early afternoon and after the tedious immigration procedures I make my way to the baggage carousel to pick up my bag. Most of the carousel is filled with cases, some of which are seemingly very heavy. My soft sports bag looks out of place amongst such expensive looking, matching luggage. A lady nearby sees me haul my bag off and says to me, 'Travelling light, I see.' I laugh it off by saying the bag contains all my worldly possessions.

I make my way to the Transit Authority train station where I will get a subway train to my destination in central Chicago. My travel agent has booked a couple of nights for me in a hotel and I have the name of the station where I must get off.

The hotel I check in to is an anodyne place. It has all that is required for a hotel stay but nothing to make it memorable. My room is on the tenth floor and I have a good view of the city and can even see Lake Michigan. Because of the time difference, it is still only early evening. I have to remember that for me it is five hours later and I had a very early start from home. The sensible thing to do will be to go to bed for a good night's sleep. I find myself drawn to the hotel bar and order what I know will be a gassy beer. I look around for someone to talk to but there is no single person available only a couple of small groups who, by their chatter and laughing, I guess know each other. Finally, good sense prevails and I go to my room.

I have never been to Chicago before and seek out an Information Centre there being no concierge at my hotel. As a result of that visit, I plan to see a few things in my short stay. The first is a visit to Grant Park. It is a lovely day and I feel I want to be in the open air. The area of the park is big and it contains many items of interest, mainly sculptures some of which are very large. I use my camera to capture the ones I want to remember. I am conscious that it will be easy to take too many pictures and must reign in my natural instinct to photograph everything.

Moving on from the park I walk to the entrance of the Navy Pier. This is a large edifice which protrudes into Lake Michigan. It is a fascinating place containing a Tiffany Glass Museum and a domed tropical garden area, not to mention an outdoor fairground which has a large big wheel and a huge swimming pool. I have a coffee in the tropical garden and, by chance, come across the lady who had commented on my luggage. She tells me she is in Chicago to attend a conference. It is her first time, too, and she is taking in as many sights as possible before the conference begins. Joan is her name and she works for IBM. 'People say that the initials are for I'm Being Moved,' she says, 'I sometimes feel that way because of the meetings and conferences I have to attend. For instance, I am only here for three days,' she says. This is my chance to get my own back about the luggage. 'I thought from what you were picking up from the carousel that you were emigrating here.' She has the good grace to laugh. I find out where she is staying and arrange to meet her later at her hotel using as an excuse that mine had nothing going for it and say, 'I am sure your hotel which is also being used for the conference will be a much nicer place.'

I have just one more place to visit. To get there I take a river boat. I am told that every March 17th green dye is put in the river to celebrate St. Patrick's Day. I know from my time in New York City that St. Patrick's Day is a big deal having once been in Fifth Avenue as a parade had passed me by on that date and I had marvelled at the large number of police in the march. Soon I arrive at my destination which is Sears Tower. Once the world's tallest building it still is quite breathtaking to look out from its Skydeck over the city and the lake. There is also a wealth of information on various noticeboards about its construction as well as guidance about the views and what you can see.

At the appointed time I am in Joan's hotel at the bar. My guess about the hotel had been correct. This is a real hotel capable of dealing with any situation. The bar, for instance, is alive with people. Most could be conference attendees, probably. It would be possible, I think, to have more than one conference here at the same time. I am conscious that I am wearing almost the same clothes that I arrived in. When Joan arrives, dressed completely differently from how I had previously seen her, I say, 'I thought you may not recognise me so I didn't change for dinner.' Again, she laughs.

We agree to go to a restaurant that is outside the hotel. I consult my Guide book. 'There are several Pizzerias recommended,' I say. 'That will be fine,' comes the reply. We take a taxi to one of the recommendations. It is busy, but that comes as no surprise. A table is found for us. It is close to other tables and, I guess, that is what atmosphere is all about. I worry that I will know more of what is being said at an adjoining table than my own. Joan is soft spoken. However, my fears are unfounded and soon we are exchanging details about our lives. She has a male partner but it seems the arrangement is a very loose one. No children are involved because both, it seems, are career oriented. They had made the decision some time ago and stuck to it. For my part, I concentrate on my job and try to steer the conversation to my forthcoming trip. However, I let slip, at some stage, about my American exchange to New York. Immediately, Joan is on my case. 'You must tell me all about New York,' she insists. I find that I am now doing most of the talking which is not what I wanted to do.

On returning to the hotel, we head for the bar. I am now calculating my next step. This is made easier when Joan says, 'Do you want to come to my room? It is on the fortieth floor has a magnificent view.' I need no second invitation.

The room, indeed, does have a fabulous view, made all the better by the twinkling lights of the city. I can recognise Grant Park and the Navy Pier and see the vast expanse of Lake Michigan. 'I did not need to pay to go up Sears Tower,' I say. 'this view is just as good. Also, it has the additional bonus that there is another lovely view closer to hand.' 'Flattery will get you everywhere,' Joan replies. This, I realise is going to be an unexpected bonus to my trip. I had hoped that perhaps I might meet an American female with whom I could relax. I had not anticipated someone closer to where I lived. I find out just how loose the arrangement is between Joan and her partner. It is nearly two in the morning before I make my way back to my own hotel. Joan knows that I will soon be on my way to the other side of the continent. We make no further plans to continue our relationship once we are both back in England.

My hotel room telephone rings and I am informed that my car has been delivered and there is some paperwork to be completed. I go down to the lobby and meet the car agent. He knows my itinerary because it is a one-way hire, or rental as he says. 'I really think that you would enjoy the trip far more if you had a bigger car. We have a special deal at the moment which will only add five dollars a day.' I am persuaded. An hour later a larger car in the Cadillac range is brought to me.

The journey begins as I find my way out of Chicago joining the Interstate 55 at exit 277. Three exits later I pull off the major road and take the first of many Frontage Roads. These roads follow the course of Route 66 in many States and I soon get used to the idea of driving on what I consider a normal two lane road whilst alongside me cars and trucks whizz along the main highway. At first I am concerned that the trip may all be like this but soon I am out of sight of the Interstate and begin to get the feel of the start of an adventure. The guidebook I had purchased in England before the trip describes the main feature of each small town that I drive through. There are many preserved pieces of evidence from the earlier years, especially gas stations. Because I have the guidebook I feel I do not have to note all of the features I see, although occasionally I stop to take a photograph. One photo I definitely want is of the huge Paul Bunyon statue in Atlanta, Illinois. Shortly after, I am passing Lincoln which is named after the President, who was a lawyer here. Allegedly Lincoln christened the town by spitting water melon seeds on the ground, I read. Already, even after only a few hours, I am beginning to realise what Route 66 means to the Americans. There are constant reminders that this is the road you are travelling on. Eventually I reach my first scheduled stop, a hotel in the capital Springfield, that I have prebooked. I wonder if I may have made a mistake when I see a large number of motorbikes in the car park.

On registering I am told the bikes belong to the police and that there is a meeting the following day to be held at the hotel. Although it is late afternoon, I want to visit the state capitol if possible. On reaching the entrance, I am told it is closing time. However, detecting my English accent, one of the guards takes pity on me and she says, 'I am about to lock up the various sections. You can come with me, if you want.' The guard is a black woman who is definitely overweight but has a sense of humour and a generous spirit, taking me around as she is. I see all the relevant tourist bits and have an added bonus of some of the off-limit sights too. In fact, when we get to the Governor's Office she suggests I might want my photo taken whilst sitting in the Governor's chair. How can I resist? Thanking her profusely at the end of my private tour I make my way back to the hotel, where I briefly join a hundred or so policemen in the bar.

It is at breakfast the following morning that I am told a tale which illustrates to me how recent American history is. I am being served by an old black woman of indeterminate age. 'Have you lived here all your life,' I query. 'Oh, yes,' she says, 'my family have always lived here. In fact my grandfather, when he was a boy, used to run errands and do odd jobs for Mr and Mrs Lincoln. He used to tell us that one day he had been naughty and Mrs Lincoln chased him down the street with a broom.' I do a quick calculation and realise that her story could actually be true. Sitting here, at breakfast, I have a direct link through the waitress to Abraham Lincoln.

A little while later I am at the Lincoln's Home National Historic Site. It is a wonderful museum using holograms to depict major events. The site is large and no cars are permitted. The Lincolns lived here until 1861, I read, before moving to the White House.

On the road again there are as usual many historical features and I again am made aware of how relevant this drive is to become imbued in the American story. I pass a drive-in cinema, a memorial to Mother Jones erected for a labour activist who organised protests against the local mine bosses in 1931, and yet another gas station at Soulsby which is said to be the oldest on the route. Finally, for the day's drive, I cross the mighty Mississippi River. A little further on, I make a detour as suggested, and reach the Chain of Rocks Bridge. This is a very worthwhile detour to see a bridge over the Mississippi River that is a mile long using the rocks in the river for the bridge's supports. The bridge was closed to traffic in the 1960s.

Shortly after I reach my next overnight stop, St Louis. There is a riverboat casino that advertises accommodation and they have a vacancy. I will not have too much time in St Louis. There will have to be a decision made as to what site I want to take in. The Anheuser-Busch Brewery I discount because I have visited breweries in other places. The Cardinals Hall of Fame has no appeal and the Transportation Museum, which has relics from the Route 66 probably contains no more than I have seen on the route itself. Sitting in my Casino Queen room, which is on the

Illinois side of the river, I have a perfect view of the Gateway Arch on the other river bank in Mississippi. That will be my destination tomorrow, I decide.

It is a good decision, I think, as I ascend the 600 feet tall edifice in a four minute lift ride. The view is breathtaking with the whole of St Louis set out before me and the mighty Mississippi River running north and south. I am set up for another day on the road. This day follows the pattern of the other days. Meremac Caverns have been a holiday destination for many years. Having been to Cheddar Gorge and other similar places, I am quite happy to give them a miss. Following Route 66 I realise takes me again on the Frontage Roads in many places. They differ in their descriptions using all cardinal points of the compass, sometimes I am on South Frontage Road, at other times it could be West Frontage Road. On this day I am intrigued to see that one of the sights is a Stonehenge replica. When I pass it, I am reduced to laughter. It is probably the ugliest site anywhere in America. It stands near a road intersection and looks so woebegone that I did not even stop the car for a longer look. It is a group of grey coloured blocks arranged in a circle.

Over the next few days I come across roadside sculptures, umpteen museums from Civil War days or well-known characters like Jesse James and Will Rogers and odd items like an old log jail. I stay overnight in Tulsa, which despite having art deco buildings, does not come up to what I imagined it would be like whenever I listened to the song '24 Hours from Tulsa' even though once recently it had been voted the USA's most beautiful city, if I am to believe an article I read in the hotel.

I visit a diner for a quick evening meal. It is very busy and the only seat is at the end of a bar because all the booths are full. I nod to my neighbour who, like me, is eating alone. It turns out he is a traveller who visits Tulsa often. I remark to him about the art deco style of buildings and the number of them. 'They came about,' he begins to tell me, 'as a result the town being so prosperous with oil. In fact, it was once described as the oil capital of the world. However, the fact that there are so many buildings like that is because of a riot that took place here when thirty five city blocks were destroyed. No one likes to recall the events of the early 1920s. They have been glossed over.' We continue with the conversation and I find out that currently Tulsa is actually going through a Depression of its own. 'Oil prices have dropped so much in the last ten years and it has affected business here. I sell far less here than I used to. I don't know what Cyrus Avery would think of it.' 'Cyrus Avery?' I query. 'He is known as the Father of the Route 66,' I am told, 'he was a Tulsan businessman who campaigned for a road to Chicago and Los Angeles.' I tell the man that I am currently on that road. We part having had the opportunity to share lifestyles and the next day I leave Tulsa.

Oklahoma City is passed through and now I begin to see the countryside that I relate to whenever I see or hear music from the Rogers and Hammerstein musical 'Oklahoma'. I am now also in the territory so graphically described in John Steinbeck's *Grapes of Wrath*. A place called Sayre boasts that some of the *Grapes of Wrath* film was shot here, but there is no evidence.

Soon I am in Texas and come to a place called Shamrock, apparently named after an Irishman who settled here. The main feature is a roadside gas station that has a diner attached. It is a feature because it is also built in Art Deco style and looks completely out of place in the open countryside.

After leaving Shamrock I am driving across the Panhandle where cattle ranches abound, the country is flat and all I can see in the nearly two hundred miles I drive are utility poles, windmills and tumble weed. I look at the thermometer on the dashboard and see that it is nearly one hundred degrees outside. I also realise how wise the car rental man had been when he had suggested a bigger car.

On my sixth day of the trip I reach the midpoint of Route 66. A billboard at the side of the road tells me that I have 1139 miles to go before I reach Los Angeles, having already driven that distance to arrive here from Chicago. There is more driving on the Interstate to follow as the Frontage Road ends and I make good progress before passing the Last Motel in Texas and entering New Mexico. And what a swift change it is because it is not long before I espy adobe houses the like of which I have not seen before on this trip. I am encouraged by the guide book to detour a few miles every so often and I have to be selective as to which trips I take, bearing in mind the overall length of the journey. Tucumcari is actually on the route and gives me an immediate feel for the fact that I am now in Indian Territory. I pass a Best Western Hotel which calls itself the Pow Wow Inn. Later I do detour a few miles to visit a small town called Las Vegas where I read Butch Cassidy, the outlaw, tended bar.

The countryside is now far more interesting. I have just come to a town called Santa Fe which is seven thousand feet above sea level. All the way along the trip there have been brown signs depicting historic events. Here I read that quite a few Civil War battles took place. The town itself exudes evidence of Mexican, Spanish and Indian influences. There are several museums with an Indian flavour. I book into to a motel in the centre of the town and spend the evening looking at various menus displayed outside restaurants before settling on one that serves, as most do, Mexican food.

The following day sees me once again driving on Interstate roads and local roads before I reach the next town which is New Mexico's biggest town by far, Albuquerque. I park and walk around the old town, yet more adobe buildings. Just up the road is the Sandia Tramway which takes passengers to the top of a mountain. I do not have any inclination to do that and so follow a convoluted route, although well-signed, out of the town. Route 66 does seem to take a pride in making sure you keep to its road. I have chosen to take the route that most favours the historic route and keeps to New Mexico signed roads. The alternative would see me on Interstates for some of the trip. Soon I see signs to my old friend the Frontage Road. I come to a small hamlet called Grants and decide to get out of the heat for a while. To do this I can visit the Uranium Museum. I am the only visitor and after signing in make my way to a lift which takes me down one floor and into the reconstructed mine. I am met by a guide who tells me that he used to work in the actual mine. It is wonderfully cool in the mine, which I am told was not the case when it was a working mine. 'We get few enough visitors as it is,' Wayne tells me, 'if it was not air-conditioned I don't think we would get anyone.' I do not tell him that I have come to the museum to get out of the heat myself. All too soon I am back in that same heat, gratefully in an air-conditioned car.

I am still taken by the mix of cultures, Native American, Mexican and Old West as I continue to drive through more rugged countryside. Next I come to a town called Gallup and begin to pick up references to Hollywood stars. Walking along the main street to stretch my legs I pass a hotel that boasts 'John Wayne and Humphrey Bogart slept here'. There are more Frontage Roads to drive and once again I find myself alongside the Interstate Highway with trucks and cars zooming along at a far faster pace than me. Then I arrive in Arizona and one of the first places I note is the WigWam Village Motel, a further sign of local culture. I do not bother to take a detour that would lead me to the Petrified Forest and Painted Desert but continue straight on to Winslow where I will spend the night.

The obvious choice for an overnight stay is La Posada Hotel. It is built in Spanish- Colonial style, I read, and previous incumbents have included Albert Einstein and John Wayne (again). Each room is named after a movie star, and

I am allocated the Shirley Temple Room. I discover that the town is at the end of a railroad line that once brought film makers to this area, especially in the era of Westerns. The hotel is annexed to the railroad station.

On the next day's drive, I do take a recommended six mile detour to visit the site of the meteor crater. I am glad I do because it is quite extraordinary to look at. Imagine, I think, if this meteor had landed in a populated area. Next on my journey is the town of Flagstaff. From here I could detour to the Grand Canyon. I would do that had I not visited the Canyon a few years ago after my teaching stay in New York. Then I had travelled the country by Greyhound bus and spent a couple of days in the Grand Canyon.

Another town boasts trips to the Grand Canyon as I arrive in Williams. Much of the downtown still has historic buildings from when the town was first founded. The Grand Canyon Railway takes visitors to the Grand Canyon rim. I continue on and come to Seligman on a stretch of road that is not much changed over the years. This is followed by miles of rolling hills and canyons which seem to go on forever. I will spend the night in Kingman which was established in 1880 and still has many buildings from that and later years.

As I drive through Sitgreaves Pass on the following morning the road begins to twist and turn and I am suddenly alerted to another phase of the past as I see a sign to Goldroad Mine. Two miles past the mine I enter Oatman. This place is the old Wild West come alive for tourists. There is a boardwalk in front of the shops, wild donkeys, descended from the earlier pit donkeys, roam the streets and there are lots of false-front buildings. Next month, I read, there will be the annual sidewalk egg frying contest. It is already very hot here and I am not surprised that egg frying will be possible. The hotel boasts that Carole Lombard and Clark Gable spent their honeymoon here. On the road again, I check the car thermometer and it reads one hundred and four degrees in this high desert area. Soon I come to the California border and am surprised to see what looks like a Customs Post.

It turns out to be a Customs Post. I am asked if I have any fruit or meat products with me. Apparently California is very protective of its fruit, in particular. Luckily, although I had not been prepared for the process I was in the clear. Alongside me there were huge trucks going through the same procedure as well as private cars like me. Ahead of me is the trek through the Mojave Desert and there are plenty of warnings about the need to have water with you and to be aware that the road surface of the Route 66 is to be driven carefully because of potholes and the like. I ignore another detour that would take me to the Joshua Tree National Park. Eventually I arrive at my overnight destination the sleepy town of Barstow. After checking in to a motel appropriately called Route 66 Motel, I cross the road to a diner for a meal and then go to the cinema next door to spend a cool evening in the air-conditioned building. I note in the morning that there is yet another Route 66 Museum, and I wish I had made a note of how many I had now passed.

Leaving Barstow once again I am crossing part of the Mojave Desert and seeing the usual remnants of Route 66, especially the old gas stations and Route 66 themed gift shops. I am intrigued to see that should I wish I could visit the Exotic World Burlesque and Striptease Hall of Fame. For a while I have to rejoin the Interstate Highway but soon I can turn off and begin a drive that takes me out of the desert and into the highlands. Eventually I reach Summit Point which is over four thousand feet above sea level. Now I am in higher, cooler regions and soon I come to San Bernadino. Route 66 signs abound and a sign to California's first winery is passed as I drive through the town. Continuing on along a far more interesting section of the trip, I stop for a coffee at a small place called Arcadia. I ask the server in the diner if this area has any claim to fame. 'Well,' she replies, 'just down the road we have Santa Anita Park and that is where the Marx Brothers filmed *A Day at the Races*. Other than that, nothing much has happened around here.'

My trip is nearly over as I enter Pasadena along its main, well-heeled street. Suddenly I am in a very civilised looking part of America which comes as a contrast to the rugged parts I have been through quite recently. After checking into one of the bland motels that stretch along Colorado Boulevard I look at the usual rack of local attractions displayed in the foyer. It seems that once a month there is the Rose Bowl Flea Market which claims to be the largest in the land. 'Too right,' says the motel clerk when I question him about it. 'You wouldn't be able to book in like you have if you did not have a reservation when the Flea Market is on.'

The next day I propose to enter Los Angeles and make my way to Santa Monica so that I can complete the Route 66 trip. I will have a couple of days in the area before my flight home and have prepared a sort of wish list, some of which I have done before. Hollywood Boulevard and Griffith Park are top of the list and I might try and take in one of the movie studios as well. Whilst sitting on the pier at Santa Monica I take the opportunity to think back over the last couple of weeks. I would recommend anyone to try the same trip if they want to get a feel for America.

CHAPTER THIRTEEN

There is one message for me on the answerphone when I return that requires my immediate attention. This very evening, after I have just spent a sleepless night on the 'plane, there is a basketball match. Brian's message says, 'I hope that you are back now. Tomorrow evening we have a game and because of holidays and unavailability at the moment we only have four players and one of those is the young son of one of the players. Let me know if you are available.' I deal with this call, which was left yesterday, first. I put Brian in the picture but finally I am persuaded that I can help out and agree to be at the court at the stated time. Secretly I hope that it rains and because the court is outdoors the matches will be cancelled. I decide to go to bed and set the alarm for early afternoon.

Another message interests me, but I decide to wait until I have recovered from my jet lag to deal with it. The message is from someone I do not know who says he has been given my telephone number by the college. This alone is rather disconcerting as I think the college should not have given my number, but when I hear the message I realise why they have. The male voice continues, 'I am ringing on behalf of Graeme's wife. She is very concerned that she has not heard from him since the end of term and wonders if you have any information as to where he might be.' He concludes by leaving me his telephone number. Whilst thinking about it, and before I drop off to sleep, I remember the Cheese and Wine Party and the attention he was paying to Sally.

I turn up for the game at the time I was told to. Brian is grateful I am there and tells me that so far our team is unbeaten, having played three games. 'Just our luck that we have a game this week when so many players are not available,' he says. 'I'm really not available,' I respond, 'I feel as if I'm still in the air somewhere.' 'Don't worry, I'm sure everything will be alright,' Brian continues. In fact everything is not alright. The referees who are on a referees course are using the matches for practical exam purposes and they blow their whistles for every small infringement. The result is that with five minutes remaining we only have two players left on court. Brian, Colin and myself have each reached our five allowable fouls. Just Norman and Colin's son remain on court. Colin's wife, as arranged, has come to pick their young son up at the end of the game which will allow Colin to join us at the post match drink at the local pub. She is somewhat surprised to see her son and one other player competing against five other players. Our unbeaten record goes and we repair to the pub. Brian assures me that this is a one-off situation.

The next day I decide that I had better address the Graeme situation. First of all I contact a college colleague. 'Do you know anything about Graeme?' I query. 'Nothing definite,' Eddie replies. 'I know that he was fond of Sally and really upset when she got another job some fifty miles away.' 'When you say fond, how fond are we talking?' I question. 'Fond enough to follow her to her new work place,' Eddie responds. 'I think he may have left his wife and I also believe he handed in his notice here, but I can't confirm that.' With that information, in the early evening I dial the number that I have been given. After explaining what I have been told, the man at the other end of the line sighs and says, 'We thought something like that might be the case, but we had no definite news. Thank you for finding out what you have,' he concludes. I utter my condolences at the situation and assure the man that, even though I worked closely with Graeme on one course, I had no notion of the situation. 'He is a grown man and you could not be expected to be his keeper, I'm just sorry that his wife is so upset at the developments. She thought that his working away from home would just be temporary and she may have had an inkling about something when Graeme kept putting off any idea of her moving to be with him,' he concludes and puts down the telephone.

Once this would have been the start of a long vacation where I could do things that pleased me. Now I have to get down to preparing an Induction Course, a Post Graduate Course and see if there are any Conferences I can belatedly attend. I am in luck with the latter when I find that the First Year Experience Annual Conference is being held in Scotland at St. Andrew's University in two weeks' time.

I go into the college to do the paperwork for the course and submit it to the Staff Development process. As luck would have it, Edgar is actually in his office and I can explain to him the reason for the application which he has to countersign. 'A bit of a change for you,' Edgar comments, 'usually it is for some form of coaching course that you take off in the summer.' I reply, 'The Director is anxious to change my life altogether. At the moment I feel a bit under pressure to come up with the goods that he wants.' 'Don't let that worry you,' Edgar replies, 'we are all under similar pressure to change our ways. Increase the student numbers, run more courses, get new courses to attract a wider student base, all these are the mantras that we are being bombarded with. That is why you can find me here today. Normally I would be away from this place at this time of year but this year it looks as if I may not get a holiday at all.'

It is not unexpected therefore when I visit the cafeteria to see Don in consultation with another of the Union Representatives. 'We are concerned at developments,' Don says when I express surprise at finding him in the college during the holiday season. 'The Director has just returned from an overseas trip and now we hear he is about to go on another. Our concerns centre over the management of the college. We think the Director has become too powerful and has no one to keep him in check. The Governors do not seem interested in what is happening here. I questioned one of them the other day and he was unaware of the scale of our overseas operations. He had been told that franchising was one way of meeting Government targets and thought the Director was doing a good job in attracting foreign customers. He knew nothing about the scale of our ventures or the seeming lack of quality control that we have in some cases. He is a typical case of a representative of a big business concern who acts as a Governor as part of his job rather than having a close interest in what the college is doing. As I expected when I questioned him he has had little or no training for the role of Governor and no background at all in understanding the education setting. He believes everything the Director says and tells me the other Governors rarely question anything. Even our own staff representative on the Governors is in the Director's pocket it seems.' I can sense a lot of hostility coming from Don and his colleague. Perhaps, I think, this is not the time to inform him of developments in my area that put me outside the usual Administrative process to be reporting directly to the Director.

Finally on this visit to the college in the holiday, I go along to the area where alterations are being made for me to have an office and the Media Resource staff to be located close by. I pop in to George-Henry's office and he is there. 'Settling in?' I query. 'Thank goodness you have come in today,' George-Henry immediately replies. 'I needed to get in touch with you last week to tell you about the interview for our secretary. It is scheduled for tomorrow and I thought I would have to do it alone. The shortlist only has three people on it. Seemingly Personnel did not make the job attractive enough.' I comment, 'My use for a secretary at the moment is very limited, probably just taking bookings for the Media Resources and typing up a syllabus. I guess there will be letters also as I try to pull this Post-Graduate Course together. You probably will have far more work for her than I will. I will have no objection if you interview them yourself, although now you have told me, I can come in tomorrow if you like.' 'That would be great,' says George-Henry.

Once again I find myself going into the college in mid-summer, something I had rarely done before. The builders are everywhere, altering classrooms as well as constructing offices, such as mine. We have managed to find a small tutorial room for the interview. George-Henry is already there when I arrive and he has set out the furniture for the interviews. There are three chairs set out behind a desk, one for Andrea from Personnel who is coming to make sure we accord to the correct procedure for the interview, and for George-Henry and myself. I immediately suggest a change. 'The desk is a barrier,' I say. 'The whole set-up looks too formal for me, I would prefer a more relaxed setting with our chairs in a semi-circle and the candidate sitting opposite. What do you think, Andrea?' I ask as she arrives. 'You can have the arrangement that suits you,' she agrees, 'I can make any notes on my clipboard.' George-Henry rearranges the furniture but I am not convinced he likes the new setting. He probably has not dealt with anyone like me before, I think, and is agreeing because he is the new boy.

All the candidates are good and we opt eventually for the one who seems to have the most experience of shorthand. Her name is Vanessa. She has worked in a medical practice before starting a family and I am happy that she will be able to deal with telephone issues of booking. We ask Andrea to make sure when informing the two unsuccessful candidates that we were impressed by their presentations and the decision had been a difficult one.

After a coffee with George-Henry I make my way home because my office at the college is not yet ready and it will be better to work in a less frantic atmosphere.

I telephone Mick to see how basketball matters are progressing. He has some surprising news for me. 'I have just got the job of England Team Manager for our basketball team,' he declares. 'I applied at the end of last season after one of the England Basketball officials had a word with me when we went to Melton Mowbray.' 'Congratulations,' I say, 'you certainly kept that quiet.' 'Well,' Mick continues, 'I did not think I had a chance, but I threw my hat into the ring. Nothing ventured, nothing gained, I thought. It is a job I really wanted. It is a chance to be with the best players in the country. I might even persuade some of them to come and play for us.' I know he is joking about playing for us, but nonetheless it will do no harm to our club's profile in the National League. I ask him about players for next season. 'Nothing definite yet,' he replies, 'I have a few irons in the fire and will let you know of any developments.'

There is another telephone call I have to make. The organisers of the First Year Experience work at Teesside Polytechnic and after several fruitless attempts I manage to track one of them down. 'Terribly busy at the moment,' I am informed by Kerry who is one of the organisers. 'You are lucky to catch me here today, I just came in to pick up some printed material for the Conference.' I quickly explain that I am new to the game and would welcome some kind of background. 'Briefly,' Kerry begins,' it is obviously an American organisation but they like to combine their conferences with a holiday. Last year it was in Dublin, this year it is in Scotland. It gives the American golfers a chance to play on a Scottish course, I guess. The group deal with first year students, as their name suggests and the speakers are staff who have come up with various strategies to help students through their first year at college. It is a friendly group and we got involved here a few years ago and act as their British representatives. There are not many Brits that come though. There are only a handful this year, despite our advertising it as much as possible. Look, I must go. I look forward to seeing you next week.' I feel better for having actually spoken to someone about the event. All I need now is to hire the car through the college and prepare to meet a group of Americans who may just have come for a jolly to our shores.

I play another outdoor basketball match later in the week. This time we have seven players, all of whom complete the match. In the pub after the game I inform Brian that I will have to miss the next game as I will be in Scotland at a conference. 'What some people will do to avoid running up and down on a concrete surface,' is all he can say.

CHAPTER FOURTEEN

The drive north is uneventful. Instead of basketball players all I have for company is a series of radio stations I tune into as I go along. Now it is a Scottish burr I am listening to as I pass through Edinburgh. I look for directions for Dundee on the A91 and soon St. Andrews comes into view as I drive past the Royal and Ancient Golf Club which was founded in 1754 and where the Rules of Golf were first drawn up. In the distance, on the clifftop, I can see the ruins of the Cathedral but, more importantly for me, I pick up the signs that have been posted to direct me to the conference registration.

I finally meet Kerry, with whom I had spoken over the telephone recently. 'You were a very late applicant,' he says, 'but we have managed to squeeze you in to one of the Halls of Residence that we are using. Here is a detailed programme for the three days, if you need any further information don't hesitate to ask. This desk will be manned throughout the conference until nine o'clock at night.'

My room is a typical student's room. There is no en-suite and I check out the facilities which are pretty basic. Still, it is only for a short time. The college map shows me the location of the Student Bar and I make straight for it. I am pleased to see it is well populated and noisy. As an outsider I wonder if I will be welcomed by anyone. I need not worry. Soon I am exchanging details with several people. Coming from England has its advantages in this company of mainly Americans. I am particularly taken by a small group of people who come from George Mason University. They are a lively group and laugh a lot. My involvement with basketball is of interest. 'I did not think there was any basketball in England,' one says, 'let alone a National League.' This opens the door for me to tell them about the

American players who I have dealt with over the years including the one who said he was told by God that he should return home. 'We were only a few matches into the season and he was proving not as good as we would hope,' I relate 'I think he had bitten off more than he could chew,' I continue. 'Once he had made his announcement no one tried to dissuade him, but it had proved an expensive mistake on our part.' I also pointed out that the Americans were not alone in thinking that there was no National Basketball League. 'Football, or soccer as you know it, and rugby rule the roost in winter and most English people are probably unaware of our Basketball League.

On the first evening there is a welcome dinner. I am ready with my tactic that I use on these occasions. I have employed it with some success at Open University conferences. When a friend had heard about by forthcoming attendance at an Open University week at Bath University he had said, 'Those events are full of bored housewives looking for some kind of outlet.' I had taken what he said with a pinch of salt. However, by concentrating my attentions on a particular female who was in my work group, I had developed a good relationship by the middle of the week. On the last night we were going out for a drink, when she asked me what my student's room was like on the pretext that she was staying in the older part of the university whereas I was in a new hostel by the golf course. We never actually went to where we had set out for. Soon we were in the single bed cementing our relationship. I walked her back to her lodging place at three in the morning. The course finished at lunchtime the following day, but she did not appear in the morning, and I never saw her again.

It is time to employ a similar tactic but this time there will be no working group because there are just general workshop type events where a speaker leads the session but everyone is free to join in. The dinner event shows me that there are far more women than men in this movement.

Perhaps I should have realised by its nature of caring as an underlying principle that this would be the case. There are certainly many women at the dinner and also in the bar afterwards. Moving away from my newly met George Mason University friends, I manage to annexe an attractive looking brunette and introduce myself. 'Oh, good,' she says, 'someone who is not American. Are you here for the golf too?' 'No,' I reply, 'I have just found out about this movement and am about to start a new role at the college where I work. So I have come to see what you are all about.' 'Likewise me,' she replies. 'I am a student counsellor at a university in St. Louis and this is my first attendance at this group's conference.' Immediately I have an opening. 'I was recently in St. Louis,' I say, 'driving on Route 66. I stayed on a casino houseboat on the river.' 'I know the one, it is not far from where I live.' I notice that she does not say anything about anyone else who might live there. From my experience, which is admittedly limited, family members are only brought into the conversation if someone does not want the relationship to develop.

Time will be very limited in this short conference, so I will have to move quickly. 'I see there is a free afternoon tomorrow,' I say,' would you like to go for a drive to explore the local area?' 'Why, yes,' she replies. 'I have not hired a car and I am a bit concerned about driving on the wrong side of the road, as you do.' I let that pass but say, 'No wonder so many people got upset with me on Route 66.' We arrange to meet outside the Student Union at two o'clock the next day.

In the morning I look through the programme. Some of the titles of the sessions are a bit strange and the whole programme seems to have a touchy-feely theme dealing with potential first year student problems. There is one title I am attracted to that is about helping students who are falling behind in the early days. The setting is quite bizarre. The room for the session is a chemistry laboratory and we sit on stools behind benches which have Bunsen burners and various taps and gadgets on them. The main speaker is a matronly woman and is introduced by a casually dressed man, who looks as if he is prepared to go onto the golf course as soon as possible. There are some good ideas that come from the short time allowed for the session but I am rather taken aback when at the conclusion another matronly type women goes up and hugs the speaker and says, 'That was so wonderful. Your university is so lucky to have such a caring person.' Clearly some of these people are far more demonstrative than the average British person.

I attend four sessions in the morning and am quickly becoming aware that these people are, indeed, caring. Also, I wonder how much is altruism and how much is commercially driven. Each student brings in money and failing to keep them on a course will result in a loss of income. I can even hear my Director's voice in my head as I think these things.

No matter, I think, as the first free afternoon is on us and Rachel is waiting outside the Student Union as I pull up in my hire car. She comments on the newness of the car and I don't bother to tell her it is a hired car. 'Let's just look around the town first,' I suggest, 'then we can drive up to Dundee and explore a bit.' We do just that and Rachel seems to be impressed by everything, especially the Firth of Tay when we arrive in Dundee. We quickly take in Discovery which was Scott's exploration ship and is plain to see from the road. I drive out to Broughty Ferry where there is a castle museum. It also has a swimming club called Ye Olde Amphibians. 'A relative of someone in my family was the first person to swim across the Tay and back,' I tell Rachel. What's more there is a picture of him floating in the local dock with his full beard prominently displayed as he poses for the picture by lying on his back in the water. We loop back to St. Andrews visiting Cupar on the way where, I tell her, 'A nine hour play was performed here in 1535. It was an attack on the Church of Scotland. The same site is also where a theatre was built by French prisoners of the Napoleonic War at the beginning of the 1900s.' Rachel is blown away by this information and the dates I have quoted. 'So much history,' she exclaims. Little does she know that I looked up the information the day before when selecting a few local leaflets from the entrance of St Andrews University.

My attentions eventually pay off when Rachel tells me she intends to stay on for a few days after the conference before she goes on to a guided tour of France. I telephone the car hire company to extend the loan by a few days.

One late afternoon I find myself in the High Street and decide to have a drink at one of the pubs. I recognise a fellow conference attendee who is sitting with a pint in front of him and smoking a pipe. He looks well settled in. I ask if I can join him and then question what he thinks of the conference so far. This seems to open up the floodgates. 'Someone at my university, where I am Registrar, suggested to the Vice Chancellor that this group might be useful in suggesting ways of keeping students from dropping out. Well, I wasn't keen on coming but pressure was put on me. All I can say is that I wish I had put up more of a defence. I don't play golf so that was not an attraction.' He then goes on to describe the first session he had attended. Interestingly, it was the same one I had been to in the science laboratory. His take on the hugging of the speaker was that he was flabbergasted. 'She had one or two ideas,' he acknowledged, 'but the reception at the end when the other woman hugged her and said that it was the most moving address she had ever heard was ridiculous. And it has gone on every day. I get the feeling that this is a very touchy-feely group who spend their time boosting one another. An outsider, like me, finds the whole thing too incestuous. Mind you, I will be more positive when I report back to the Vice Chancellor.' In part I agree with him, but, nonetheless,

I have picked up some strategies that we could apply at the college. However, there will be some costs involved and I wonder if that might have an effect.

I venture to Rachel that she might like to have me show her some other parts of Scotland before she flies out from Edinburgh. We still have not shared many personal details. Even after several days in her company I do not know if she is married or has a partner. I have found out quite a bit about her childhood, her college years and the jobs she has had but precious little about her private life. Rachel tells me she will think about it because she had already made some plans of her own. 'We can stick to them, if it does not involve anyone else,' I say. 'I am willing to drive you anywhere you want to go.'

On the last day, Rachel approaches me and asks, 'Is your offer still on?' 'Of course,' I reply. We make arrangements to meet the following day and I spend the evening at the social event saying my goodbyes to several people I have got to know quite well. The group from George Mason University are together as I approach them to say my farewell. 'You must come and visit us,' they say, 'we will get you to sing yet.' This is a reference to a short outing we had made on a free afternoon to a local distillery. On the way back several people had taken the coach's microphone to sing various folk type songs. I had considerable pressure put on me to add to the entertainment but managed to resist, knowing the limitations of my singing voice. My decision had been confirmed to myself when the person who did get up next rendered an operatic aria at full volume and, as far as I could tell, in tune.

Rachel confides in me as we drive away from St. Andrews that she had been hesitant to agree to my offer because her original plans had included going with two other women from the conference for the two days. However, they had now agreed to meet up at Edinburgh Airport to continue their original itinerary to France. 'Do you still want to follow your original plans?' I ask. 'No' Rachel replies, 'I am entirely in your hands. My friends are going to continue with our planned trip by taking the train to Glasgow and exploring that area before returning here to catch the plane.' 'In that case,' I say, 'we will stick to this part of the world and go up the east coast to show you something of Scotland that is not a huge city like Glasgow.'

The first part of the journey takes us along the familiar road to Dundee and then I pick up the A92 and proceed to Arbroath. In a local café near the ruins of the Abbey the owner tells us about his town. 'We have a football team here that plays in the Scottish League,' he says. 'It is known as Arbroathnil.' He laughs at his own joke and I have to explain to Rachel that it means that the team does not score many goals. When the locals listen to the football results on the radio it will be something like Forfar two Arbroath nil.' I am not sure Rachel understands what I am talking about. He also mentions the smokies, haddock smoked over an oak fire, and to my surprise Rachel has heard of them. As we continue north I tell Rachel some of the history that I know about. We are close to the sea and Rachel is fascinated by that. Living in St. Louis, she tells me, one is rather landlocked. We reach Aberdeen and I explain all about the greyness of the city and we look for somewhere to stay the night. We have not brought up the subject of one room or two at a hotel. 'One room will be cheaper than two,' Rachel says, 'and despite this being your summer I feel a little cool, being used to temperatures much higher than this, so perhaps one bed would be a good idea so we can share our body heat.' I think how tactful Rachel is and go along with her wishes. Once we dump our luggage there are places to see and we drive to the dock area and I point out the wealth of handsome buildings of grey granite flecked with mica that glitters like silver when caught by the sun. We are staying on Union Street so are immersed in the feel for the city.

Then we make our way to the area where there are beaches and find a restaurant overlooking the beach and sea.

I find there is a lot of pent up passion in my brunette girl companion when we eventually return to the hotel. 'I am married,' she finally admits, 'but it is not in the happiest of states at the moment. My husband wants a family, but I am not ready yet. I reckon I have a couple of more years at work, which I love, before I must settle down.' The night passes and is filled with an endless series of kissing and lovemaking. We are nearly too late for breakfast which is extended to ten o'clock at the weekend. Eventually we leave the hotel and Aberdeen and make our way north by way of the coast road. Six miles out of Inverness we come to the site of the Battle of Culloden and we pay a visit to the museum and the battlefield. Rachel is amazed to see the small thatched cottage which remains almost as it was when the battle was being fought around it in 1746.

My suggestion is that we stay the night in Inverness which will give us an opportunity to drive through the Cairngorms on the A9 for her to meet up with her friends at the airport. 'You will not have a chance to explore Edinburgh,' I explain, 'but that will give you a reason to return one day.' I tell her that I intend to stop and see my birthplace on my way home and this leads me to disclose more about my upbringing. Rachel seems intrigued and tries to fathom out why I should have remained unmarried. I steer the conversation away from this topic to the choice of hotel we might make. We settle on one that is a stone's throw away from the cathedral and close to the river. It is a perfect setting for our last night together which follows a similar pattern to the previous night. This time I set the alarm on my travelling clock because we will need an early start.

The Cairngorms do not disappoint. We stop at Perth for lunch. Rachel has seen the original film *Thirty Nine Steps* and I tell her that the author, John Buchan, was born here in Perth. I also tell her that I think the plot of the film is better than that of Buchan's book. There is just too much Scottish history connected with Perth and, as Rachel will soon be departing, we spend the time in small talk instead. 'Hopefully, I may see you again at a future conference,' I say. 'That depends on whether or not my husband gets his way regarding a family,' Rachel sighs. 'Time is passing and he is so persistent.'

Rachel asks me to drop her at the Departures entrance at the airport so that there will be no fond goodbye.

I decide to call in to Wallsend on my way home and visit Mary. She had been a cousin of my mother and when I had found out about my natural parents she had been the one who I had contacted. Her name had been on one of the fostering forms. She is at home when I call in. 'Sorry you could not get to the basketball game in Sunderland all that time ago,' I say, once a cup of coffee has been placed in front of me. 'Yes, I remember that day, too,' Mary replies, 'I couldn't see a hand in front of my face because of the fog, and I am nervous of driving anyway. Still it is lovely to see you now. Is there a purpose for your visit?' I explain that I am on my way home after a conference in Scotland. 'Do you want to stay the night?' she enquires. 'No, thanks,' I reply. 'I have to get back to work because of lots of changes there.' Already, I know most of my story about an absent father and a mother who could not support me. Mary had told me in the past that the rest of the family knew nothing of my mother's moves to have my sister and I fostered. At the time, she had said, the families had not been close. This had continued and eventually our mother had died. 'There were very few at the funeral,' Mary had said, 'and to be honest very little thought was given to contacting your sister or you because we reasoned that it might be upsetting for you. It came as quite a surprise when you did finally get in touch. I am so pleased you have done so well. Jackie, my husband, always said, before he died, that he thought you would find your way in the world.'

As I leave, I feel glad that I have made the effort to see Mary. Although now a widow, she has some relations living nearby and is a staunch member of the local Catholic church where most of her social life takes place. I also happen to remember that she likes Sequence Dancing having once on a visit north been taken to a club where the dancing took place. I had felt quite out of place there but the regulars had made me very welcome and I remember I did not have to buy a drink all evening.

CHAPTER FIFTEEN

Home again and I go into college. The workmen are still in evidence. There seem to be more academic staff around than I would expect. I know I used to absent myself for most of the summer vacation and that some staff are involved in research and come in to use the new computers and library but still I did not expect to see so many. Soon I am made aware of why so many staff are in college.

'The Director has gone too far this time,' Don tells me in the cafeteria. 'He has employed an ex-CID man to find out who is responsible for the publication of The Lies. The ex-detective has been busy looking into staff workrooms and examining filing cabinets. Word has soon got round and quite a few staff who we do not usually see in the summer are now coming in to check on what is going on. All the Union people have been interviewed last week. No one is saying anything. The Director is keeping a close eye on things, although I hear he is going off again in a few days to Greece. Something about another franchise, I hear.' 'I may know something about that,' I interject. 'The father of one of my basketball players told me he had business with the Director. The parents had come to see how their son was doing, they said, but I was suspicious there was more to it than that, especially when the father said he was going to see the Director at a later date.'

The college is no place to be at the moment fomenting with distrust, an investigation and workmen everywhere. I do go to see the librarian, though. Mike is supervising an extension to the library and I have an idea partly brought about by my recent attendance at the Scottish conference. I am interested because the extension to the library includes a separate room, outside the actual library itself. 'Mike,' I say, 'could this new room be a multi-purpose room where some teaching could take place as well as storing books?' 'It is already a nightmare,' he confesses, 'it is outside the library as you can see and means that we will have to monitor its opening to safeguard the books and avoid pilfering. This could be partly a solution by limiting the opening hours when we will have to man it.' I decide to push my luck. 'Could it be carpeted, too?' I ask. 'We can bring in stacking chairs with armrests for the students and carpeting will avoid any noisy movement of the desks should group work be encouraged. 'My budget just might stretch to that,' Mike replies, 'I will keep it in mind.'

For the next few days I work at home, taking time to review my thoughts on the First Year Conference I have just attended. Brian telephones and reminds me of the next basketball match and says that because of holidays we will be struggling for numbers again. 'This is why I asked you, should we decide to enter the local league, if you could always have a pool of student players that we could dip into. Mind you,' he adds, 'I am thinking of calling our team Seniles so that everyone knows what we are. The odd student will look out of place but I am sure the other teams will realise the necessity to have some form of back up.'

July is fast approaching its end. I decide to talk to Mick about how the team is shaping up for next season. 'No signings so far,' he reports. 'I am going to see a player who has come from Nigeria and is making a good impression at the local club he has joined, although they are not competing in any summer league at the moment. If he is any good I will try to get him to come to pre-season training which begins in three weeks' time. As far as I can tell, most of last season's team will be available which will give us a good mix of experience and youth. I am going to the Annual General Meeting of the Basketball Association in Sheffield next week. Do you want to come?' In fact, having just relinquished the local secretary role last year, I do not want to go. This will be one of the advantages of not having that job. However, a thought crosses my mind. Graeme had come down from Huddersfield when he joined the college and I wonder if I should go and see his wife to give her my condolences. It would also give Mick a companion for the journey. I could drop him off at the meeting, go to Huddersfield and pick him up on the way back. I suggest that to him and he seems very agreeable to the notion.

Another defeat for our team follows. We only have five players and are playing against a much younger team who constantly switch players from the bench to the court. Brian is still optimistic about entering a team into the local league next season. 'I have interest now from about ten of the old team that used to play regularly. They all agree that they need regular exercise. I still have the old team kit at home and a couple of serviceable basketballs. All we need to do is get a scorebook and a clock that can be seen by both teams. My wife says she is quite willing to do the scorekeeping so we only need someone to operate the clock.' I note the use of the word 'we'. 'If it can be arranged,' I say, 'then we can alternate match nights with the college team and use the college sports hall. In that case we will have a scorebook and a clock. However, we will not be able to practise at the college.' 'That is marvellous,' says Brian. 'Once the season begins we will not want to practise anyway. One game a week will be enough. We will just need somewhere for a bit of pre-season work outs.'

The day comes for my trip north with Mick. We leave early enough to have time to stop at a motorway services to have a bite to eat. While we are there, Mick elaborates on his England team manager's role. 'It is something I always wanted to do, 'he says. 'I miss the involvement with basketball at the top level like we used to have. Luckily I still have good contacts with those who are still in the National League. I think that is why I have been given the chance to do the manager's job.'

I drop Mick off at the venue for the Annual General Meeting. We are in good time and I have no doubt Mick will soon be in the room working on the contacts that he told me about. Mick, I know, loves that sort of networking. I tell him that I will be back in plenty of time to pick him up for the return trip. Graeme's wife lives further north and I make my way to her house. I have not announced my intention to visit. If she is not there, I will return to the Annual General Meeting, I reason. However, she does come to the door when I ring the bell. I introduce myself and am invited in.

My first impression is that Graeme's wife is older than he is. I am soon told that this is her second marriage and there is a teenage daughter from the first marriage. 'I had no idea that Graeme was having any involvement with another member of staff,' I begin. 'Your telephone call came out of the blue. Graeme and I had been teaching on a course for this last academic year, but he was not involved with me in any other way. We did not share a work room. I had to go and ask other members of the college staff to try and find out where he had gone after you had got in touch.' She takes all this in and then offers to make me a cup of coffee, which I accept. Whilst she is out of the room I look around and see photos of her with Graeme and a young girl. I also see the same girl in another photo with his wife and another man. This man is definitely older than Graeme's wife and a lot older than Graeme himself.

As if realising what I have been doing, I am told, when she returns, that her first husband had died a few years before. Graeme's romance had been quite a whirlwind affair, it seems. 'I should have taken longer to think about my circumstances,' she says, 'but my daughter, I felt, needed a father. Then he got a job with you. He promised me we would move but I have my whole family here and could not bring myself to agree. He came home whenever he could, but it was an expensive train journey every time and soon his visits came less and less. My daughter is heart-broken to lose a second father, although not as grief stricken as she was when her natural father died.'

Our discussion is interrupted by a new arrival who, I quickly learn, is the man who had telephoned me originally about the fact that Graeme was missing. There is a warmth about the relationship I am now observing. The man is older but clearly interested in the welfare of Graeme's wife. I feel that her status will soon be one of a married woman again once any divorce has been resolved. Funnily enough I think that the situation is resolving itself in the best way possible. Graeme will lose an older wife that he has grown quickly estranged from and she, in turn, will gain a more age-compatible husband.

With this thought in mind, I bid my farewell having been thanked for taking the trouble to call and explain the situation as I see it.

I drive back to the location of the Annual General Meeting, park the car and find my way to the room where the meeting is being held. The room is fairly full with fifty or so representatives from the world of amateur basketball. Mick sees me arrive and comes across to waylay me and lead me outside the room. 'I have a request to make on behalf of the Basketball Association,' he begins, 'it is quite a contentious matter and your help is needed.' Knowing that Mick can be a wheeler-dealer at times and at other times will only tell you part of a story to persuade you about some course of action, I am on my guard. 'In short,' he continues, 'they want you to be a candidate for Vice-President of Development for the Association.' This is quite a bombshell. I had only come because it gave me a chance to see Graeme's wife. 'What's the story?' I ask. We are still outside the room of the meeting but Mick speaks in a low voice as if he is worried that he might be overheard.

'There are big changes afoot in the way things are run,' Mick begins, 'it is something to do with funding and the Sports Council. The current Vice-President of Development had one more year of his three to run, but has resigned. It is because of ill-health, I am told. The Association needs someone to come in on a one year term but because this has happened so recently, they don't want to have to call another meeting, which will be expensive, just to elect someone for one year. The Secretary approached me before the meeting to see if you would be interested. He did not know you had brought me here and would be coming back later on. He said that the Executive had discussed the matter and had you in mind as a recent winner of the Administrator of the Year Award. If you are agreeable they will be able to pass the motion for you to take the position at this meeting. They are at pains to point out it will be just for the year. All you will have to do is work with the professional staff member who is in charge of Development. You will not be expected to be involved more than as a sounding board for the amateur side of the game.' This all sounded very straightforward, but I am suspicious based on Mick's description and his past record not always disclosing the whole facts of a situation. Mick, I know is a company man when it comes to basketball, having recently got the England manager's job. However, I have had dealings with most of the basketball officers over the years and am sympathetic to their plight. Besides, I think, if it does become all too much I can resign as well. I agree to Mick's request and we go into the meeting. I notice Mick gives a thumbs up sign to the Secretary and my fate is sealed.

After the meeting I am thanked for agreeing to the position I have. They ask for my details so that Calling Cards can be printed and sent to me. I have a brief chat to the man who holds the professional post of Development and we exchange telephone numbers and I am assured that the job will mainly be a rubber-stamping of initiatives coming out of the main office. I am told in a clandestine way that big changes are afoot and my position will only be temporary.

'I hope so,' I reply, 'I have enough on my plate at work to keep me occupied at the moment.'

Mick is full of the contents of the rest of the meeting as we journey south. He has always been a political animal when it comes to analysing basketball administration and the main players involved. I cannot get enough enthusiasm to concern myself about such goings-on but hope I am a good listener and ask a few desultory questions to try and show an interest. Despite all he has to say, he still breaks off when on the motorway we pass the radio masts and aerials to tell me about the significance they played when he was a radio operator at sea.

Once home, I forget all about my new role in the basketball world because I have more pressing issues to deal with. Once again I find myself in strange territory by going into the college in mid-summer. I am now trying to piece together a programme for the new members of staff. Some of my suggested contributors are still at work in the college. I manage to track down the Safety Officer, who complains that with the building work he is busier now than when the students are present. He agrees to lead a short session for me. Mike is in the very quiet library where I count just three people. He will do an input for me on the library and I ask him further if he will take some of the newcomers on a guided tour of the buildings. 'I think there will be too many for just one group to go round,' I say. 'We can work out an itinerary for each of us to avoid clashes.' After that my luck runs out and I have to leave messages with several Administrative departments about what I am hoping to involve people in. I stress that it is important that, if possible, the Head of the Service does the presentation. I cannot give numbers that will be attending at this stage until I get the list from Personnel, but I assume because of our rapid expansion there will be quite a few.

There is virtually no lecturing staff to be seen as I traverse the buildings. The few I do see are all aware of the existence of the CID man and are all of the same opinion and condemn the action of the Director. It is he who I go to next about his involvement in the Staff Induction Programme. I am thwarted. Apparently his trip to Greece has been extended. His secretary informs me that, once again, his wife has accompanied him. 'They are probably taking the chance to tour the country whilst they are there,' she says, 'but he has telephoned me to say he will be back next week in time for the Governors' meeting.'

Obviously, I have to settle for this. But I want to involve him in my latest thinking for helping the staff and students, realising that expense will be involved. With such an increase in student numbers I reason there must be money available for some initiatives. We still have the goal of Polytechnic status and we will be shown in good stead to the Quality Council if we come up with ideas to retain students on their courses rather than have a huge drop-out of students in their first year.

On the front page of the *Times Higher Education* paper there is an article about the new legislation about to go through the Parliamentary process that would affect the college. In it, it is suggested, that the existing Polytechnics will be allowed to become Universities if the legislation is passed. No mention is made of colleges like our own although much is made of the effects on colleges of Further Education where it intimates that lecturing staff will be put on new contracts requiring them to work longer hours for more pay. Those who refuse to sign, it appears, will remain of their current salary with no increase in the future. Dark days lie ahead for them, I think. I do not know what to think about our situation. I will need to consult the Union members who always have their ear to the ground on such matters.

CHAPTER SIXTEEN

Dave calls me and is surprised when I answer. 'At last,' he begins, 'I have tried several times recently, all to no avail.' 'I have been away,' I tell him, 'but I have been back for a while, so I guess we must have just missed each other.' 'Perhaps you could come tomorrow evening when we have a directors' meeting of Starbrite. We have missed you recently and need to know how basketball matters are progressing regarding the playing side. I have been busy trying to get interest from some local businesses and have had some success. It has helped that we are back on the national scene, but we still need to hold our own in it if we are to attract sponsorship.' I tell him about Mick's appointment as England Team Manager and he is pleased to hear about that. 'It can't do us any harm to have such a high profile person connected to the club. Do you think he might be able to attract players for us?' 'Probably not while we are in Division Three,' I counter, 'but you never know. Also I might be lucky in getting players through the college. We are increasing our student numbers considerably and it may bring in some players like the one we have just lost who has finished his college course.'

As soon as I put down the telephone I call Mick, only to get his answerphone. I leave a message asking him to call me telling him I need an update on the players for the meeting I am going to the following day. Then it is back to thinking about my strategy for my upcoming new working arrangement. No sooner do I sit down than it is Brian on the telephone. 'Don't forget our game tonight,' he says. 'It is our last one and the good news is that all the lads are keen to enter the local league next season. We are going to have a meeting about it over the weekend. I have sent in the entry form and the fee. I have taken the liberty of accepting your offer of playing at the college when the college has no game. I hope that is alright?' 'I am sure we can work something out,' I say. 'The college team can always have a practice session before our matches start if you say that our games will begin at 8.00pm. The college team can practise from 6.30 to 7.30pm. That way I will always be available for home games, at least, unless the college has an away game on the same evening when I will have to go and coach.'

I play in the last game of the outdoor league where we have not distinguished ourselves, but do manage to win this time. In the pub afterwards the talk is all about our last throw of the dice, as we call it, by entering the local league that we had last played in almost a decade before. Then the team had not been able to continue as most of the players had become fathers and had family duties or they had jobs that took them away from time to time. All of them express their commitment to the team and a date is arranged for a get-together to divide up the tasks that are involved in playing regularly.

Basketball continues to dominate my evenings when I attend the directors' meeting the following day. Dave is on good form and shows an ebullient attitude as he looks forward to being in the national league and running a successful team which will attract sponsors and a good following of local support. No one at the meeting wants to appear negative, it seems, and are quite happy to let Dave have his way. After the meeting we repair to a local Indian restaurant and everyone is in a good mood. We toast Mick's new manager's job in his absence. Only later does Dave take me aside and expresses the reservation he had made the day before on the telephone. 'I hope Mick can deliver the players and the results,' he says. 'At the moment we have some good backing, but I fear that if we are not successful we might run into trouble.'

My preparations for the Induction Course continue. First of all I have to get my head around the changing structure of the college management. When the new academic year starts we will have three new posts that are to be titled Director. This could lead to confusion because of the insistence of our current leader to be known as Director. Obviously he has a thing about Directors, I think. I know that one of the new Directors will be in charge of something called Academic Operations, whilst another will be involved with Resources. The third title I currently do not know. I would like an input from the three Deans of the new Schools as well. I am beginning to think that this Induction Course should be attended by every staff member such is the rate of change we are undergoing. A template letter is composed to be sent to those I want to contribute to the course. I emphasise that those attending will be in danger of information overload and ask the speakers to restrict their input to ten minutes at the most and allow time for questions. I drop the draft off at the college and give it to George-Henry for our new joint secretary, Vanessa, to type when she joins, next week.

Finally, I manage to get to see the Director. He wants to know of my progress in my new job. 'I have lots of ideas,' I tell him, 'but some will cost money.' 'Just tell me what you have in mind,' the Director replies, 'and let me worry about the finances if I think any of your ideas are worth pursuing.' I begin, 'From the literature I have read and attending the First Year Conference, one big issue is the dropout rate. Every student who drops out means income lost. Usually the drop outs are because the student falls behind with the work and quite often it is related to general issues, like maths, rather than the specific subject knowledge of the course being studied. I wonder if we could introduce something along the lines of a Study Assistance feature. I think we might have two people who will have office hours to meet students who have problems. They need not be on the lecturing pay scale, to keep the cost down.' 'Do such people exist?' queries the Director. 'I don't know,' I answer honestly, 'but we could advertise and see who applies. If no one responds or we cannot find any suitable candidate then I will think again. The other main issue is that of teaching. We are constructing lecture theatres and taking on many more students. A lot of the staff have been used to small group teaching of mainly part-time students. I think the staff will need a lot of help to change their methods of course delivery. To help that I would like to appoint a person in each of the nine Faculties who can work with me on teaching delivery. They could be released from their lecturing duties for, say, three teaching hours and the Faculties will be given money to employ part-time staff to cover for them. Their job will be to help disseminate good practice that we can discuss at team meetings. I have other ideas but these two are my main concern for the moment.'

I think the Director is sympathetic towards my suggestions, especially when he tells me to get in touch with one of the new directors who has been titled, Director of Academic Operations. 'You are both starting a new era,' the Director says,' and you will need to work with Alan who is taking up his post next week.' I guess that in the future I will be dealing with Alan and not the Director. This is perhaps an indication of how we are growing as an institution. The Director is employing a Praetorian Guard of people making access to him more difficult. I can see the sense in the move, but I wonder if it could backfire as staff feel more and more isolated from management. For the moment I can make no more progress on my ideas until the new member of staff arrives.

The Hampshire Hoops have begun training in earnest now. There is one disappointment as Eddie has failed to put in an appearance despite several telephone calls. Mick has spoken about an American player he has heard of who is stationed in England. 'As I told you earlier, he would be expensive to sign, but at least we would not have to pay transport costs and accommodation,' Mick says. 'I will invite him along for training and get him to play in a pre-season friendly before making a decision whether to sign him or not. I have arranged a pre-season game against Plymouth.'

On Saturday, we travel to Plymouth, but the American player is not with us. 'He couldn't get away from his service duty at short notice,' Mick observes. We are also without Eddie, who has still not appeared, and Jon who is away training with the England Under 22 team. It turns out to be a low scoring affair and we can only muster 47 points, losing to our opponents by nine points. On the way back, Mick tells me he has one more pre-season game against an American Services team which is going to be played at a naval base.

The Induction Course for new staff takes priority in my activities in the following week. All the contributors turn up and we are treated to a whole range of short presentations, as I had suggested. The new staff ask sensible questions and I feel that the course has gone well and ask those who have just taken it to give me any feedback over the coming months. At the end of the session which includes the Director of Academic Operations, I manage to sideline him and suggest we have a meeting as soon as possible. 'I know what you want to talk about,' Alan says, 'the Director has filled me in. He is all for your suggestions so we had better get together to see how we can make it work.' This is good news for me. I have already drafted an advertisement for the local newspaper for the Study Assistance jobs which I will be able to take to Personnel as soon as Alan agrees. The other matter, of staff from the Faculties being released to help me, might take a little longer to put in place because part-time staff will have to be sought to replace them.

Mick reports back that he has decided not to sign the American player. 'He was nothing special so I've decided to go with the local lads. I am still interested in the Nigerian player, though. The National League fixture list has given us three away games to start the season. When it was first published I had made a telephone call to the league offices to complain about the lack of balance to the fixtures but had been told that nothing could be done about it. The first fixture is against our old rivals, Crystal Palace. The story of that team mirrors our own. We were once great rivals when we were among the best teams in the country. Like us, Crystal Palace has just come out of a period in the wilderness.

I recognise some of their support staff when we arrive to play the match. It is like a joyous reunion. Ken and Mike had been part of that era and the occasion is especially poignant for them. For our younger players there is evidence of nerves as we take the court in the National Arena that is Crystal Palace. The game is very low scoring and Hampshire's one point lead at half-time is as a result of only scoring 25 points. There is also a one point difference at the end of the game, but this time the advantage is to Crystal Palace. Our return to the National League has ended in a defeat.

On the following Monday, I meet with the Media Resources team. The building work has finished and the team is pleased with their new accommodation. I introduce Vanessa to the team and also get each of them to say a small autobiography. I have laid on coffee and refreshments for a mid-morning break and then we discuss how the group is to operate. I make the point that we are in a period of change, especially regarding the increasing student numbers and that things may sometimes go wrong. There is also the advent of technological developments and that this will inevitably affect the work Media Resources does. Staff Development will help, I tell them, and they should keep an eye on any short course that could help them. 'You have two weeks before the main body of students arrive to get everything up and running,' I conclude.

The week passes and I have meetings with the Director of Academic Operations and firm up my plans. He is optimistic that I will get my way. I am invited to join the management team staff training event on the following Friday afternoon. I sit down beside Mike the librarian. The event concerns itself with staffing issues and is led by a woman and man from some employment agency. All goes well for the first hour when we are given small tasks to do, in pairs, concerning issues that arise at work. We have a short break and it is after this break that our peculiar circumstances of working practices is brought into focus. The woman leading the session refers quite often to the 'glass ceiling' that exists for female employees. It is after one of these references that the Director, who is sitting some distance from the woman, slaps his hand hard down on the table we are sitting around and says, 'There is no glass ceiling in this college.' I look around the assembled group of managers and count fourteen men and one woman, Judy the Head of Personnel. The action of the Director has only reinforced my feeling that power lies in one person only when it comes to policy.

The second away game follows for the basketball team. We have a long drive to Cheshire. I have noticed over the years that long trips often take their toll on players even before the trip begins. Excuses used to come thick and fast when we were in the National League before. Quite often it concerned slight injuries which could be exacerbated by having to sit for hours in a minibus. I am glad to see, therefore, that no such excuses come from our young English lads and even Ken is up for the trip. At last we gain a win with a powerful display. The only blot on the performance is a knee injury picked up by Jon near the end of the game. I go in search for any ice that I might quickly apply. The bar staff are less than helpful claiming they need all the ice they have but point me in the direction of the ice rink which is next door. I hurry across the car park to the ice rink only to find out that they have no ice that can be used for my purpose. They do not even have a bar I can try. Luckily after a quick departure we call into a petrol station that has a shop and I buy a packet of frozen peas for Jon to apply to his knee for the long trip home. Welcome to the National League of a minor sport, I think.

After getting home I compose the press report about the game and send it to Lorelei at the local newspaper. It is three in the morning before I get to bed. However, by Monday I am ready again to face whatever the college throws at me. I am told that the advertisement for the two part-time staff I want will be placed in the local paper in the coming week with a suggested date for interviews in a couple of weeks' time. 'It is important to have them in place as soon as possible,' I urge. 'We really need to show the students that we care if they have any difficulties.' These words are said to the Personnel member of staff responsible for placing the advertisement. I am not sure she agrees with my sense of urgency, but promises to give the matter her full attention.

I shut myself in my new office and begin to think about the strategies I might employ to give myself a profile in my new job. I look through the feedback forms that I had distributed at the end of the Induction course. I am pleased to see that most attendees are positive in their responses. As I expected, the most commented on feature is the ability to put names to faces of the various management staff and the chance to mix with people outside their own discipline. There is no clue for me in the comments about what my future role might be with the teaching staff and I think I might have added that as a question.

Pete comes to visit and one topic he raises is about Trevor's forthcoming retirement. 'I won't miss his constant railing about management,' he says, 'although sometimes he does talk a lot of sense. I will miss his presence, though. He has been a good friend to me whilst I have been here. We will have to organise a 'do' for him at the end of term. I am thinking of applying for the Head of Section job. What do you think?' I give Pete my whole backing and ask him to let me know if there is anything I can do to help. 'Now you are in with management, you might put in a good word for me,' he replies. This remark shocks me. Are people beginning to think of me in that way? I have already fought with the Director about staying a member of the academic staff but it looks as if my card has been marked, if even Pete thinks I have moved to the management area.

Vanessa, my shared secretary with George-Henry, comes to tell me that Peter, the course leader of the National Board of Supervisory Studies, telephoned whilst I was out of the office to say that six people have enrolled on the course who want to take the Recreation option. I need to call him back to firm up which of the three two hour slots in the week I would like. The option will be one term in length but I will be needed also to supervise any project the members might choose if it is in recreation. I telephone to arrange a meeting so that I can find out more about the students and also, to be honest, to get a feel for the course as a whole about which I know very little.

At the end of the week I pick up the minibus for Hampshire Hoops next away game. This is our longest trip and it is to Sedgefield. I am not in the least surprised when telephoning Mick the night before the game and he tells me that there will only be seven players travelling. Eric has tonsillitis and Marc an ear infection, I am told. Mick then drops a further bombshell when he reminds me that he will be on England manager duty for the weekend and that Mike will be coaching the team.

Arriving at Sedgefield at 6.00pm on a Saturday is like arriving in a ghost town. It takes some time to find the entrance to the Sports Hall which is situated in a shopping mall, most of the doors to which are closed. Once in the hall we find that the brand new basketball backboards are causing a problem. They had only arrived the day before from Germany and the instructions to assemble them are in German. One board has successfully been erected and is in place. However, the other basketball goal cannot be moved from its twelve foot height. This provides a new experience for Mike who, at over seven feet in height, rarely has to jump to touch the basketball ring which is ten feet above the ground. Just when it looks as if the 700 mile round trip has been in vain, the backboard is finally adjusted and the game begins in front of a very small crowd. I have made a mental note to include this situation as a case study for my forthcoming recreation option. Mike, as coach, keeps faith with just five players in the first half, Ken, Jon, Toby, young Craig and himself. The new backboards and ring are unforgiving for any shot not accurate and the halftime score is just 22 – 20 in our favour. Joe and Steve are called into the game in the second half and we gradually forge ahead. Jon scores the only successful three point shot of the game and we are able to come away with a twelve point victory. Of our three away games two have been won and one lost, and that by a single point.

    The journey home is made by even less players than had come up. Toby's father works for the railways in some capacity and we drop Toby off at the railway station for him to make his own way home, presumably in a more comfortable way than in a minibus.

CHAPTER SEVENTEEN

College affairs dominate my life in the following week. The buildings are swarming with students which makes the place feel so different after the lack of them during the summer. Perhaps they had not been missed so much this last vacation since they had been replaced by the builders who had seemed to be everywhere.

I go to see Mike, the librarian, and he proudly shows me the newly carpeted room just off the main library. He has put the small selection of education related books we have on the shelves. 'You can order more,' he tells me, 'now that we are thinking of running a Post-Graduate Course for our staff. Since we have no undergraduate teaching courses there has been no call for education books.' He also goes on to give me a recent anecdote about what has been happening. 'I was in here the other day sorting out some of the stock and had a pile of books that were dated and about to be thrown out. One of the Directors looked in and asked about them. I told him I was throwing them out whereupon he said I should not do that. The books could be used in the library that we were setting up in our new Greek campus arrangement. Some were about the Craft courses, it is true, but a lot were out-of-date Business books. He was about to visit the Greek college and would take some books with him and send some others by sea. I shudder to think what is happening out there,' he concludes. I tell him that I have a sort of connection with the Greek college and that one of the proprietors has a son who plays in my college basketball team.

Positioned in the corner of the room is a stack of portable student desks. 'Is this what you wanted?' Mike asks. 'Yes,' I reply, 'although I notice that the table tops are not interchangeable and all sixteen are for right handed people. Still, it's a start.'

In the Refectory the talk is still about the changes that are happening at such a fast pace. Don says, 'Dennis, who our Union representative on the Governors, says that we have now established governance arrangements that give considerable power to the Director. The Director himself has got the Governors to agree to a strategy to achieve Polytechnic status in the shortest possible time. He has reduced the number of separate Governors committees from five to two and now sends resumes of committee meetings instead of the full Minutes. By doing all that he has given himself carte blanche to do whatever he wants with no one to challenge him. Most academic staff members don't know what is going on and care less. They are overwhelmed by the amount of work they have to do dealing with the increased student numbers. The Union has tried to meet with the Director on several occasions but he seems to be forever out of building travelling to franchise colleges or other jollies. Our guess is that he has the internal auditors under his spell as well. How he does it we just don't know, but we reckon these franchises are beginning to cost us rather than adding to our income.'

Freshers Week is just beginning and I decide to contact Yannis to see that he makes sure the basketball club is represented and try and find out if we have any basketball talent arriving. Trevor is in his office and is in a philosophical mood. 'This is my last term,' he begins, 'and I never believed I would see so many students wandering about the building. I long for the days when we serviced the mainly part-time courses and the few full time students. I don't know if we have the facilities to satisfy the new demand. There have been requests from quite a few clubs who want time in the Sports Hall. Your Basketball Club time is safe, but you may have to be prepared for some changes in the long run.'

I make a point of getting in touch with Dave to keep him updated about Hampshire Hoops first home basketball match which will be against North London. One thing I am able to tell him after talking to Mick earlier, is that we will have a new player for the game. It will be the Nigerian player who Mick had told me about some weeks before and has been a regular attendee at training.

Saturday evening arrives and I am grateful to see over 600 supporters at the game. It really is gratifying to know that so many loyal followers are at last getting to see their team in a home game after three games on the road. We start confidently and build up a fourteen point lead half way through the first half thanks to Jon, Toby and Mike scoring freely. Mick then introduces our new signing, Masai, into the game. He makes a dramatic entrance by soaring above the basket and scoring with his first touch to bring the crowd to their feet. Hampshire Hoops win by thirty points which is exactly the same as Jon's individual contribution. As a bonus for me, Mick has found a team manager he wants to work with and I am relieved of the duties of taking care of the kit. I warn the new incumbent not to leave the bag exposed in his car to avoid the possibility of being robbed!

The Director has returned from his latest trip and I get the call to visit him in his office. He listens as I tell him of my experiences over the summer and the fact that this week I am interviewing candidates for what I am currently calling Study Assistance. He then counters by requesting me to make a visit to one of our franchise courses. 'It is in Cartagena in Spain,' he begins. 'We have to demonstrate some sort of quality control over the course that we franchise out. One way is to run workshops on how we teach courses. You can go the day before, run the workshop and return a day later. Keith will make all the arrangements for you.' I have dealt with Keith before when I have hired cars but this will take things to a new level for me to include flights and hotel accommodation. The trip will be taken in a couple of weeks' time, I am told, and the Spanish college will arrange the workshop. Just outside the Director's office I come across Edgar and tell him about my forthcoming trip. 'I had to go to Ireland recently,' he says, 'to check on the progress of our Business Administration degree. I found the whole experience surreal. Their library is inadequate, the course content seemed unbalanced to me and the staff did not seem to be adhering to the syllabus as we would do here. They had a different emphasis on some of the subject areas. I told the Director this but he seemed quite complacent about it. He was more interested in the numbers of students taking the course. What I did not expect was to be given a brown envelope addressed to the Director containing money which the college said was the course fees for the students. I gave that to the Director and told him I thought it highly irregular.'

My next task is to interview the shortlist for the Study Assistance post. I had wondered when I put the advertisement together if there is anyone who will feel suited to taking on a job like it. It will require a wide range of skills. In the event, although not actually being snowed under with applicants, there seemed to be quite a few people who will be prepared to accept the challenge. I ask Mike, the librarian, if he would interview with me. I feel that student study support is in his field. He is only too willing to help. We spend the morning interviewing the four candidates I have chosen from the applications. Once again Andrea is present to make sure we get the process right. Mike and I agree on the most suitable person for the lead role without much discussion. Ethel has a strong education background having worked in schools and a college before raising a family that has occupied her for fifteen years. She has tutored in that time and says she is particularly strong in Maths and English. As a strong advantage she can start work immediately. Rather than appoint a second person I think it better to leave Ethel to be involved in the process. We leave the formalities to Andrea.

At the first basketball practice in the college Sports Hall we are overrun with players. Yannis has done a good job advertising the club but has been less successful in weeding out recreational from competitive players. We still have a recreational session in the early evening one day a week and it is not long before we are suggesting to some of the keen but not competent players that they might enjoy that session more. It will take a few weeks before we can settle on a squad, I think. Brian has already contacted me about when our own team can practise. I suggest to him that we hire a space somewhere for a few weeks before the season starts in October. We have worked the fixture list so that there is no clash with my own use of the Sports Hall for college matches.

The Media Resource staff are fully occupied and getting on with their jobs with no interference from me. I am negotiating for a space where the Study Assistance work can take place and think I have found a suitable small tutorial room that can be used during most morning and afternoon sessions. In time I hope to find a purpose built facility capable of accommodating several students at once and with space to fit any equipment that may be required, bookshelves and the like.

In no time at all it is the weekend again. I have not been able to attend training for the National League team this week. We are at home again for the match at the weekend. It is a National Trophy game. This competition is for Second and Third Division teams. The last time we played in it we were the winners, but that was ten years ago. Now we are to play Mid-Sussex Magic. We play as if we want to win the Trophy again and easily win by exactly the same margin as the previous home league game. There is no sense of the crowd being bored by the ease of our victory and they file out after the game in a good mood.

The following week sets out the pattern for a term time week. The office is busy responding to the demands for

Media Resources, I spend time preparing for the various new facets of my academic life and two evenings are given over to attending basketball practices, both with the college team and with Hampshire Hoops. The latest staff newsletter contains a notice of the intent to hold a Christmas Dance. It is being organised by Jaquie who now has moved into the office of one of the new Schools. I meet her in the corridor one day and comment on the task she has given herself. 'Well, it is about time everyone stops moaning and we begin to pull together,' she says. 'We have the Main Hall available for events, so let us use it.' I agree with her notion and wish her well. Apparently she has a team from the old General Office who are going to work with her. 'Do you ever hear from Meryl?' I enquire. 'Only once after she got back to Australia,' she replies. 'She has got a job and all seems to be well.' 'Give her my best wishes if you write to her anytime,' I say.

I have now noticed that no bulletin is being issued by the Director any more. 'The Truth' has seemingly been put to bed, or else the Director has not been around to write it. There has been no success for the detective in finding out about the rival publication, 'The Lies', and rumour has it that he is no longer employed looking for the source. I can only hope that this might be the beginning of a truce between management and the staff.

Over the past few months I have been able to keep up my regular runs that I enjoy. From the college I have several routes that take about thirty minutes and from my flat there is woodland nearby that offers me a range of routes also. Occasionally I can join in with the college basketball training and as a result of all my activities, I feel I am fairly fit for my age. Certainly I will be able to play my part in the forthcoming local basketball season. So when one of the staff approaches me with the opportunity to join the staff football team he is getting together, I jump at the chance. He explains that the matches will be played on Sundays and the opponents will be carefully picked to match the ages of our team. 'There are quite a few teams around who are looking for fixtures with other veteran teams,' Peter, from the Social Studies teaching group, says, 'We will not play every week and once winter sets in, we probably won't play at all,' he adds. That suits me fine, I think.

Our next National League basketball match takes us to Chiltern and brings back memories of our return to our own whole sports hall to play them in a cup game in the previous season. We win the game but are considerably helped by the indiscipline of the home team who gift us fifteen free shot points in the second half because of infringements.

Dave invites me to another evening session at the pub with the bar billiards. After my usual defeat we sit with our pints in front of us and he tells me how he has snared another backer for the club. 'It is a local building firm,' he says, 'and it shows our wisdom in having someone from the local Planning Department as a director of the club.' I know what he is getting at, but really do not wish to find out more. What with brown envelopes with money in at college and now an intimation of favours perhaps within the basketball world I feel a sense of becoming involved with things I do not wish to know about. Dave scoffs at my reservations when I express them.

At college I am pleased to welcome Ethel and I spend a mornings with her talking about her approach to her new job. I also tell her about some of my other ideas for helping students by addressing the course delivery given by the lecturers. 'We are increasing our student numbers so quickly that we have to take measures to stay on top of the situation' I observe. 'You will have an important part to play. But first you will need an assistant. We have the names of the other three we interviewed and wonder if you had formed any opinion of them whilst you were waiting? Our letter to them, telling of your appointment, left it open that we might be in touch later.' Ethel replies that she had been impressed by one of the male candidates. Andrea is contacted to ask the man if he would be able to come in for a follow-up interview.

It is time to get more serious about the nine lecturers I have suggested I will need. I talk with Alan, the Director of Academic Operations, and we agree on the wording to be distributed to the Faculties. It will be a case of the Faculties putting forward a candidate rather than a chance to select who I might want. Obviously I would prefer to choose staff who I know would be effective but I am told that I would have to respect the autonomy of the Faculty Heads. We hope to have the system up and running by the end of the first term. This will allow for replacement part-time staff to be appointed as cover. My main concern is that the job will be given to members of staff who have a light timetable. The light timetable in turn could come from being a less effective lecturer and these are people I would not want. It is important, I think, to have role models who are respected for their teaching. I have to rely on the Heads of the Faculties being sympathetic to my notion of dealing with the changing role of the lecturers and wanting to help them in that. Nominations are asked for by the end of the month with the system being in place in the new year. The Director himself, I hear, has just gone off to Malaysia on one of his recruiting missions. I wonder if Governors approval had been sought for this latest jaunt. Will I be expected to run a workshop out there?

Thinking about that, I realise that I need to finalise my preparations for the workshop in Cartegena. I visit Genevieve who teaches languages mainly to our Personal Assistants course. She kindly offers to translate the main points I wish to make into Spanish and put them on the acetates that I will use on the overhead projector in Spain.

As I am doing this I suddenly have the thought of how things have changed for me over the last year. It is like I have become a different person concerned now not with the physical, as I have been over my professional teaching life, but with academic matters. It is like a new dawn.

Keith supplies me with the information for travelling and I take the plane from Gatwick to Alicante. After clearing the customs and immigration area I walk out into the area where people are holding up cards with names on them. I see my name and look at the two men who are standing together. They look just like two Mafia type personnel but I guess it is just their natural colouring from living in a sunny climate. In any event they are pleasant enough and can speak a smattering of English. I studied Spanish as a two year course when I had a limited timetable in the Sixth Form many years ago. The teacher was nearing retirement and had a habit of falling asleep whilst the other boy and I, there were only two of us in the class, worked out any translation he set us. Once we had perfected the translation, using a dictionary quite often, and were ready to read out our effort we would make a noise which would bring him out of his slumber. He always then said, 'Again,' as if he had not caught the first rendition. He must have thought we were very good.

That was then and since then I have not spoken the language other than the occasional holiday dialogue. I do not want to admit to my previous learning of the Spanish language and so the car journey to Cartegena is conducted in a sort of hybrid English. I am taken to a hotel and spend a half hour with the two men who I realise are the proprietors of the college. They will not be present tomorrow but are at pains to tell me that they have employed a translator to help me run the workshop. I am told that several of the attendees do not speak English. Someone will come and collect me in the morning, I am informed.

The workshop is to be conducted in a classroom which contains basic furniture, but does have an overhead projector I am glad to see. After the usual preliminaries I take the translator aside and say, 'I don't need to understand all that is being said. If what I say sparks a conversation among those present do not stop them talking to tell me what they are saying. You can give me a précis later on. I would rather the staff talk about their teaching methods to one another quite freely.' I then give my exposition, bearing in mind that we are talking about my own college run course that has been approved to be delivered as per our quality controls. This, I tell them, entails a variety of delivery methods which I then explain using acetates that Genevieve has made for me.

At the end of the session, which I think goes better than I could have expected, we repair to a local wine bar. One thing I learn there is that the staff, including the ones who supposedly do not speak English, all have a good command of the English language.

As the owners take me back to the airport I ask them if any woman are teaching on the course since I had only men present for the workshop. I am told that there will be women in the future but at the moment it is only men involved in the delivery of the course which has mainly men as the students. 'Talking of the course,' one of the owners says, 'please take this box for you Director. It contains the outstanding course fee payments.' My heart stops as I recall Edgar's comments after he had returned from Ireland. Am I now to be complicit in some sort of illegal action? What will the future hold for all these franchises?

PART TWO

Development

CHAPTER EIGHTEEN

I still shudder when I think of accepting the brown box to be delivered directly to the Director those eighteen months ago. I remember giving it to his secretary with a short message, something like 'A present from Cartegena for the Director. I don't know what it is.' I was trying to distance myself from the arrangements for the college franchises based on the suspicions of some of the Union officers, Don in particular.

So many things have happened since that time. The biggest event was the confirmation eventually of the government's plan to do away with Polytechnics and make the existing Polys into Universities. We had not achieved that status at the time of the decision. Needless to say it caused much heart-searching and the staff were called together to be told that University status was now to be our aim. Arrangements had been made to liaise with an existing university, one that our Director of Academic Operations had a close connection to, having worked there for some years. It would act to help us through the processes necessary to establish University status.

If my professional life had not been as smooth as I would have wished, some other parts of my life had been very successful. The Hampshire Hoops return to the National League proper had ended with us winning the league and then the Championship Play-Off at the Wembley Arena. Unfortunately the subsequent promotion to Division Two had coincided with the loss of several key players. As a result we had struggled through the season and finished tenth out of twelve places with only five wins to our credit. Luckily the sponsors had remained faithful and Dave kept reminding me how useful it was to have a council Planning Officer on the Board when the main sponsor was a local building firm. My main problem was my broadcasts in the Sports programme of the local radio. We were suffering quite a few defeats and I had to try to be optimistic about our next game whilst holding some credibility as to my knowledge of basketball. Sometimes I just knew we were going to lose but I never let my feelings rule my predictions.

I had enjoyed playing basketball in the local league again for the last two winters, but began to feel that age was catching up with me for such an energetic game. The staff football team had provided me with more enjoyment playing against similar aged players and at a slower pace.

And then there was work. It is hard to believe how much had happened on that front and a lot of it had sprung from my connection with the First Year Experience. I attended the annual conference which took place in Dallas. I looked out for Rachel but she was not there. I guessed her husband had finally got his way. However the ladies from George Mason University were there and I quickly picked up where we had left off in St. Andrews.

I took a trip out on my own to visit Dallas Baptist University and talked my way in to find out about their teaching methods and support for students, using the fact that I was attending the conference nearby. Whilst in the library I noticed what looked like oil paintings of distinguished figures scattered around the room. On enquiring who they were I had been told that each was a winner of the Lecturer of the Year Award voted for by the students. I made a note to mention that to the Director as a way of highlighting the role of the lecturer. I had no idea of what that would lead to at the end of our next academic year.

The Conference hotel in Dallas was the usual palatial building with very comfortable rooms. I managed to isolate a female staff member from an establishment on the West Coast who was attending for the first time. She was all alone, looked about to be in her mid-thirties. After a few opening remarks about the location and number of people wandering around I managed to persuade her that she might like to see more of the immediate area in my hire car. 'You mean you have rented an automobile for your short stay here?' Beverley had enquired. There was a chance, I realised, that anyone following my attendance at the First Year Conference might consider that I was doing it to make contact with members of the opposite sex. Whilst there was an element of truth in that, I was nevertheless getting some good practical ideas for implementation at my own college from the content of the workshops.

One idea I had picked up was to get workbooks for each course module. There had been a decision made to alter our timetable from terms to semesters following the American model. In essence parts of the whole course were divided up into thirteen week sections followed by one week of revision and one for assessment. The management team had originally held an almost farcical meeting when we were trying to suggest dates for the two semesters which had to be separated by a week to allow processing of results. In one scenario we would have begun the year in early September to allow a natural break at Christmas. It would have also meant ending the academic year in April. Eventually sense had prevailed but it still meant some awkward implementation with Christmas and the movable Easter breaks. However, for me the breaking up of the course into modules lent itself perfectly to Workbooks. After discussion with the Director I was able to introduce the idea and it was so successful that eventually a separate bookstore location was set up to sell the books. The two staff employed came into my section. To encourage the production of the workbooks I had also introduced a scheme that I had called Teaching and Learning Projects.

In effect this scheme released staff from their teaching commitments for a few hours a week. I had set in place a system whereby staff could apply, with the permission of the

Head of School and a panel would assess whether or not to support the proposed project.

I have explained all of this to Beverley to convince her that my attendance at the Conference is driven by a professional approach to retaining students who might otherwise fall by the wayside. 'So is that what you want from me,' Beverley has asked, 'a discussion on keeping students from leaving?' 'Not really,' I reply, 'I think I have got enough ideas from this Conference about that.' Once we have agreed on that subject we feel free to explore other aspects of life. I ask her if she is satisfied with her life and receive the surprising reply that she regrets that the size of her breasts is not bigger. I feel the need to comfort her on this issue, especially as we are in her hotel room at this time. I expound on the notion that her blue eyes, blonde hair and engaging personality far outweigh anyone thinking about the size of her breasts. One thing has led to another and Beverley, it seems to me, is ready to explore the notion of getting to know one another in a physical sense. Later, as we dress, Beverley, unlike Rachel from the Scottish time together, tells me that she may book for the next Conference which is to be held in New York in June, the following year, 'If I know you will be there,' she adds.

By then, I realise, I will have completed the first year as leader of the Post-Graduate course in Teaching and Learning in Higher Education. It certainly is a long title but, at least, it is descriptive. The process of validating the course had been tortuous. In particular the external member of the panel had been scathing of some of my earlier attempts to put the course together. It had been a painful learning experience for me when I came to the conclusion that some people are so fastidious in matters of course writing. No statement went unchallenged in the syllabus that I was putting forward. In turn those statements were usually coming from perusal of the Standing Conference on Educational Development. I began to think that the externally appointed man concerned, who had been brought in by our overseeing University to guide us through the process, had some vendetta against the personnel of the Standing Conference. Indeed, one conversation I had at a meeting in London, seemed to confirm my suspicions. Apparently there had been a parting of the ways between my external source on the Validation Panel and the organisation of the Standing Conference. To make matters worse for me I was not getting the support from the Director of Academic Operations that I needed. He seemed to side with the external member quite often, even though he had agreed with what we had thought to offer at the Validation meeting.

The situation had resolved itself in a dramatic way when the man had died. He had suffered heart problems, of which we were unaware. His replacement, from the same University, was far more sympathetic, having no axe to grind and our course was validated in short time. Seventeen members of staff have enrolled on the forthcoming course.

I have a staff of three Academic Development Leaders who are working with me part-time to help deliver the course. To these have to be added the two Study Assistance personnel, nine part-time teaching representatives, one from each of the Faculties, the two bookshop workers, seven Media Resources staff and a semester-time receptionist to deal with bookings. Vanessa, my shared secretary with George-Henry, had become his full-time secretary and I am about to get a full-time secretary for myself.

There will be a Management Conference at the start of the academic year which will be in Bournemouth. Hopefully it will be less fraught than the last one. Then, with most of the senior managers at the conference, there had been trouble back at the college. Matters concerning the rapid expansion of student numbers, the building programme for both the college campus and the student accommodation, the number of overseas franchise programmes which had to be monitored and the government's decision to limit pay rises had all combined to give a situation of unrest. The Union officials still blamed the Director for his gung-ho approach without taking time to put into place a system that could deal with the changes. Whilst the managers were away, the Union had taken the opportunity to lay out their concerns to the one director who had remained on campus. He, in turn, had telephoned the Director to explain what was happening. The Director had wanted to talk to the Union officials over the telephone but they had refused. Several of the managers had been dispatched back to the college immediately. The result was a conference that lacked any focus other than what might be going on back at the college. Eventually everything had blown over. The Union had made their stand and for a time the Director had seemed in a conciliatory mode whilst still taking off to visit franchised colleges. We now had arrangements with seven overseas bases, the latest of which had been the establishment of two courses in Malaysia. These were at sub-degree level but still the Director had felt in necessary to visit the colleges concerned for a couple of weeks accompanied by his wife and a staff member who had joined the college shortly after the Director's appointment and had come from the same college as the Director had worked at. This staff member had also taken his wife.

Before the Management conference, I have to concern myself with the Hampshire Hoops situation. Strangely having finished tenth out of twelve in the previous season in Division Two of the National League, we now are about to play in Division One. This has come about because of the creation of the Basketball Premier League which has automatically led to the renumbering of all the other divisions. Sponsorship has continued to flourish thanks in part to Dave's contacts in the world of business. There are also an excellent backroom staff who promote matches and help out at the games including selling merchandise. Mick has persuaded a physiotherapist to give us his services and

Derek is much in demand by the players. On the playing front Mick has signed a player approaching the end of his playing career who wants to develop his coaching attributes and is promised the opportunity to do that by Mick. Toby, the club's Player of the Year in the season before last, has been persuaded to come out of his self-imposed retirement. The possibility of an American player is also mentioned, but that will require money we cannot be sure of having. As it is, we still had the Colombian player who had returned the year before to work locally. His registration fee to play in the league already dipped well into our financial resources.

Thankfully my tenure as Development Officer for the Basketball Association came to an end at the recent Annual General Meeting when the favoured nominated candidate got the job. I had made virtually no impact on the national scene in my year at the post, but this was in accordance with the understanding I had when I let myself be put forward for the role in the first place.

There is plenty happening in my life anyway and it is difficult to find time to see Sharon and the family still in Kings Lynn, but I do manage the odd trip to the Fenland. I always steel myself to be ready for the inevitable talk about settling down with a wife. 'Soon it will be too late to think about a family of your own,' Sharon constantly tells me. I make sure I get a visit in before the start of the academic year in 1993. Little do I realise the events that will unfold in the coming year.

PART THREE

Denouement

CHAPTER NINETEEN

We are all gathered for this Management conference in a hotel in Bournemouth. I wonder if the location has been chosen should events arise like they had at the last conference. Several of the staff have intimated that they could stay at home because they live nearby but the Director has been firm about everyone staying in the hotel. We have an outside speaker to start the ball rolling and it soon becomes obvious that this conference is going to be centred on the notion of us becoming a university in our own right. We are asked for suggestions of what type of university we would like to be and I, because of my American influence, say, 'A Sidewalk University, where people feel we are part of the community.' I feel quite pleased with that contribution, especially as it is so short and counters some of the other contributions which try to include various facets of university life and become quite convoluted. My other contribution to the conference is more representative of my approach to matters where I know it is of no use following any course counter to the Director's thinking. We have just returned from a group session and have to report back our findings. The subject is contentious and I know the Director's views from a previous conversation I had with him. And I feel most people knew his views. Despite that the reporter for one of the groups, Mike the librarian, launches into a course of action contrary to that favoured by the Director. He is not even allowed to finish before the Director intercedes and launches into a diatribe that confirms my view that his mind is already made up on this issue. My action is to take a small piece of paper and put a black dot on it and send it with Mike's name on surreptitiously along the staff members sitting between me and him. He grins on its receipt.

The rest of the conference passes without incident and we return to the college buildings to prepare for the forthcoming semester, as we must now call it. I meet with the Director. 'I have given some thought to your suggestion about Lecturer of the Year,' he begins, 'I think we might broaden the concept and include other parts of college life including the administration side. I am thinking of things like Secretary of the Year and rewarding other contributions to college life. I will get up a working party to consider it.' 'We don't want it to become a means of upsetting staff,' I counter. The lecturer idea can be voted by students, but the Secretary award will depend on the advocate who is putting forward the person. That will be far more personal.' 'That is something for a working party to consider,' the Director says as he concludes the interview.

My attention now switches to the basketball team and I make my way to the BBC studio to start my regular contribution on the Sports Programme. I talk about the new season, the teams we will meet and the players we have. Bearing in mind last season's poor performance overall, I try not to paint too glowing a picture, conscious of the fact I may have to eat humble pie regularly over the season.

The next evening I am heartened by the display of the Hampshire Hoops team in a pre-season friendly match against Worthing. Last season they had been national champions, and were now part of the newly formed Premier League. Their squad had only recently come together to train for the new season which begins several weeks after ours. Hampshire took advantage of that situation and in the end Worthing had to hang on for a one point win. Mick is heartened by his squad's performance and especially the nineteen points scored by the Colombian player.

On the following morning I am involved in the staff soccer team. The mix of players means that I have a chance to find out what staff members are thinking across the college when we are in a bar after the game. The mood is good since we have just won another game. 'I've been asked to join a working party about rewarding staff,' one of the players says to me, 'is this anything of your doing?' 'I suggested to the Director that we might consider acknowledging lecturers who students think are good. It is an idea I picked up whilst at a conference in the USA. However, he seems to have decided that the notion should run throughout every facet of college life. I fully expect to hear that we will have a Caretaker of the Year award.' 'I hope money is not involved,' says my companion, 'I think that will make the whole thing divisive.' 'Exactly what I think,' I reply.

It is back to reality in the following weeks as the students return and my staff are fully involved in dealing with staff and student issues. I put the finishing touches to the Post-Graduate Course in Teaching and Learning in Higher Education. Already I have conducted the Staff Induction course and received favourable feedback. Several of those attending that course will soon enrol as part of the seventeen strong cohort for the first time the course is to take place. The Director had spoken strongly in its favour when he had met with the Induction Course members, stressing the importance of having many lecturers with a teaching qualification if we were serious about our bid to become a university. I notice that one facet of our college that is notably not mentioned is the existence of the franchise arrangements. I take it that it is the Schools that will appraise their staff of any dealings they might have with other colleges.

The room that Mike and I have prepared for teaching, but which is part of the library, is now ready for use and will provide an excellent teaching base for the course that is designed for staff members. The carpeting has already been noticed by other staff and there is a lobby by some for a wider use of carpeting. On the grapevine I hear that one storey of the building is in line to be carpeted later in the year.

Saturday evening sees me once again as the commentator at the basketball match. It is our second friendly, pre-season game. Only it is not so friendly as feelings rise in the encounter with Swindon Sonics. Toby receives a bloody nose and Craig a gashed hand in the game we win by twenty four points.

The next morning's football match is at our own playing field and for the first time we use the bar facilities. The bar is under the management of the Student Union and previously they had not opened it for staff matches. However, there was a student event later in the day and it had been agreed to open the bar for us also. Pete was the liaison with the Union. He did not play regularly for the staff football team and previously had shown no interest in the post-match situation. We had usually gone to a local pub but an opportunity to drink at the clubhouse was very welcome. Once again I am involved in conversations about the Reward Scheme which has now been announced through the previous week's college newsletter. I again protest that my idea has been expanded and I should not be held responsible for any developments outside my original thinking.

Sport also dominates the next week at college as we hold trials for the basketball teams. Yannis has been good to his word and a couple of very useful Greek players show themselves. Yannis also tells me that the Director has met with his father in Greece and that some sort of business arrangement has taken place. He is vague as to the details but it sounds to me like another franchise, probably at sub-degree level and maybe offering places at our college on completion of the course. I believe that some Greeks may still come to avoid military service.

The atmosphere at the college of the established teaching staff is still one of suspicion. The goal of university status is generally accepted although the disappointment of having the Polytechnic goal taken away has not been forgotten. Our new status means that we are subservient to another institution and this is a cause of concern for many who would that we were masters of our own fate. Don is especially vociferous on this matter. 'It means that the Director can hide behind the external influences,' he says, 'how do we know what the top brass are playing at? And I get the feeling that we are being played. Already one or two of our courses are being threatened because our guiding university already has similar courses that are under-recruiting. We will have to keep our eye on that situation. Also there is such an increase of red tape. Everything we do must be done in duplicate to satisfy the Administration.'

George-Henry drops into my office. 'My job is changing,' he tells me. 'I am now to record the joint meetings of our guiding university and ourselves. As well as that, I have been told that I will be the Minute Secretary at our own Board of Governors.' 'At least you will know what is going on,' I retort. 'That will be very useful to me if you can ever share any information. I'll be particularly interested if matters of teaching are discussed.' 'Don't worry.' George-Henry replies, 'I'll let you know anything that might concern you. I owe you that, at least for taking care of me when I arrived.'

A bit later in the morning, Pete comes to visit. 'Fancy a short round of golf,' he queries. 'We can go to the local municipal course and hire some clubs. I'm free after three o'clock if you can make it.' I look at my diary. 'Yes, I can,' I say, 'but I have not played golf for quite a while.' 'Don't worry,' replies Pete, 'I don't consider myself any good. It is a lovely day and I need to get out of here for a while.' We arrange a four o'clock start and I work through my lunch hour to justify to myself slipping off early, after giving some pathetic excuse of a dental appointment.

Pete is already in the car park when I arrive and we go to the golf shop to hire the clubs and pay for the nine hole course. It is still a glorious day and surprisingly there is only one pair of players waiting to tee off meaning we will only have to wait a short time. I go to an area where I can practise my swinging which is a little rusty because I have not played for so long. However, I am unprepared for Pete's next comment. He has been doing the same as me when he suddenly announces, 'I forgot. I play golf left-handed. I will have to go back to the golf shop to exchange the clubs.' When he returns I accuse him of gamesmanship. 'Of all the tricks to play,' I begin, before he interrupts me to say, 'Honestly, it has been so long I genuinely forgot.' It is no surprise when I lose and I blame it on his ploy at the beginning as an excuse. In fact, neither of us has played well and I am reminded of Mark Twain's comment about golf that it was a good walk wasted. In the clubhouse afterwards, Pete tells me about another of his forthcoming assignations and I begin to see why he wanted a round of golf with me. 'If you come with me you will enjoy yourself, I am sure,' Pete says, 'although you might not end up like you did with Meryl.'

When the weekend comes I am pleased to see a good following for the basketball team. The visitors are Sheffield Forgers and that brings back memories of our only home defeat two seasons before. To add to that, Sheffield had won their division in the previous season. They were obviously an in form team. We were without our Colombian player. He had been disqualified for fighting in a match at the end of his previous spell with us and it was his punishment to sit out this game. Luckily for Hampshire, however, Sheffield had failed to register their new American player/coach in time for the game. Despite a scare in the first half when Sheffield went briefly ahead just before half time, we pull back the deficit and go on to win by ten points. The crowd has watched an exciting game and their team has won. After last season's miserable performances at home games, I am pleased for the fans. Dave is at the game and afterwards introduces me to the owner of the building firm that is now our main sponsor. His name is Diego and it seems he is a second generation member of an immigrant Spanish family. He tells me that some of his extended family members have played basketball in Spain. 'It is played everywhere there,' he explains, 'and two of the family are still playing in the Spanish League where thousands watch every match and many games are on TV.' He knows the same is not the case here and I wonder if his sponsorship is driven by the thought that eventually there will be a wider acknowledgement of the game or is it more that he wants to be in the market for local business using our current member of the company. I notice he goes back to his table in the bar with Dave to join Derek, from the local Planning Department, probably to discuss more business.

George-Henry and I have had several evenings out in local pubs since his arrival. Over that time I have discovered that he is now divorced, though amicably it seems, since he sometimes goes to visit his ex-wife. Two sons are involved, one being at university and the other working. We get on well having been rather thrown together at work. When he arrived he stayed in a bed and breakfast for a while but now he has a flat not too far from where I live. We do not discuss work on our evenings out but rather stick to general events and sport. However, I sense that he wants to unburden himself about his new position that brings him into contact with the higher management team and the governors. But, all I can get out of him on our latest meeting is that something seems amiss. 'I obviously can't talk about what I suspect, because I may be way off the mark. I am too new to the centre of operations to have an informed sense of what is going on, but I worry that not all is well. More I cannot say,' he concludes. I do not push him on this matter knowing that when the time comes he will probably unburden himself. I hope he feels he can trust me with his suspicions. As for my own feelings, I have sensed for some time, thanks in part to the Union officials, that not all is well.

All of that is put behind me when I meet with Pete for our next night out, the one arranged at our recent golf game. Our companions are two of the Marketing staff, Liz and Sarah, both in their mid-twenties and fairly new to the college. Pete's lack of imagination means that we are eating in the same restaurant as we did with Jacqui and Meryl. This time it is to the flat occupied by Liz that we return. It only has one bedroom and when Liz and Pete eventually go into that, I am left with Sarah. I can sense that she is very apprehensive. To lighten the moment I ask her about her husband. 'He is a builder who is working on a contract in Germany at the moment,' she replies, 'he will be away for another couple of months. The money is good and we are saving up for a deposit on a house.' We chat a bit more and she relaxes slightly but becomes taut again when Pete comes back into the room to retrieve his jacket, before disappearing again into the bedroom.

I ask Sarah about her previous job. 'I worked for a firm that sold yachts, including very big ones,' she says. 'The trouble with that job was that the potential purchasers usually thought that I was part of the sale and they could flirt with me as they wished. I only lasted three months.' 'You don't have that problem at the college, presumably?' I say. 'No, the college problem is that the leader of the department has not got a background in Marketing. Apparently he came from the same college that the Director worked at shortly after the Director started here. They must be good friends because he often goes on the trips to our overseas colleges and takes his wife also. We never get a chance to take a trip to do any marketing abroad.' I could see her cast glances at the bedroom door and wondering about how she might get away. It was getting quite late.

'Can I give you a lift home?' I enquire. 'Yes, please,' comes the relieved reply. On the way back she tells me that she has only known Liz for a few months and had agreed to come out with her tonight just in case things did not go well. 'Once she went into the bedroom, I guessed my role was no longer needed,' Sarah says, and we laugh together. Later when Pete checks on what happened between Sarah and myself I ask him why he had come for his jacket. 'Did you think I would see if there was any money in it?' I ask. 'No,' he replies, 'I had left my condoms in one of the pockets.'

CHAPTER TWENTY

Although Hampshire Hoops had beaten Sheffield Forgers, it was not to prove a sign of what was to come. In our next home game, against Brixton Topcats, we suffer a defeat. The visitors are far quicker on the court and hustle the Hampshire ball handlers to good effect. We are unable to settle down and play to our rhythm. Trailing by fourteen points at half time and despite the encouragement of the home supporters, we are unable to match the Brixton total. Mick, our coach, is despondent in the bar afterwards. 'I must find at least one more player who is good enough to match the best we have,' he says. 'It is a pity there is no money forthcoming.' I can only sympathise and tell him that I will mention his wish when I next see Dave.

Meanwhile at the college it is becoming obvious that tensions are rising between the management and the lecturers. One complaint put to the Director of Academic Operations is that the continued expansion of student numbers is in direct conflict with the latest Government action which has been to impose controls on the student numbers of home and European students. Don, as usual, sums up the general feelings when he says, 'We should now consolidate, decentralise the power base and create a culture of collegiality.' When put to the Director, he is quick to counter with the news that the British Council is encouraging overseas expansion by British universities and colleges. As such he announces a free standing income-generating company to now control the overseas franchises we have. 'My foresight has been rewarded,' he says at a staff meeting, 'we are in a strong position to approach the Privy Council for our own degree-awarding powers and hence, university status.' He also announces that his contract has been renewed.

This latter news leads to more frustration for the academic community. In my next evening out with George-Henry I hear his views. 'The contract was renewed on the strength of the views of the Chair of the Governors,' he says. 'No one challenged the decision. In truth, I don't think the current Governors know enough about what is going on. Government policy changes don't help. The Director has announced a meeting of his senior staff to plan for the future. I know some staff feel that this pursuing of overseas students will put at risk any chance of embedding academic quality further in order to achieve degree-awarding powers.'

Peter from the Social Studies group who runs the staff football team asks me if I am up for a trip north, to Clitheroe, to play in a football match to be organised by an ex-member of staff who has moved to a university in the area. 'His father was the headteacher of a school in Clitheroe,' he says. 'I already have nine players, you will make ten. We only lack a goalkeeper. Unfortunately, I cannot make the trip myself so Jeff will be in charge.' I check the dates with the basketball fixture list and see that the team is not at home for the planned date and make a decision that a change will do me good.

The next staff soccer match finds us playing new opponents at Canford School, Dorset. Canford School is blessed with huge playing fields and the changing room is so distant from the pitch that the team decides to change 'al fresco' to avoid wearing ourselves out in walking to the pitch.

Each team has thirteen players with substitutions being allowed on a rolling basis. The opposing captain apologises for the presence of two young players who were 'staying for the weekend with one of the team'.

Half time finds us trailing by five goals to one. The home captain asks us if we would like to 'borrow' some of their team for ours to make the game more even. The compromise reached is that their younger players will be withdrawn until the last five minutes of the second half.

Our organiser for this match, Jeff, tongue in cheek, warns the opponents that we are a second half team. The opponents promptly score two more quick goals to leave us trailing by seven goals to one. Twenty minutes later the score is seven all! Their younger players are re-introduced considerably before the last five minutes and the home team nets twice more. A late further rally by us results in a final score of nine – nine!

Over the many years of the combined history of matches played by all the players in the game no one can quite recall either as many goals in a game nor a fightback of such magnitude. Our team even has the energy to walk to the changing room on foot for a celebratory shower before returning to our cars in the distant car park. In the pub afterwards the talk is of the forthcoming tour to Clitheroe, being a new experience for the college staff team.

We are still talking about the game several days later in the staff Refectory. Don puts a damper on our light-hearted comments by saying that the Director has some scheme in mind to alter the structure of the college yet again. 'This will be the final straw,' he says. 'Only last year we were reorganised and some of the problems that threw up still exist.' We ask on what evidence does he base his suspicions but he will not divulge any more information and parts with the words, 'Watch this space.'

It is now widely perceived that the changes from Divisions to Faculties, now under three Schools, has been superficial and that no devolution of authority had ever been intended. Only a few months ago one of the three Deans had tendered his voluntary redundancy notice. This, it was mooted, came directly as a result of that Dean leading a deputation of senior staff to the Chair of the Governors saying that they had lost confidence in the Director. The academic staff, he had said, would prefer to embed academic quality further in order to secure degree-awarding powers rather than put that in jeopardy by having so many franchise courses.

As a result of the resignation and the appointment of a successor, the Director has held a two day senior management team-building event. However, if Don is to be believed, the Director has suddenly announced yet another management restructuring. It is, according to Don, only a year since the last restructuring and 'without any consultation involving the Deans who he has only recently spent time with on his team-building exercise.'

So Don's prediction has come true and we are called to a staff meeting to hear about the changes. The Director outlines his plan and, as far as I can see, I will be unaffected by the changes, which are mainly managerial. As I leave the meeting with all the other staff I find myself walking alongside Sarah who I have not spoken to since our evening out with Liz and Pete. I ask about her husband. 'Is he home from his overseas work yet?' I enquire. 'Not yet,' she replies, 'but he is due back in a few weeks.' 'So, if I want to see you again I will have to act quickly,' I joke. 'Yes,' she replies, in a way that makes me believe that a meeting would be possible. Now there is a dilemma. Apart from the age difference, which I guess to be about fifteen years, she is a work colleague and, so far, I have avoided any involvement with that situation. I remember only too well Graeme's ultimate fate. However, he was married and I am not. I make a quick decision, 'How about tomorrow night,' I venture. 'Fine,' Sarah replies. ''I know where I dropped you the last time. Shall I pick you up there?' 'No,' she replies, 'too many neighbours. I will be in the supermarket car park nearby at 7.30pm.'

The next day passes quickly and I make my way to the supermarket car park which, much to my surprise, is still busy. Sarah is already there and joins me in my car. 'Any preferences?' I enquire. 'Only that you find somewhere quiet and away from here,' she responds. I drive out into the country to find a pub that I know has a restaurant but where you can also eat in the bar area. The restaurant is nearly empty and Sarah suggests that we eat in the bar area where there is more atmosphere, as she puts it. I am conscious of how she had reacted when being left alone with me when we were with Liz and Pete. 'Sorry about that,' she says, 'Liz had not told me about what her intentions were with Pete and it came as such a shock when they upped sticks and left for the bedroom. I did not know if I was meant to do a similar thing on the couch. Thank goodness you acted so kindly.' I then tell her about Pete's retrieval of his jacket where he had his condoms. 'I'm not too sure that Pete expected Liz to act as forthrightly as she did, although I know he would not turn down a chance that was given to him that evening.' Before we can continue the conversation we are asked to select from the menu and spend the next hour or so talking generally about work and the food we are eating.

After the meal I ask her how her job situation is. 'Has your boss got the hang of his job yet?' I say. 'Things are just the same,' Sarah replies, 'he is off again next week to Greece. I can't think why he has to go so often to our overseas places. We need to make an effort to encourage more British students to come to the college. I have attended several events now in this country. In fact, I go when others could but because they have family they don't like to spend nights away. Liz is always up for trips as well, so we tend to do them all. I have a short time before my husband comes back. There is one event I am going to shortly. It is in Manchester, next week.' Almost without thinking and very quickly I blurt out, 'Would you like some company for the overnight stay?' 'Can I think about it?' Sarah replies and we move on to other topics. Eventually, I drop her in the supermarket car park where we had met and give her the briefest of kisses on the cheek as we part.

Mick, the basketball coach, is apprehensive about our next away match. 'We need a win to raise spirits,' he says, 'but our next opponents, Coventry, are unbeaten and to make matters worse, it is an away game.'

His fears are compounded on the night when we lose Toby with a bloody nose, courtesy of an opponent's elbow early in the second half and, to make matters worse, Eric is fouled out with twelve minutes left. This means we have lost our outside shooting capability. For me, I am intrigued by the match commentary. There are guidelines for the commentators of which I am aware. It is the same Coventry commentator that I remember from a few years before and he is still encouraging the home crowd to make a noise when we have a free throw. I have spoken to several players about what effect the crowd has on any free throw and the general consensus I reached was that it had no effect at all. Therefore, I do not bother to mention the guidelines to the Coventry commentator who would probably not change his approach anyway. Eventually we lose by ten points. 'Our next game is a home National Trophy match against a team from a lower division, this will give us a chance to pick ourselves up.' Mick optimistically points out.

At our next college basketball training session, I ask Yannis how his father's connections with the college are progressing. 'He never talks to me about such things,' he responds, 'but I know several of the staff from here have been to visit him.' I put the college situation out of my mind after a telephone call from Sarah. 'Were you serious about coming with me on my next trip?' she asks. 'Certainly,' I reply. 'I have the hire car booked for that day and I can pick you up at your flat at 10 o'clock' she says. 'That will be fine,' I reply. 'It will only be for one night away,' she continues. 'The event is for schools in the Manchester area and is in the evening. We will be back here early afternoon on the next day.' I tell her that my diary allows me both days to be possible.

Just two days later, punctually at ten o'clock, Sarah arrives at my flat and we begin our trip north, with Sarah driving and for me a chance to look at the countryside on a trip that I have made so often whilst driving the basketball team minibus. We stop at a pub for lunch and as Sarah is parking the car she nudges into the wall. Luckily there is no damage to the car, it having been only the slightest of bumps. 'I'd better take over driving for a while after lunch,' I say. Sarah agrees but not after saying, 'I've never done that before, it must be nerves.'

Nerves are not in evidence when we find the hotel and go to check in. 'Leave this to me,' says Sarah. I go to sit on a couch in the entrance lobby and soon Sarah is by my side with details of the room which turns out to have a four-poster bed in it. 'A bit over the top,' I decry. 'Where's your romance?' Sarah is quick to respond. Her event is close by to the hotel and in a short time she is ready to leave. 'Do you want any help?' I enquire. 'No, thanks,' she replies. 'It will be better if you don't attend and then I won't have to explain why you are there. We marketing people are a close-knit group and everyone knows everyone else. Just be patient and I will be back as soon as possible.' 'I should have brought my running gear,' I respond.

It is ten o'clock before Sarah returns. The event finished at nine, but she tells me she had to socialise with her colleagues for a while. 'I hope you have not been too lonely and bored,' she says. 'I am sure I will get over it,' I say. 'Are you tired or would you like to go to the bar for a nightcap?' 'No nightcap,' she says, 'and yes I am tired but also looking forward to relaxing in the four-poster.' 'Let's just do that,' I agree. I am thinking about the previous time we were together in a room and how apprehensive she was. I wonder what has happened to bring us to this situation. Nevertheless when she appears from the bathroom and is ready for bed I am quickly following her. As she snuggles up to me she starts to talk about what is happening. 'I married my childhood sweetheart,' she says. 'I have no regrets because we are good for each other although I am sorry that he has to work away so much, but we need to save money for a house. I think I missed out by marrying young. Although I told you about being harried at the boat selling job, nothing ever came of the proposals that were made to me. I spurned all the advances. However, with you, it is the opposite. You were so kind to me on that evening with Liz and Pete and even recently when you took me out for dinner. I feel I can trust you and that I can lay to rest the demons that haunt me about missing out by marrying young.' 'Wow, that's a tall order, Sarah,' I say. 'I am so glad you allowed me to come with you and promise you I will respect any wish you may have about our relationship.'

We grow quiet and do not speak for a while. Occasionally I feel Sarah tremble as she lies in my arms. Eventually I break the silence and say, 'Look, if you now consider this a bad idea I am sure I can find another room.' 'No, please don't do that,' she says, 'I am the one who suggested this whole scheme and it is just that I am being silly. You have come with me and I don't want to appear as if I have led you on. It just takes some getting used to, that is all. Other than my husband you are the first person with whom I have shared a bed.' I try to lighten the situation by saying, 'All you are going through in your mind and conscience, the feelings, the situation, the predicament and yet you can still say 'with whom' I have shared a bed'. Fortunately, Sarah laughs and immediately relaxes. I feel her whole body lose its tenseness as she turns to face me. 'Thank you,' she says, 'that is just what I needed. After all, this is just for one night but it is one I will remember for a long time. Also, it is the first time I have slept in a four-poster bed.' 'That's the trouble,' I reply, 'you will remember the four-poster bed long after you will remember me.' That seems to do it and now Sarah becomes a compliant bedmate and we eventually fall asleep in each other's arms.

The journey home is uneventful. There is perhaps a slight awkwardness between us as we are not sure about what we have just done. For me it is a new departure to sleep with a work colleague. For Sarah it has probably a much deeper significance. I feel sure we will both be able to handle the work situation since we rarely come across each other in the workplace. That is an advantage, I guess, of working in a large organisation. By the time we reach home, Sarah is again at the wheel of the hire car and drops me at my flat. There would be no clue to anyone watching that it was not anything other than being dropped off by a car driven by a woman, other perhaps than me reaching for my travel bag which is on the back seat.

CHAPTER TWENTY ONE

I have missed the basketball team practices this week and so I telephone Mick, the coach, to find out any news. I will need some information for my broadcast on the local radio the next day. He reminds me that it is a National Trophy game and we are playing Guildford Storm who are in the division below us. We should be at full-strength he finishes. There are no telephone calls from the college on my answerphone, so I assume that all is well. I want to spend the evening at home going over the experiences of the last twenty four hours. I am tempted to telephone Sarah, knowing she will probably be alone also, but eventually I decide not to call her.

We manage to win our match the following evening, but not as easily as we would have hoped. The visitors are fast and agile. Joe fouled out and Toby, despite Mick's full-strength assurance, was suffering from a heavy cold and took no part in the game. It was only three minutes from the end before we took charge. It had been exciting for the crowd and that was about all the comfort I could take from the evening in my match-promoter role.

Back at work on Monday, it is evident that things have run smoothly in my absence. My immediate task is to prepare the next teaching session for my Post-Graduate course. I have some material that I have collected recently for discussion about the teaching methods employed at the college. Last year I had surveyed 121 members of staff about their teaching methods and the frequency of their use. It is this survey that will form the basis of my session with those on the course. The assessment of the course is through a presentation of a portfolio and the teaching contact hours for staff members on the course is therefore limited. We do not meet every week. In the survey I had used twenty one methods of course delivery and asked the respondents to say if they used the methods often, sometimes, rarely or never. Unsurprisingly lectures had been used by 98% of the staff often. Our session is lively and, once again, brings to the fore the issue of large classes and numbers of students to teach. I point them in the direction of one of the Teaching and Learning Projects being undertaken currently by a member of staff who is seconded to my area at the moment and who will be leading one of the sessions later on their course and deals with less used teaching methods.

In my office the following day my attention is drawn to an article in the local newspaper about the college. Someone is obviously talking to the Press because there are comments about unease of staff members about the management style and scope of the college. Particularly mentioned is the growth of overseas courses. News to me is that there is to be a communications audit, sanctioned by the governors, by an outside person. I wonder how I had not heard of this action. Certainly there has been no mention of it in the regular college newsletter.

I seek Don out and visit him in his office. 'Are we back to the days of 'Lies'?' I ask. 'Not as far as I know,' Don replies. 'I don't know where the Press got their information, but I can confirm that it is true about the audit. The Governors made the decision at their last meeting on Friday. It probably helped that the Director was not there. He was on one of his overseas visits. He is due back tomorrow and then watch out is all I can say. Just to add fuel to the fire there have been complaints, and I do know from whom, about the internal auditing of the college and these have been passed to the Higher Education Funding Council which has, in turn, said it will investigate. We are all in for a rough ride,' he concluded.

There is good news for me later in the week when Mick telephones to tell me he has signed another player. It is a Danish player called Steen who has played over seventy times for his country. 'We had a local league match the other evening and this six foot nine inches player was in their team. You could tell immediately that he was good. In fact, he was too good for my team. My local league team that I coach lost its unbeaten record. Anyway, in talking to him after the game, I found that he was very interested in playing in the National League. He is over here on a language course for a year. He will help us considerably. We will include him in our game against Bury if his registration comes through in time.'

One of the staff of Media Resources staff approaches me to ask if he can go on a visit to another college. 'They are doing a lot with computers,' he says, 'and I see a big future for their use in teaching.' I arrange the details for him and ask him to keep me in touch with developments in that area. It looks as if the days of the Overhead Projector may be numbered. Several members of staff, I know, are already using computers in their work and I guess I had better keep up-to-date with changes that will be happening.

I come across Sarah in the staff refectory. It is not a place she often visits and I wonder if she is there because she knows I might be. Liz is with her and already Pete is there giving me the perfect excuse to casually join them. I search for any signs that Liz may know about my trip with Sarah but am satisfied that Sarah has kept everything to herself. In fact, Sarah makes much of the impending return of her husband from his building contract and I can see how much she must be looking forward to it. Pete and Liz hardly listen to what we are saying. After the women have gone I ask Pete if there have been any further meetings with Liz. 'Just a few,' Pete says, 'and they have been very enjoyable, if you know what I mean.' 'Just be careful,' I caution, 'remember what happened to Graeme.' 'I can handle it,' Pete says, 'trust me.'

Later in the week there is another article in the local press, which, it seems, smells a good story. The first headline had been 'Storm Hits Local College'. This is now followed by, 'Auditors Go In To Check On College'. I remember that Don had told me about the complaints of financial impropriety but he was not too sure that the complaints would hold water. Especially since, as he put it, 'They will have to work hard to uncover any evidence of mismanagement of funds. The Director and his aides are crafty old buggers. There was a fuss at his previous college when accusations were made about his misuse of Erasmus funds. Nothing was ever proven.' The Erasmus programme I knew was to do with funding students for European projects.

That the college is a big organisation to work in now is obvious with the huge increase in staff and student numbers. Consequently, I am taken aback when I see the main story in the Times Higher Education publication which concerns our college. This time it has nothing to do with money or franchising. It seems a member of the teaching staff has left his wife to live with one of his students. I have already experienced something similar with Graeme, but that concerned another member of staff. This time it has student involvement but to make matters worse it has an irate wife who has raised concerns about staff and student relationships. It seems she is concerned that the college does not have any written guidelines on this matter. She sees staff members, males in particular, being in danger of romantic advances made by young students. It goes beyond, she asserts, the simple affair to matters of academic nature with the possibility of favouritism in course marking and other ways. I am surprised the Times has taken this matter as its lead. Although I do not know this particular member of staff I am aware of another one, who plays for the staff soccer team sometimes. Since I have known him he has been friendly, to say the least, with two students. So friendly, in fact, that he has left his wife and children to move in with the latest one, an admittedly mature, student.

However, his wife has not gone public on the matter. I can only guess that the newspaper has other cases it can drip feed in to its articles. With our upcoming investigation by the auditors I can only think that the press must be rubbing their hands in anticipation.

It comes as a relief to be able to turn my attention to the forthcoming basketball match against Bury. Mick tells me that I can say on the local radio that we have signed a new player who will be making his debut in the match. Toby has also recovered from his 'flu and we could potentially be at full strength. Just before the game Mick admits to me that the new player Steen has not yet trained with the squad and he intends to use him sparingly. However, when the teams are to be introduced I notice that Marc is absent. So the new player is used in the game more that Mick had anticipated and he does well using his height to great advantage. Luckily for us our opponents are not very good and we are able to win the game comfortably. Our only concern is the non-arrival of Marc. When I get home, Mick rings. 'Marc's car caught fire on the way to the game, that is why he didn't make it,' he reports. 'Marc is OK and says he will be at training next week but he will need someone to give him a lift.' Training next week will be important, I know, because next weekend we have matches both on Saturday and Sunday.

Waiting for me on my desk at the beginning of another working week, amongst the pile of the internal post, is a letter from America. As is usual, a sticker on the outside of the envelope gives the sender's name and address. I am surprised to see that it is from Beverley. What she wants to be assured of is that I will be attending the New York Conference before she commits to signing up for the Conference herself. As she points out it is a long way from the West coast to the East if the Conference is the only reason to travel. I realise I am entering dangerous territory by confirming my attendance. How serious is she about our relationship which I see as casual only? I decide to wait a while before I reply to the address on the sticker. I don't want to appear too keen.

There is no follow-up in the Times Higher Education newspaper about the story of the previous week concerning the college staff member. No one has even written a letter to the newspaper it seems. Perhaps the reporters will ease off now. The Director sends an internal memorandum to the managers saying how important it is at the moment to have positive news and anyone with such news should communicate it to the Head of Marketing. Don gets to hear of the memorandum and is quick to comment, 'It is like the Dutch boy with his finger in the dyke. Sooner or later everything will come crashing down around the Director's ears and I can't wait for the day.' Another colleague, who is at the refectory table when this is said, jumps in to defend the Director. 'We need University status,' he remarks, 'and we stand a chance with all that is happening at the moment. I sympathise with the Director who has to fight against entrenched attitudes that will keep us in our current role as a college that has to report to another institution before we do anything. We need to be masters of our own fate.' I can see Don quietly seething as he listens but he only says as he gets up to depart, 'There are ways to do something correctly and there are ways to get us into trouble by doing things wrongly.'

Through my regular attendance at the weekly hour's staff three-a-side football that takes place in the Sports Hall I am able to keep in touch with staff feelings across various sections of the college in an informal way. I still have the sense that everyone on the academic staff is working so hard to deal with the rapid expansion of courses and students that Don's worry about correct or incorrect ways holds little water with most staff. Most do not have time to look beyond their immediate concerns and are not too interested in the bigger picture. I am still taking a lot of stick about the Staff

Awards programme and I occasionally try to defend myself by saying that my original intention was very small scale and has now been blown up out of all proportion.

The weekend arrives and Hampshire Hoops have a home game against Plymouth Raiders who are bottom of the league. Toby is absent, and would be for the game the following day, although I could get no reason from the coach as to why. However, he is not missed as we win the game easily. The next day I drive the team to Cardiff. Mick is sure after the game, which we lose, that it is tired limbs that have cost us the match which took place only eighteen hours after the end of the game the previous evening. 'Just seven points,' he says, 'we ran out of steam.' I remind Mick that I will not be available for the trip to Nottingham the following week as I will be in Lancashire with the staff soccer team. I also point out that I had to miss a staff soccer game today to drive the team to Cardiff, just in case he thinks I am being selfish for missing next week's basketball match.

CHAPTER TWENTY TWO

The week has passed and eight staff football players, not nine as promised by Peter, meet in the college car park on Saturday morning for our trip north. We will be augmented when we reach the venue for the game by the brother of one of our team and an ex-colleague through whom we have arranged the game. One notable absentee is still that of the position of goalkeeper. We are hoping to persuade someone when we arrive to take that position. Three cars are needed because two of the players have brought a guest with them. The guests are female and I am informed by one of our team that neither of the women are the wives of the players concerned. Those four will travel together and I will use my car for two others whilst another driver will take the remaining two members of our squad. Jeff, who is now in charge of the tour now that Peter cannot be there, then issues instructions that we should travel in convoy and keep one another in sight as much as possible.

Jeff's idea of keeping together proves difficult to carry out. A few road works with temporary traffic lights plus a lot of traffic in total means we soon lose sight of the other two cars. Suddenly, on the M6, there is a complete hold up of all traffic and we remain stationary for at least five minutes. 'Take the next exit,' Stuart, one of my passengers says. 'I used to live up here and know the roads.'

Stuart then guides me onto the A460 to Cannock and then we pick up the A34. After a while we come to a sign indicating the Cannock Chase German Military Cemetery. 'This was opened in 1967 when I lived up here,' Stuart informs us, 'and there are over 4,000 Germans buried in the cemetery.' 'I did not know about this place,' I reply, 'but it just goes to show how informative our football tours can be.'

Eventually we rejoin the M6 and find that the traffic is flowing freely. After about fifteen minutes we pass a veteran car travelling quite slowly. 'We were behind that car when we turned off the motorway, Stuart,' I tell him, 'that must have been some detour we have just made.'

We arrive at John's house just outside Preston and find the other two cars have been there for some while. 'We were about to send out a search party,' comments Jeff. After a quick drink we move on to a Chinese restaurant where we meet up with Stuart's brother, who is a local bank manager. All ten players plus our two team followers are present for the meal which proves to be a jolly occasion. When it comes to paying, we elect the bank manager to be in charge of working out the details. He suggests dividing the total by twelve irrespective of what everyone had individually. We agree to this and all add ten percent for a tip. This proves too much for the bank manager. 'This is way more than we should leave,' he expounds and we are given change back so that the tip is more like five percent. Stuart pipes up, 'Your customers must feel safe with their money in your hands, no irresponsible financial outgoings.' I wonder how Don, at the college, would respond to this example of parsimony after all he has said about the financial skulduggery he suspects. Still, we are a long way from the college and I am surprised at myself for thinking about it. I do not raise it with the others.

After the meal we move on to a local club recommended by Stuart's brother. It is like so many others of its type, dimly lit with excessive noise that masquerades as music. It is almost impossible to hold a conversation without shouting, but from the evidence around me conversation is not top of people's agenda. We split up into three groups each having our own alcove. We are conscious of the fact that we still do not have a goalkeeper for the forthcoming match. When Colin detaches himself from his lady friend from the adjoining alcove it is to tell us that an ex-student of his is in the club. 'Can you persuade him to play in goal tomorrow?' Jeff asks. 'I don't remember him as a sportsman,' Colin replies, 'but I will give it a go.' He returns a bit later and says, 'He is not willing, but he has a younger brother who might be interested.' Jeff tells Colin to give his ex-student details of the venue and time and says, 'Tell him we will give him back any expenses he incurs.' 'That reeks of professionalism, doesn't it?' Stuart jokes.

We do not have a late evening after such a long day and with another long day facing us tomorrow.

The game is to take place in Clitheroe and we meet at John's house again so that he can lead us to the venue. It has been a cold night and there is still a biting wind as we climb the hill toward Clitheroe and we see evidence of snow on the ground. The pitch we notice on arriving at the ground is covered with a layer of snow. The groundsman has thoughtfully brushed away the snow covering the lines of the pitch and everyone seems content that the game can go ahead. We meet the young lad who has been volunteered by his brother to help us out although there is no sight of the brother.

In the changing room, Jeff produces a new team kit to replace our usual blue shirts and shorts. It is a garish green and white chequerboard design for the shirts. 'Our opponents will find us less than formidable in this outfit,' someone says. Jeff tells us that the kit had been obtained by Pete at the college from his usual supplier at a good rate. 'That's because no one else would think of buying a strip like this,' moans Stuart. Our guest goalkeeper then pipes up, 'At least none of you are like me and having to wear lilac-pink.' At this we burst into laughter and make our way to the pitch.

John has warned us that the opposition contains an ex-professional footballer who is now physical education teacher at the private Grammar School. He is playing on the right wing which means he is on my side of the pitch. Our opponents kick off and quickly move the ball out to their ace player. He makes off down the wing with me in pursuit. Behind me, at full-back, is Joe. Joe is a dour Yorkshireman who for some reason known only to him supports Barnsley Football Club. Joe, himself, has no pretensions to any football ability, but relished the chance to have a trip north. He is now faced with an oncoming winger moving at a quick (for us) speed. Obviously, not being a regular player, Joe has just one pair of football boots and they are more suitable having short rubber studs to dry, hard grounds. As he takes a pace to try an intercept the winger he slips on the snow and falls to the ground. The winger probably cannot believe his luck as he waltzes by the prostrate Joe. He then crosses the ball into the goalmouth where another, younger, member of the opposition is placed who thumps the ball into the goal. I mutter to Jeff, 'We should have told the goalkeeper that he has no defence in front of him. This looks like it might be lambs to the slaughter.'

Shortly after, we have a bit of luck, as the ex-professional player limps off to be replaced by another player. 'Thank goodness for that,' I hear John say, 'I was going to warn you about him before you came, but I thought you might think twice before travelling here.'

It is cold and we have already agreed to knocking twenty minutes off the normal match time. With their star player gone, the home team seems to lose heart. One player even departs at half-time muttering about other duties. His replacement is actually a school pupil who has been drafted in for such an eventuality, we are told. Although young, he is unable to make an impression on the game and gradually we gain the upper hand. However, by now we are two goals down and time is running out. A speculative long shot by Stuart's brother skids off the snow and gains pace which fools their goalkeeper and we are back in the game with the goal that results. As the game enters its final minutes one of the opponents is adjudged to have fouled Stuart in the penalty area. I wonder at the decision. The foul was marginal, I consider. Does the referee take into account our long journey up and back and consider a draw might be a humane decision, assuming we can convert the penalty? As usual at such times with our team everyone is looking at someone else to take the responsibility of the penalty kick. John cracks first probably feeling it his duty to try and level the scores so that we can depart with some honour and dignity. He has no opponents for the penalty kick role. He manages to convert the penalty and after a few minutes more the full-time whistle is blown.

When we emerge from our changing room it is to find that all our opponents have disappeared. 'So much for northern hospitality,' I exclaim to John. I have suffered many times at the hand of Pete at the college about soccer players' lack of sociability. He is always quick to tell me of the camaraderie of the rugby fraternity and especially their post-match celebrations. I hope he never gets to hear of our current round trip of about 300 miles when the opponents were nowhere to be seen after the game. Using John's local knowledge we climb further into the Pendle Hills and find a pub which plays on the local Witches of Pendle story.

Our time there is limited with a journey home to contemplate. I have to restrain myself to one Shandy drink and remember the time when the basketball team stopped at a pub in the Midlands and I found myself in a similar situation. One piece of information that astounds me is that Joe is the member of staff about whom the Times Higher had written the article quoting the angry wife. Joe is quite open about it. 'I thought you knew,' he says, 'in fact, I thought everyone knew.' Since Joe was not a regular player for our team, I guess I had missed out on that piece of information.

As we journey home down the M6 a car cruises by. It is caked all over with mud but we can just make out a painted number in a circle on the side of the passenger door. Stuart says, 'That must be one of the cars in the Lombard Rally which goes through Wales on forest tracks mainly. There is no way we can match that one for speed.' Sometime later we pass the same car on the hard shoulder and notice the occupants are busy changing a wheel. 'A classic case of the tortoise and the hare,' I say to Stuart as we leave the motorway some time later not having seen the Lombard car again.

It is just after nine o'clock when I return home. The first thing I have to do is find out about our cup tie basketball match against Nottingham. I telephone Mick. 'It was a close run thing,' he explains. Nottingham are unbeaten in the league programme in the division below us. They were full of confidence and established an early lead. However, we did not panic and eventually won by six points. Luckily for us Steen has now blended well with the others and was an important factor in our winning this game. Toby came back for the game after a three game lay-off because of his ankle injury. He did not take much part in the game and looked unhappy throughout the whole journey and the match itself. I just wonder if he will be available for our next away game at Ware Rebels.'

After that call I pick up the few messages that have been left on my answerphone. One is from my sister telling me that her family is going to a hotel over Christmas and leaving me details in case I want to join them, although, she points out there may not be any availability at this late stage. There is still nearly a month, I think, how can they be full up?

Later in the week I am pleased to see that Toby will be travelling with us to Ware, although, as Mick has intimated, Toby tells him that he does not feel he has the commitment to continue playing for the team. Mick takes me aside and says, 'This is a major blow. We are bound to miss him as he is a class player.' The only good thing from the game, apart from the ten point win, is that Jon has just made his first appearance for the team after his enforced lay-off. Mick had used him sparingly in the game. 'I had promised to ease him back in,' Mick tells me, 'he has only had a few training sessions with us.'

We have difficult games ahead of us but all that has to take a back seat as once again I have to immerse myself in the college situation where the auditors are about to give their findings and Don is stirring up the staff to show more interest in our franchising policy.

CHAPTER TWENTY THREE

The Audit Report from the Higher Education Quality Committee did contain a number of negative points aimed mainly at the overseas franchises. It also indicated that the Director had made attempts to prevent the publication of the situation by not speaking to the local press. Not forgotten, also, and stated in the report, was the voluntary redundancy of one of the Directors. The question had arisen about the reason for the redundancy application. Had it been, the report asked, because he had led a deputation of directors and staff to complain about the management style of the Director and Governors?

In fact in the last three years, the Report continued, there had been two Funding Council audits of internal controls at the college prompted by complaints from the Funding Council itself. Whilst the complaints proved groundless the Funding Council was concerned about the press damage these allegations were doing to the college. The Funding Council found that there were still issues to be investigated.

'So he is still not off the hook,' Don was quick to point out when expounding in the college Refectory. 'I think they smell a rat,' he continued, 'and good luck to them. They haven't missed much and there is still the report of our internal communications which is being undertaken by that supposedly neutral person from another college.'

For me life continues as before with the double tasks of the Post-Graduate course and the National League basketball team. Also, I still have the coaching of the college team to consider. One activity that is in abeyance for the time being is the staff soccer team. We have reported back to Peter on our trip and result. 'That means we are unbeaten this year,' he says, 'but it is time to take a break. No one wants to go out in this cold weather to play recreational football,' he adds. I agree, 'It was a bit nippy on the snow covered pitch with a cold wind blowing. I am much happier that we should arrange matches over the summer. Perhaps it is an age thing?' He makes no reply to that suggestion.

Things are quiet at work in the college. Don is still vociferous with his criticisms of the management but he can find little Union support as everyone waits for the report of the person looking into the communication situation, hoping that it will highlight other problems of which people are aware. In fact, even Don concedes eventually, that there is little advantage in trying to change anything at the moment. With Christmas coming up, most people are not thinking of rebellion but ways to have a good time. I find that my sister is right after I have made a telephone call to the hotel she had recommended and find that it is, indeed, full for the Christmas period. In one sense, I am not disappointed. I can at least tell her I tried. But, to tell the truth, I am looking forward to a break from my everyday life. We have just lost two home basketball matches, one of which was a National Cup game. At least we had good attendances which much helps our club finances.

I am surprised when one of the Crystal Palace officials approaches me after the game that we had just lost and says, 'You may know of the International Tournament we hold over the Christmas period. We are short of an announcer for a couple of the days and wonder if you would be interested. We can cover any expenses.' After a little thought I agree because it will be a welcome break from having any involved interest in a game.

Dave is still working hard on the sponsors and we meet regularly at the pub, although playing bar billiards less and less. I guess I am just not a good enough opponent for him. All in all I think that a short break from routine will be very welcome.

This indeed proves to be the case as I return from our last away match of the year which is in Sheffield. We lose the game heavily but we are without several key players because of holiday commitments. Mick informs me on the way home that there are no fixtures for a month, although he is anxious to arrange at least one game before our next league match.

With basketball out of the way, except for my two day commentating, and a three week break from college work, I am able to do things that I cannot find time for in my usual routine. Some of these activities are simple, like reading a novel or going to the cinema.

It is fortunate that I could not join my sister over Christmas because on Boxing Day I find myself driving to Crystal Palace National Recreation Centre to fulfil my obligation as a commentator at this international tournament. I have to be there for a 10.00am game which means arriving a while before that. Luckily, I hear my alarm at 6.00am. On arriving I find the game I am to commentate on is a Women's match between an American team and one from Poland. I look at the Polish team list with dismay. One name does not even have a vowel in it. I approach the Polish coach to make my apologies for what I know will be a travesty of pronunciations of her team members. She smiles and helps me as I write the names phonetically. I make sure she knows that the team members will be introduced in numerical order so that even if they don't recognise their names they can run onto the court at the right time. In one sense it probably doesn't matter anyway since the spectators I am commentating to barely reach double figures. I start by acknowledging that and say, 'You can say you were here in future years when this game is remembered.' I actually hear someone laugh. The game proves a close one with just one point separating the teams at the end. By now more spectators are arriving ahead of the next game and I finish my commentary by referring back to my first remark about saying, 'You can say you were here' to the spectators, most of whom, if they notice at all, are probably confused as to why I should say that.

I have one more game where I have to do the commentary. It is mid-afternoon before it ends and, having had enough basketball for one day I head home. The following day follows a similar pattern. As I go to leave, the organiser comes to me and thanks me for my services and asks me how much I want for expenses. Knowing the parlous state of the basketball world I waive any claim and wish him well with the rest of the tournament which goes on for another two days.

A week's laziness follows during which the only decision I make is to write to Beverley to tell her I will be attending the First Year Conference in New York. I know I will be able to get funding for it since the Director, when I last spoke to him, encouraged me to keep in touch with the movement.

So it is with a refreshed attitude that I attend the first training session for the basketball team of the new year only to be confronted by a major crisis.

Russ, our most successful point scorer and rebounder announces that he no longer will be playing for the club. As we stand by the courtside at the training session, he says, 'I told the coach at the beginning of the season that I wanted to step down from playing and be used for coaching. Mick promised me he would take me under his wing and give advice and encouragement in a coaching role. This has not happened. My role as Assistant Coach has been minimal, nothing like that of Mike who did the job before.' Mick immediately blusters as he expresses surprise at what Russ has just said. 'You have never said anything to me about your frustration. In fact, with you playing so well this season I thought that you were happy not to have any other responsibility. Look, I can change all that if you reconsider your decision.' However, Russ is adamant that he has been let down and wants no more to do with the club.

A match has been arranged for the opening of the Banbury Sports Centre against a team from the lower division. This is Mick's chance to prepare for life without Russ and he states that he is going to try to persuade Toby to come back, although he is not present at Banbury. The game is won and a pleasing feature for Mick is that Jon scores freely and Steen seems to be in good form and not suffered a drop in fitness whilst living back home in Denmark over Christmas.

At college the Communications Report is finally issued. It is highly critical of the Director's management style and the frequent administrative and academic reorganisations. Even a couple of the Governors weigh in to reinforce the findings of the Report. The Union, and Don in particular, express their backing for the findings. 'Will anything happen now?' Don asks as several of us join him at a table in the Refectory. 'We've had so much criticism as an organisation over the past few years, surely something will happen. It is ironic, too, that the Director and the Head of Marketing are at this moment on another of their jaunts to one of our franchised colleges. I wonder what his reaction will be on his return?'

Liz and Sarah come into the Refectory and this is the first time I have had a chance to talk to Sarah for some time. 'Did you husband get home for Christmas?' I ask. 'Yes,' she replies, 'we had a good time with both his and my family. He is about to go off again for a short contract in Germany.' I try not to show my feelings that I am glad he is going away again and mutter something about her being left alone again. 'Yes, but we need the money,' she says. Liz then pipes up, 'Talking about going away, our boss has gone again with the Director. They have both taken their wives but we are wondering if that will continue.' 'Why,' I ask. 'Well, Jack, our boss, seems to be getting very close to the Amy who is the secretary of our Marketing section. They have been spotted together a couple of times in a local hotel and they give all the signs at work of being more than just professional colleagues.' As Liz tells me this I think of quite a few other trysts that even I know about and wonder if anyone has commented on Sarah and myself. However, I feel quite safe in that since I haven't seen Sarah for some time. That is a situation I would like to change now with the latest news I have just received from Sarah. I will have to find out exactly when he is to go away again.

  I go for a drink with George-Henry and he rocks me with a few disclosures. 'As you know,' he begins, 'I have had my role changed several times since I was appointed. As a result of one of the reports that has come out recently it was decided that I should be clerk to the governors but not by that title.' I tell him that I remember the conversation we had at the time.

  George-Henry continues, 'This means I attend all the meetings and they trust me to report them carefully and confidentially. This has put me in a very awkward position because I have become party to information that I think is damaging to the college and is not good practice. However, my hands are tied.' I don't want to encourage George-Henry to tell me anything that would compromise him and so I respond, 'Well, I'm sure Don and his henchmen will have sources of their own and will find out what you know.' 'I'm not so sure,' George-Henry continues, 'nothing seems to have happened yet.' 'I'm not a political animal,' I continue, 'and goodness knows I have enough on my plate with the machinations of the basketball team and the day-to-day managing of the service I run. I would rather leave the bigger picture to others. I get the sense that they enjoy taking management to task as well as having, as they think, altruistic motives. However, if you want to share your worries, your secrets will be safe with me.'

  'With government encouragement,' George-Henry continues, 'all colleges have now been tasked to increase their student numbers, as you know. We have decided to go down the franchise route as well as upping the home student number. The Director has been on many overseas visits, usually taking his wife and quite often the Head of Marketing and his wife also. The Governors have not been involved in the decision to franchise so many courses and are unaware of the quality control issues that might arise if we continue to spread ourselves so thinly. Apart from the quality issue there is the expense of these overseas visits. I can see a big storm arising because the internal auditors have begun to look at the situation.' 'There you are, then,' I respond, 'you won't have to make anything public. Leave it to the auditors.' George-Henry is still not convinced. 'I would like to think so,' he continues, 'but so far the evidence is that the Director has a way of brushing these concerns under the carpet. He is due to return from his latest trip in a couple of days, so I guess we will soon find out if he is at all fazed by the latest criticisms.'

I am able to renew my recent acquaintanceship with some of the Crystal Palace officials when they come to play us in the following week. We have not had a competitive game for over a month and have lost our main scorer and rebounder, Russ, to boot. This game is a National Trophy Quarter Final match. We can only muster 62 points and this would never be enough to overcome the free scoring Crystal Palace team. We lose by 14 points and Mick takes some comfort in this since this was the difference the last time we played them recently. That time we had our full squad. I am apprehensive about our next game which is home to the league leaders, Coventry.

In the following week I make it my business to see Sarah at work. I visit the Marketing office under some pretext of finding out about future courses that are being advertised. When Sarah and I are alone I check on whether there will be any chance of meeting her out of work in the future. 'My husband leaves next week,' she says,' you can call me at home any time after that. I would like you to do that.' I leave the office almost spring-heeled and make plans about places we can visit in the weeks ahead. I wonder if she has any Marketing trips planned that will take her away like we did before. I resist the temptation to telephone her on the internal telephone system to find out an answer to that. I don't want her to think I have a one-track mind about our relationship.

I am inclined to speak to Pete about Sarah and at the same time find out how things are between Liz, Sarah's Marketing friend, and himself. I remember how he told me that things had been under control when we last spoke. 'To tell the truth,' he says, 'I am trying to back off from Liz at the moment. She seems to be getting the wrong idea about our relationship. I wouldn't say she is stalking me, but she turns up a lot of times wherever I am. Last week, she was actually in the clubhouse after my rugby match. This would have been alright if only my wife had not been there also. It was very awkward when Liz joined our group. I tried to explain it away that she was a member of staff, but obviously she was there alone. I think I may have got away with it. My wife has not mentioned it since.' 'I did warn you,' I say. 'At least the boot is on the other foot with Sarah and myself.' 'You lucky bugger,' is all Pete can retort.

All too soon it is back to the basketball world and a home game against Coventry, who are still top of the league. Mick had high hopes that he had persuaded Toby to change his decision about not playing for us any more, but on the night he has not appeared after injuring his back in the last training session. Despite that the team plays well and at half time we are actually leading by two points in a low scoring game. The lead is mainly due to Steen who has scored half of our points. Sadly his scoring dries up in the second half and what would have been a huge upset of a result turns out to be another home defeat for us, if only by six points. Our next opponents in a home game will be another team currently near the top of the league. My concern is that another defeat might affect the number of supporters. We have a core of faithful followers but everyone knows that success in results always brings more paying customers.

Back at college, as I expected, my application for a Staff Development event in New York is approved. I write to the organisers with details of a proposed talk I can give about the work we are doing at the college to help first year students. From experience I know at what level to pitch the talk and details to give. I also know that since it is basically an American movement they will be anxious to include an international perspective. I call in Ethel who is now running the successful Study Assistance Programme to tell her I am going to feature her work in my presentation talk. 'So I need some examples of the work you have done, especially the successful outcomes,' I say, 'I am only too sorry that you will be unable to accompany me to New York but we have to watch the expenses.' She understands the situation and good-naturedly says, 'I will go next time instead of you.' I am also anxious to include examples of the Workbook initiative and speak to the two who are employed to sell them to the students. I also have news for them. 'At next year's Awards Dinner there is to be an award or two connected with the Workbooks. I would like you to think of a couple of categories that might be suggested. The Director has expanded my original suggestion of Lecturer of the Year to include so many other categories it is not true. I still have doubts about the whole scheme as he is implementing it, but he is adamant that it is a good opportunity to make all staff aware of the contributions some are making to the work of the college.' I do not tell them but I think that I will be putting a positive spin on the initiative when I speak at the First Year Conference.

At my next session with the Post-Graduate course, the staff attending are full of the most recent report that has been issued and eventually I suspend the topic of assessment that I am going to deal with. It is interesting to hear the variety of opinions offered by the new staff who have all come in to lecturing from a variety of professions. Some are used to the ebb and flow of union representation, some have no experience at all of such matters. All have views as to how the Director should react. I tell them, 'You will soon find out what he thinks as the Director has just returned from his overseas visit and will no doubt call a staff meeting, if previous form is anything to go by. Then we shall know for certain how he has taken the news.'

CHAPTER TWENTY FOUR

It is exactly as I had predicted. The staff members are summoned to a staff meeting. The Director begins, 'All of you will be aware that the college is receiving bad publicity at the moment, this will not help us in our drive to University status.' I wonder if he is going to continue to accept some or all of the blame for the bad publicity. 'We all have our part to play in making sure things run as smoothly as possible and that we are on the right track. The most recent report shows that we need to tighten up on the way we communicate so that everyone is aware of reasons for any action the Governors or Management team take.' So far, there is no intimation that it is the Director himself who is being criticised. 'In the past I issued information in the form of a newsletter, but some saw an opportunity to play havoc with that system. The Minutes from Governors' meetings and some Management meetings are freely available to be read in the Library. I have suggested to the Heads of the Faculties that they make efforts to keep you all apprised of the content of those Minutes.' The Director then goes on to more general matters and concludes the meeting with a rallying call for us all to pull together. I look forward to hearing Don's take on the meeting where no questions have been allowed under the pretext that students are waiting for their lectures to begin.

Walking back to my own building on the campus I make a beeline for Sarah who is on her way to the Marketing office. 'Any chance of a get together soon?' I ask. 'As I said last time, wait a week and then give me a call,' she says, 'I really would like to see you again.'

It is several days before I catch up with Don but he is still holding forth about the meeting when I come across him in the Refectory. 'You know what off a shovel,' he says, conscious that a couple of female staff are in the group, 'he is taking absolutely no blame for the state of affairs. When is he going to be challenged? After the meeting he refused to see the Union delegation claiming pressure of work that had built up whilst he was away. And that is another thing we wanted to bring up, why is he away so much?' I remember George-Henry's comment about the Governors being largely unaware of the number of our franchising arrangements, but decide not to bring it to Don's attention.

The next event for me is very heartening and it concerns the basketball team. The season which is now drawing to a close has not been wholly successful. I take comfort that we are still a functioning club thanks to the efforts of Dave and his success in attracting sponsors. But on the court our results have not been good and now we are facing Cardiff in front of our own spectators. Cardiff is near the top of the league and have aspirations of winning the league. Mick has found another player who at 6 feet 6 inches and may help us, especially in defence. However, with a quarter of the game remaining we are trailing our opponents by seventeen points. Suddenly things begin to go right for us and I excitedly count down the Cardiff lead to the crowd. Almost on the final buzzer we level the scores. My commentary goes unheard by the crowd of over 500 spectators who are on their feet clapping and stamping. Five minutes of overtime beckon and I can see Mick urging his team on in the team talk before the overtime period begins. Toby, on his return, has been invaluable. Steen has scored freely also and Jon has weighed in with points. But the fightback has come at a cost as three of the senior players have committed their fifth foul and can take no further part in the game. It is up to the remaining senior players and the youngsters to seek the win. The Cardiff team becomes frustrated having seen a big lead frittered away. One player in particular has a rush of blood and commits a foul in the last minute of the overtime period to send us to the free throw line. So upset is he at the referee's decision that he swears at the referee and we gain two more free throws at a vital point. It is Eric who goes to the free throw line and sinks three of the four shots. With twelve seconds remaining one of the opponents scores a three point shot to bring Cardiff to within three points but we manage to hold on to the ball to the end of the game for an unexpected victory. The crowd are still cheering long after the final hooter has blown and the bar of the Sports Centre is fuller than it has been at any time in the season. Mick has barely used his new signing and is full of praise for the squad. 'I know we have the potential,' he says, 'and things can only get better.'

Back in my office on Monday morning I risk an internal phone call to Sarah. The risk is that she will not be in the office and someone else will pick it up. I am relieved when I hear Sarah's voice. 'Can you talk?' I ask. 'Yes, I am alone here,' she replies. 'Any chance of a get together,' I continue, 'I'm thinking of a day out, if possible.' 'This week would be good,' she says, 'I am due a day off for a Saturday I worked recently at a school's function.' 'Great,' I say, thinking fast about my week ahead and if a day away from the college would be possible. Vanessa usually reminds me at the beginning of the week if I have any important meetings but she has not said anything today so I gamble and say, 'How about Thursday? We can meet in the large car park outside the local supermarket, say at 10.00am.' I have chosen the time just in case I need to go to the college first to deal with any emergency, although I feel confident that none will arise. Sarah agrees and we end the call.

By Thursday I have informed Vanessa, my secretary, that I will be out for the day and make my way to the car park of the supermarket and park a fair distance from its entrance. Promptly on time I see Sarah driving around the car park looking for me. She joins me in my car. 'There is a four hour time limit for parking here,' I say, 'but I am sure that you will be able to park for longer without anyone noticing.

I thought we might go to Bath for the day.' 'Lovely,' she replies, 'I do not know that town at all well.'

After a drive where we chat about things in general, I park in a Sports Complex, pay for four hours parking, and we walk across a bridge and into the centre of Bath. 'Time for a coffee,' I remark, 'and I know just the place.' We make our way into the Pump Room where we are greeted at the door and escorted to a table. Sarah is impressed by the fact that there are two musicians, a pianist and a violinist, playing in the venue. 'I certainly did not know about this' she exclaims. 'What a lovely surprise. How did you know about this place? Have you brought unsuspecting females here before?' 'Of course not,' I bluster. I do not want to tell her that I have resorted to my old tricks of researching ahead of time any place I visit. I remember how well it had worked when I took Rachel on a tour of places in Scotland.

My new found local knowledge helps pass the time in Bath when we visit the nearby Roman Baths and then stroll up to the famous Royal Crescent followed by walking through The Circus to the Assembly Rooms. All the while I am making comments about the Georgian buildings. She seems most impressed when walking along Great Pulteney Street where the tall, handsome houses bear plaques telling of former tenants such as Napoleon III, William Wilberforce and Lord Lytton. Finally we cross Pulteney Bridge with its quaint shops and make our way back to the car.

The journey home seems to fly by and I sense that Sarah has had a good time. Certainly she has been good company. I have found out several things about relationships at the college. She, like me, is concerned about her colleague Liz and her friendship with Pete. 'She is always talking about him,' Liz says, 'and making plans to be where he is so that she can accidently bump into him.' In turn I tell Sarah about Liz turning up at one of Pete's rugby matches when his wife was there. 'I am not surprised,' says Sarah. 'And then there is my boss,' she continues. 'It is becoming embarrassing to watch him and Amy when they are together. I hope Jack's wife never appears on the scene when Jack and Amy are up to their usual shenanigans.' 'And I hope the press don't get hold of it,' I add. 'I recently found out that Joe, who plays in the staff football team, was the one who hit the headlines when his wife complained to the press.'

As I drop Sarah at her car she says, 'Do you want to follow me home? It is the least I can do to give you a meal after all you have arranged today.' I do as I am bid and after a short journey I park in the road outside her house. She excuses herself and goes to prepare a meal. I hear the microwave working and in a very short time we are eating a pasta dish and drinking a red wine. After the meal, Sarah goes into the kitchen and clears away the dishes and other items involved in the meal. I take a seat in the armchair. When she reappears she makes straight for where I am sitting and seats herself on my lap. 'You don't mind, do you?' she asks. 'Not in the least,' I reply, 'especially as you are so slim and not likely to stop the blood circulation in my thighs.' As time progresses we explore one another's lips and bodies, but it is evident that we will not be going to the bedroom. I sense that there may be a taboo about that in her own home and do not press the point. At ten o'clock I say, 'You need your beauty sleep after such an exciting day.' She sighs and thanks me for taking her to Bath. 'I have had a lovely day,' she says, 'and I will let you know if I have any more overnight stays coming up for work.' 'Please do,' I respond.

I have had to miss the basketball training this week but when I telephone Mick to check on the weekend arrangements, he is full of optimism. 'Training went well this week and I reckon we will be able to defeat Bury on their court. Like us they are struggling in the league at the moment and after last week's performance against Cardiff I am full of confidence. You can quote me on the local radio when you do your bit this week.' My bit, as he describes it, is usually done in the week at my convenience. I telephone the radio station and arrange to come in at an appropriate time. This week it is on Friday afternoon. Sometimes, if we are travelling within the local radio's range, we have the radio on in the minibus and the players can hear my comments, so I have to be careful with what I say, not that I would criticise anyone on air. This week they will not hear what I say because we will be leaving earlier than 6.00pm when my piece is on air. Bury is one of our longer trips.

After all the build-up and hype that Mick had given me, and with me predicting a win on the local radio, we disappointingly lose by five points with Steen the only player who was scoring well in the game. The trip back is, as usual, very long after a defeat like that.

The following week is filled with my usual duties of overseeing my Service, meeting with the Post-Graduate course and dealing with issues of my staff members. All that is college connected and outside of that I attend the two basketball training sessions. The season for my own college team has now ended. It has been a mediocre season and Yannis, the Greek captain, is disappointed. 'My father has been taking a close interest in our results,' he says, 'now that he has a connection with the college.' I guess that the close interest has something to do with a franchise. I have heard that there is a Greek connection to the college but do not know any of the details.

I try to explain away our recent defeat against Bury in my next radio interview and hold out a hope for better things in our next home game against Stockton and away match at Crystal Palace the following day. What I had not anticipated is that Stockton would only arrive with six players, blaming their lack of numbers on illness and injury. I am somewhat sceptical knowing from experience that long trips in a minibus quite often leads to the lesser players bringing out excuses for not travelling. Anyway the six put up a good fight and a close game ensues and it is only a purple patch by Jon that means we lead by one point at half time. The scores are still close as the game nears its end. I hear Mick tell his team to get the ball to our new six foot six player when he is close to the opponents' basket. Acting against instructions the tall player does not go to the basket but tries to score with a three point effort from a long way out. By some miracle he scores to seal the game with seconds remaining. The team, with the exception of Toby, has played well. It comes as a surprise when Toby announces he is unavailable for our next day's trip to Crystal Palace leading Mick to comment to me, 'Toby needs to make up his mind about commitment to top flight basketball. It is against the odds when we lead at half time against Crystal Palace but we cannot sustain the intensity and gradually the home team takes control and run out easy winners.

At the start of the following week I come across Don once again in the Refectory as I take a mid-morning break. He seems agitated but in an excited way. 'The National Audit Office has decided to institute enquiries into the planning and conduct of our overseas operations,' he says, 'if they do their job properly there is no way the Director can justify what he has done. I know for a fact that some Governors have no idea of the scale of our undertakings nor the number of trips he has made over the past few years.' He is about to expound even more but I see Sarah leaving from another table and am anxious to talk to her. I make my excuses, quoting work issues, and hurry to catch Sarah. 'Sorry I did not get a chance to talk to you last week,' I say. 'Have you any free time week?' 'Sorry,' she replies, 'I have several events to cover locally at schools in the evenings, so I am fully occupied.' 'Can I meet you after one of those events?' I enquire. 'The nearest one is on Thursday and finishes at nine o'clock, if that is not too late,' she says. 'Give me the details and I will be there. Would that be too late for you to eat?' I question. 'Yes, I'd rather go for a drink and perhaps you might come back to my house. I have been feeling lonely lately.'

Thursday eventually arrives and I find myself outside a school at nine o'clock to see the parents and children streaming out. Sarah soon arrives and tells me to follow her. This I do as she drives to a pub on the way to her home. 'This is far enough away from where I live for there to be no locals in, I hope,' she says. 'I could be a work colleague who has been with you at the Presentation tonight. In fact, now I come to think of it, I am a work colleague and we have just come from the Presentation,' I reply. There is no need to go through this charade anyway as the pub is quite empty and there is no one we know in it. 'It went well tonight,' Sarah continues, 'there was a lot of interest in our college in particular.' I express my delight for her and that she thinks the effort has been worthwhile. We have a drink and then Sarah asks, 'Are you still willing to come home with me?' 'There is nothing I would like more,' I say.

I park a little way down the road from her house so that no one will hear me drive off later. 'That is thoughtful,' Sarah says, 'are you practised in these matters?' Luckily the smile that goes with the comment makes me realise she is not being serious. This time, instead of sitting in the armchair, I put myself on the rather large settee. I remark to Sarah, 'This is rather a big item of furniture.' 'Yes, but these older houses sometimes have bigger rooms, so it does not seem out of place. We had to get it in through the French Window, though, it would never have come through our hall. Anyway,' she continues, 'it is more than a settee for me. When I'm alone here in the winter evenings I bring a blanket and a pillow and quite often spend the night in here where it is warmer than the rest of the house.' 'From the temperature outside tonight, I would say it is still winter,' I remark. 'In that case,' Sarah is quick to reply, 'I will go and get my blanket and pillow.' Remembering my last visit it is clear to me that I will not be going to Sarah's bedroom. She is quickly back but in the short time away she has changed into a nightdress. 'Do you want to join me on the settee?' she asks. 'Nothing I would like more,' I say as I undress down to my underpants and snuggle under the blanket with her. After a while she sits up and pulls her nightdress off. 'Now you can keep me warm with your body,' she says. Her body is firm and her nipples are prominent as she moves even closer to me. 'You only invited me out for a drink,' I murmur, 'and this is the best invitation for a drink that I have ever had.' 'Just be here for me,' Sarah whispers, 'at the moment I lead a lonely life.'

It is past midnight when I eventually emerge from Sarah's house. It is cold, and I am almost tempted to go back and see if I can stay longer. I manage to resist the temptation and later, in my own bed, I spend a long time going over the time I have just had. Her husband, she said, would be back in a couple of weeks and it may be the last time he will go away because now they have managed to amass enough savings to move to a more modern house and work is more plentiful at home at the moment. I am sorry, from a selfish point of view, to hear that news and know I will have to back off trying to make any future meetings after that time. That leaves me just a couple of weeks at the most and I wrack my brains trying to think of excuses to meet with Sarah outside of work. Neither of us can probably repeat a day outing but Sarah has mentioned a big event in Birmingham in the weekend of her husband's return. Her sense of duty means that she will go, despite her husband arriving home over the same weekend. I have already checked the basketball schedule. It is nearly the end of the season and we have an away game so I am free if I wish to be. And I do wish to be.

CHAPTER TWENTY FIVE

Just two days later I am sharing the driving of the minibus on a trip to Stockton, the team we had played only one week before. We manage to take more players than they brought to us, but Toby was not among them much to Mick's annoyance. The trip itself is uneventful and we arrive in good time and in good heart. Stockton, we notice, now has a full squad of ten players including the four who did not make the journey down to us. They are just above us in the league table but our away form has been poor with just one victory all season. That is not altered as a result of this match and, once again, we are faced with a long journey home. Next week we have another long trip to bottom of the league team, Plymouth. Normally we would have looked forward to a certain chance of winning but recently Plymouth have had a change of fortune with a win over Crystal Palace in the National Trophy semi-final. That meant that they were playing Sheffield in the Final tomorrow. Mick, the coach, is obviously concerned too. He telephones me on Sunday evening to say that although Plymouth lost in the Final it was only by two points. 'We must win next week to make certain of staying in this Division,' he says.

However, the tribulations of the basketball team take a back seat after I read the evening edition of the local paper the next day. The headline is *Storm Hits College*. The paper seems well informed about the National Audit Office and its forthcoming action. Most, but not all, of our franchise colleges are mentioned as well as the rules that are supposed to govern such franchises. '*Public money is involved*' the article intones. '*Serious issues could be raised*' it continues. I guess that the Union has leaked the story and wonder how involved Don is. It is therefore surprising when I see him the next day and he denies any responsibility. 'It might be the same group of people that used to issue that publication The Lies,' he says. 'The Union has serious reservations about what is going on, but no hard evidence. We are quite happy to see the Audit Office is looking into it, because that makes us one placed removed from hurling accusations. In fact, in a complete turnaround from our usual tactics, we are going to the Director to make clear that the press article has nothing to do with us. On the grapevine I hear that he is considering a legal case against the newspaper. Remember how he took action to find out about The Lies publication? He hired a detective that time, but it did him no good. Seemingly he is ready to react again. I'll give him that, he doesn't hang about if he thinks he is under threat.'

Most staff are talking about the article, although not everyone has read it. As is usual with Chinese Whispers, information about the article is distorted on the retelling and soon I am coming across people who are recounting to me the outcome of the National Audit Office report as printed in the press. I have to tell them that the Report has yet to be published and that the local paper is just flying a kite at the moment with innuendo as its main line of attack.

There is no follow-up in the paper on the next evening but Dave is interested enough to ask me about the situation when we meet in the pub over a game of bar billiards. I give him my versions of events but, as soon as I can, I turn the conversation to basketball matters. 'Looking ahead,' I begin, 'we will hopefully have a place in the Play-Offs for the League Championship. My guess is that it will be against either Coventry or Crystal Palace. The game will definitely be away so we can't look for any income but set against that we will not have any hall hire expenses or referees' fees. However, we know that Steen has been selected to play for Denmark the weekend before and he has decided to stay home for Easter because he cannot afford to fly back here for just one game. I have spoken to Mick and he wants to see if the club officials can help us raise the cost of his air ticket back for the game. We can use our last home game to have an Appeal Fund for the fans to contribute to the same cause.' Dave replies, 'I'll look into it. It might be hard trying to persuade the others because they will say we probably have no chance of winning with or without Steen anyway,'

Saturday soon comes around and the all-important trip to Plymouth is on us. We arrive to find a huge crowd present, indicative of Plymouth's recent run of good form. The crowd has plenty of entertainment from the match as the lead changes hand twenty times in the game. We look to have clinched the game when Steen scores two points from the free throw line to give us a two point lead with just eight seconds remaining. However, we reckon without Plymouth's mid-season American signing. He weaves through our defence to level the scores. In overtime we take a six point lead before the scores are levelled again. In the end Eric's free throw shooting is the difference between the teams as we win by five points and guarantee a place in the League's Play – Offs.

The team are in good heart as we make our way home, arriving at one o'clock in the morning. Just fifteen hours later the same players are being introduced on to the court for our last league home game. Our opponents are Ware. Depending on the outcome of this match, the losers will play Coventry, who have already won the league, whilst the winners will travel to Crystal Palace. There is only one point difference between the teams at half time. Ware, who had not had a game the previous day, are able to finally take the lead towards the end of the game and for us a trip to the league winners beckons. As it is the last home game there are presentations to be made and the Players' Player of the year goes to Steen who has proved himself very popular as well as effective on court. The Supporters have voted for a young player, Mark. He is about to go off to the USA for a year at a college and, I guess, this is the fans way of wishing him well. With Steen winning his award it is a good chance to tell the fans about the Appeal we are launching to fly Steen back for our Play-off game. Dave comes up to me in the bar afterwards and tells me he is confident that he has secured enough money for Steen's air fare from a couple of the club sponsors.

It is back to the intrigue as I return to work on Monday. An early edition of the local paper is brought in to my office by my secretary Vanessa, 'I think you might like to look at the headline,' she says. *'New Blow Rocks College Director'* it exclaims. This time the information is about the frequent trips made by the Director and others to visit the franchise colleges. Someone must have been keeping a tally, I think. George-Henry had mentioned in passing once about the number of times the Director had been absent from meetings, but I guessed there were always lots of things that needed attending to in his position. I certainly never thought that he might be away from the college on all those occasions.

'I cannot believe it,' Don says to me when I meet him in the Refectory. 'The Director has just issued a newsletter to all the staff and one thing he emphasises is that we should be present at the college during working hours and not only when we have lectures. We must be available, he says, for student consultations and any meetings that are necessary. He is implying that we skive off if we are not actually time-tabled to be here. How dare he suggest that whilst he is under investigation himself.' 'Perhaps he considers the best form of defence is attack,' I reason. 'In that case, he is in for a shock,' is all Don can retort.

At training that evening I tell Mick that I will be missing the trip to Brixton this weekend. 'Still, we know our league position now, so we can prepare for the trip to Coventry.' I say. 'That will be a tough proposition,' he replies, 'even with Steen's return. It is lucky that we do not need him this weekend. The Brixton result will not affect our league position.' Fortunately Mick does not ask why I cannot be with the team this weekend, as I would have to concoct some story, probably involving my sister and her family.

Sarah and I have decided to travel to Birmingham on Friday evening. The event itself is due to start at noon on the Saturday. 'I will not be staying at the hotel where most of the delegates are staying,' she says. 'I know some of them very well and although they have never met my husband I think it will be better if we use a smaller hotel a few miles from then others.' So it is we arrive at a boutique hotel which looks just a bit bigger than a large bed and breakfast accommodation. It has about twelve rooms on two floors, but it also has a small bar and dining room. 'Very cosy,' I remark. 'Yes,' Sarah replies, 'I have used this place before. I found it by luck when I was attending another event last year.'

We have a quick drink in the bar and buy a bottle of wine to take to our room. Everything seems so natural between us as we spend the first part of the evening watching television and then get into bed, not bothering with any night attire. I do not want to mention the fact that this may be the last time, bearing in mind the return of her husband from abroad and his future plans to work in this country. All of a sudden, after some hours, there is a very loud noise which I realise must be the fire alarm. We quickly don some clothes and I am about to leave the room when Sarah says, 'Let me go first and then you follow in a bit. When we are outside don't make contact with me.' I am surprised at her words, but do as I am told. Luckily, it is a false alarm and the manager is soon apologising to everyone and saying that we can go back to our rooms. When I return I ask Sarah why she had not wanted to be seen with me. 'Just as we were coming up, I recognised one of the Marketing girls from another college checking in,' she said. 'I have spent some time with her and we have spoken about our husbands. She knows, if she remembers, that my husband and I are about the same height and also,' and here she looks coyly at me, 'roughly the same age.' 'Oh, I get it,' I say, 'perhaps I look a bit older than you.' 'As well as six inches taller,' she adds. This gives me a chance to tease her and both of us an opportunity to continue where we left off before we went to sleep. Breakfast together is now out of the question also I realise. This allows me to lie in and eventually watch Sarah as she gets in to her hire car in the car park and drive away.

Sarah's colleague has not returned for the Saturday evening. 'I checked to see if she was spending two nights here but she said she was anxious to get home,' she tells me. This means we can eat in the small restaurant and retire to our room quite early in the evening. 'I will miss being able to go to places with you,' Sarah says, as we lie in the bed. 'I really enjoyed our trip to Bath.' 'Well,' I reply, 'who knows what the future may hold. It might be possible to arrange some trips together, especially as you go on these jaunts around the country.' 'Jaunts, indeed. I'll have you know we in the Marketing department drum up the students that keep you employed.' This raises the subject of her department and I enquire about the latest situation between her boss and his secretary, Amy. 'Jack and her seem to have got very close,' she replies. 'In fact it is quite embarrassing at times, the way they look at each other and the things they say.' I use the opportunity to raise the topic of the frequent absences that Jack must have when he goes on trips with the Director. 'Some of those must be awkward,' Sarah answers, 'because he always takes his wife, but recently he has told the Director that he does not want to go on the trips anymore. He has even suggested that one of us could go to do the marketing. I know this because Amy mentioned it to me. I think she sees a future in their relationship.' 'Not like us, then?' I say and Sarah punches me lightly on the upper arm. 'I never said that,' she concludes.

I return home to find that the basketball team, without Steen, had lost its match at Brixton. In a way the result is unimportant since we already know that we will have to play Coventry in the Play-offs and we now have two weeks to prepare for that game.

The latest titbit in the local paper describes how the local MP has become involved in the college saga, as it describes the situation. There is no mention of any proposed legal action by the Director and I wonder what the current thinking is by the Director, himself. He has never openly told the staff of his intentions but George-Henry lets me know that it is one of the actions he is considering, having brought it up at a recent Governors' meeting. Apparently preliminary discussions have taken place with a local firm of solicitors. This is confirmation of the information about the grapevine that Don had already mentioned to me. I am able to tell George-Henry, who might be afraid of letting me have what he might consider confidential information, that I have already heard of the Director's course of action. George-Henry's response is immediate, 'I don't know why they instigated an enquiry about the lack of communication within the college. Everyone seems to know what is going on.'

I am on the point of leaving the Refectory where I have been talking to George-Henry when Sarah walks in with her colleague Liz. I join them at their table with a second cup of coffee that I have purchased. 'How is the marketing for the college going?' I ask them. Sarah is quick to reply, 'I have just been to a big conference in Birmingham and I think I generated a lot of interest in our courses.' 'Birmingham,' I comment, 'is there much to do when you have finished your work?' 'You would be surprised,' Sarah continues, 'but I am going to have to let your imagination do the rest.' Liz then pipes up, 'There is a lot of camaraderie amongst the marketing people,' she says. 'We meet up quite often in various places all over the country. In fact, Birmingham is one of the better venues because we usually stay overnight.' 'What does your husband think of that, Sarah?' I ask. 'He knows he can trust me,' she replies, 'and, anyway, he is away far more than I am although that is about to change now that he has returned from his latest job.' From the reaction of Liz to our conversation I am satisfied that there is no suspicion on her part about Sarah and myself. I can tell that Sarah knows that I am sounding out the situation and when Liz excuses herself to talk to someone on another table about the marketing of his course Sarah is quick to remark, 'A bit cheeky, that.' 'Just testing,' I say. She then tells me that her husband has returned as expected and that there is no further work away planned at the moment. Coming back to relationships she again reiterates that her boss and Amy seem to be getting closer than ever. 'It was only last week that he told the Director about not wanting to go on further trips and offered us the chance to think about whether we would want to go instead. Liz seems up for it but I explained that my husband has only just returned from time away. I laid it on a bit thick but the thought of going with the Director and his wife is not exactly appealing.'

Later in the week there is an unusual incident that just adds fuel to the fire that the local press are stoking up as much as they can about the college. However, the editor of the paper has obviously decided to let the public make up their minds about the state of the college and just report the incident as an incident, casting no aspersions at the college organisation itself. The report is about a lecturer being airlifted off a path on the Isle of Wight on a Thursday afternoon. I think back to the most recent edict sent out by the Director about staff being present at the college even if they have no lecturing duties. Obviously the press could not have known about this or they would probably have gone to town on it. What surprises me is that the lecturer concerned is someone I vaguely know and seems to be to be the most unlikely candidate to break a rule imposed by the Director. There are members of the teaching staff, I know, who put in their teaching hours and tutorial time at the college but are hard to find on the premises at other times. Some claim research takes them away. However, the man concerned has always struck me as a conscientious member of staff. Now he has been airlifted off a path at a time when he should have been at work. One saving grace might be that he teaches a lot of evening classes and is given time off in lieu. None of that is in the paper's report, just that he works at the college. Coming so soon after the Director's recent mandate, I wonder what action will follow. Rumours begin among the staff almost immediately. It seems the Director's son is on a course at the college and it is he who was searching for the lecturer concerned on several occasions. He must have told his father, the rumours have it, who then issued his statement about staff attendance. The rumours may or may not be true but it does not bode well for relationships between the lecturers and the management.

There is no basketball game this weekend and I use the time to catch up on some reading and go for a longer run than usual. Pete has recently come to me with his latest hare-brained scheme. There is to be national event for healthy living which will involve as part of it something called the Great Britain Fun Run. It will cover the whole country and each day over about two weeks in early June will have about a hundred mile run divided up into ten stages. The nearest leg of the Run for us is from Weymouth to Portsmouth. He has asked me if I am interested and, foolishly, without thinking about it too much, I have agreed to take part.

Pete has obviously got the bit between his teeth about the Run. I have been working late in my office looking at some of the portfolios being forwarded by some of my Post-Graduate course members. I decide to visit the staff bar which is located in the Refectory before going home. The bar operates at lunchtimes and in the evening until 9.30pm to cater for any evening class attendees. Lee is the main server for the five day week that the bar operates. One habit he has, which I admit is a good one to check what someone orders is to repeat the order as soon as it is said. Being in a mischievous mood, I say to Lee, 'I am going to order a drink, but I don't want you to say what that drink is when I order it.' 'OK,' replies Lee. 'Now remember,' I reiterate, 'I will say the drink I want but you mustn't repeat it.' 'Yeh,' Lee says. 'Alright, Lee, I would like a pint of bitter, please.' 'A pint of bitter,' Lee responds. Another battle lost, I conclude.

Whilst I am drinking my bitter at the bar, Pete walks in. I listen as he places his order, which is repeated by Lee. It is now that he begins to talk about who might want to take part in the Run. In his physical education role he has a good idea of some of the staff he might approach. I want the team to be college wide,' he says. 'We need someone from Administration and the Support staff as well as lecturers.' 'Don't forget the students,' I add. 'Yes, yes, of course,' Pete agrees. 'Also,' he continues, 'this will be chance to raise the profile of the college, so I will talk to the Marketing girls.' 'You mean Liz in particular, don't you?' I say. 'Is she still following you around?' Pete puts up a brave show by saying, 'This is a college issue, nothing to do with what there is between us.'

We are now alone in the bar at 9.15pm and Lee seems anxious to close up. However, he admits to overhearing about the Run and says that he knows of a part-time member of the bar staff who is a runner. 'He has taken part in the Paris Marathon last year, I believe,' Lee adds. 'Great, that will cover the part-time staff,' Pete responds, 'ask him if he is available and if so I will get in touch with the details.'

I am still in college mode as I drive home and thinking of my presentation that I will be giving in New York at the First Year Experience conference. There is plenty to talk about, I think. As well as my overall function of trying to facilitate the change from small group teaching to teaching large numbers, I have now put in place the Study Assistance scheme with its two staff, the Workbooks to help with various topics of study and a network of staff dedicated to consider learning delivery as part of their job. The Post-Graduate Course for Learning and Teaching in Higher Education is also part of scheme to increase the profile of teaching. I will need to mention the Award Scheme also but I will concentrate on the teaching awards and Workbooks rather than introduce the notion of acknowledging secretaries and other categories.

More immediately, there is the Play-Off game for Hampshire Hoops at Coventry. Our chances are slim, but with Steen flying back to join us we will be at full strength. One piece of good news we have is that Jon has just been awarded the March Divisional Player of the Month Award. It must be rare for a team finishing eighth in the league table to receive an award such as this. The award is based on the statistical analysis of each game played and includes many facets of the game not just point scoring. It is a pity there will not be another home game to present the award.

Although it is after ten when I arrive home, I still telephone Mick, the team coach. I know he is a night owl so will not mind being disturbed. 'I see Jon has got an award,' I begin, 'it is a pity we do not have a chance to present it.' 'I've been thinking about that,' Mick responds, 'we could have a Mayor's Charity game. This would be useful when we beat Coventry, reach the semi-final, win that and then have a two week delay before the final at Wembley. We could put the game in on the weekend before the final and do the presentation then.' 'I admire your optimism,' I reply, 'even if we don't make the final a Mayor's Charity game sounds a good idea and I will put it to Dave. He might even find a sponsor for the court hire.' So it is, I think, that my life looks to be busy for the next few months.

CHAPTER TWENTY SIX

Mick's optimism about the end of season arrangements is conveyed to the players as we sit in the changing room prior to our quarter final match at Coventry. Steen has returned after his game for the Danish national team and managed one training session in the week. Mick has been upbeat at that saying to the team that we had the resources to worry Coventry. However, only five minutes into the game it is becoming apparent that a damage limitation exercise is the only viable option. In front of a sell-out crowd, Coventry offer us little respite as they build a commanding lead at half time. Despite Eric's twenty two points we still lose by twenty five points. It is, I consider, asking a lot of a team that has finished the season with just seven victories to beat a team that has only lost twice over the twenty league matches. However, arrangements are in hand for a Mayor's Charity game for our club so, as long as we plan carefully, we can end the season on a high note. Already the notion has been put forward that we can invite celebrities to join us on the evening. That way, at least, if we mix the teams up, there will be no disappointing defeat for us.

With basketball nearly out of the way for a while, I can concentrate on my college work although the college itself is not a comfortable place to be at the present time. The press attention is unremitting. The local paper is bad enough but now we are attracting the interest of the national papers. All of this is before the Audit Report is issued. The Director and his wife, unbelievably, have gone off on another visit. This time Jack, the Marketing manager, has not gone and it looks as if what Sarah told me about his relationship with his secretary, Amy, might be the reason.

It is Sarah herself who provides me with news that I had not been expecting. She actually comes to my office and makes sure that the door is closed before announcing, 'I think I am pregnant.' Luckily I am sitting down when I hear the news. 'How can that be?' I enquire, 'we took all the precautions we are supposed to.' 'It may not be yours,' she replies. 'When I returned from Birmingham it was early evening and my husband had been waiting for nearly two days for me to arrive back. He insisted on making love that night.' 'So, you have been unfaithful to me,' I weakly attempt some humour. 'It is no laughing matter,' Sarah retorts. 'Although we have accrued money for a better house, I will still need to keep working for a while to furnish it.' 'Well.' I say, 'the first thing you have to do is confirm your suspicions. When you have done so, let me know the outcome and I promise I will do all I can to help.'

Peter is on the telephone a few minutes after Sarah leaves telling me that the staff football team is about to begin its matches again. 'Are you up to playing for another season?' Peter asks. 'Certainly,' I reply, 'I am looking forward to it.' 'Well,' he carries on, 'we have arranged a game against a local factory side to be played in the evening next Wednesday on an all-weather pitch.' 'Not too good for my knees,' I respond, 'but send me the details and I will be there.'

Work issues and conversations with some of the Post-graduate course members take up most of the rest of the week. I recognise the writing on the envelope that Vanessa brings to me just before the weekend. The letter is from Beverley and she is, once again, making sure I will be there in a couple of months' time, adding how much she is looking forward to it. I have a certain apprehension, especially now that Sarah has given me her news.

George-Henry has been off work for a week or so but when he returns, saying he thinks he has finally shaken off his bad cold, we agree to meet for a drink in his local pub. 'Things seem to be going from bad to worse at the college,' he begins, 'I have only been off for a week but I can sense a complete change of atmosphere in the Administration offices. Everyone is on their guard. Several have been spoken to by the Audit Office staff and it seems that they know quite a lot about what has been going on.' Finally, I think it best to come clean about my reservations. 'I have not been spoken to,' I tell George-Henry, 'but I wonder if I am called if they will ask about my visit to Spain and, in particular, about the box I had to bring back for the Director.' 'What box?' George-Henry queries. 'I was given it just as I was leaving. It was presented to me by the owners of the Business School and I was told it contained the course fees of those taking the course. I was apprehensive about doing it but as I was just about to get on the 'plane I could not enter a discussion about it. I also have a second concern. Yannis, my basketball captain at the college, has a father who is doing business with the college. It is located in Athens and I am suspicious, without any evidence, of what is going on. We have to tread carefully at the moment about quality issues with our bid to become a university so it came as a surprise when the librarian told me his story about the Greek arrangement. Apparently he was sorting Business books out to throw away because they were dated when one of the Director's colleagues saw him. Eventually, he says, the books were boxed up and sent to the library in the Greek college.'

I have not seen Sarah for a few days when I learn that she, too, is off work although no one seems to know the reason. With her husband now home, I am reluctant to telephone without a good reason to do so. Soon I am fielding calls about the basketball Mayor's Appeal game. Apparently the Mayor's office has contacts with several well-known personalities who are willing to take part in our event. There is even a prominent DJ who, they say, has offered his services to compere the evening. This is good news for me because although I am happy to explain basketball matters at any actual game I still find it odd that I commentate on what is happening in front of everyone and which they can all see for themselves. My happiest commentary moments are when the game is exciting and the crowd takes over with its noise. I have a front row seat and am in the centre of the action and do not have to say anything because it would not be heard. In one of the calls from the Mayor's Office I confirm that I will be on the local radio as usual advertising the game. They inform me that they, too, will be having inputs into the local media.

 Wednesday arrives and I turn up at a local all-weather pitch to play football for the staff against the local factory team. It seems to be a clash of cultures. Odd comments are made by some of the opposition about our status as know-alls. The factory team seem to take delight in goading us verbally but they grow increasingly quiet when we score our second goal to lead by two goals to one. Peter, who has arranged the match, is full of remorse at half-time. 'My contact at the factory is a drinking buddy,' he extols, 'he never told me what a coarse lot he has as players.' 'Don't worry,' responds one of our team, 'we won't hold it against you. Let's just play the match out and get away as soon as we can.' The advice about playing the match out is sound, but unfortunately it is Peter himself who changes the whole tone of the game. He is bundled over in a very rough tackle. As he sits on the ground nursing a sore leg he complains to the one who tackled him calling him a bastard and then giving him a further description. 'Oh no,' I say to our nearest player, 'now we are for it.' Sure enough from then on our opponents are out for revenge. Luckily they quickly score two goals and once in the lead slacken off on their animosity. The game ends and we agree to go to a local pub rather than stay in the sporting venue's bar where our opponents will be drinking. We probably seem like bad losers by doing that, but we are in no mood to kiss and make up. I remember Pete's words about rugby players and the socialising that goes on after the game despite having spent eighty minutes knocking seven bells out of one another and think how pleased I am he is not here now.

In the bar I am able to find out what other staff members think about the Audit visit. To my surprise most of them are quite laid back about the situation. In the main they seem to be concerned with teaching their courses and the problems that arise with students. In a way this is not surprising since most of them do not have to deal with extraneous college matters. Soon, however, I think they will become more involved as I hear that there is a petition circulating about the necessity to remove the Director from his role. There has been unrest before, but I sense that this time things are about to get nasty with action being demanded by the staff. The petition is bald in its demand, but there is a leaflet that accompanies it which sets out some of the reasons for the action. The main thrust is the misuse of public funds which will give the college a bad name and hinder its progress to being awarded university status. This to me seems rather premature. True at the moment we are being investigated by the Auditors but no report has yet been issued and I wonder if the Auditors get to hear of the petition if it will sway their thinking. I know the National Audit Office is particularly looking at the overseas operations and I feel they will be able to come up with something, especially remembering my own part in it.

The next day I meet Pete in the Refectory. It is just the two of us at a table eating a lunch. 'I've got to do something,' Pete begins, 'the situation with Liz is getting worse. I have told her that we ought to take some time away from one another and she has taken it badly.' 'I thought you said you could handle the arrangement,' I tell Pete. 'I thought I could,' he replies, 'but she is more insistent than any of the others I have spent time with.' 'That's an interesting way to describe it. Look wife, it was just an arrangement that I was involved with, you could say' 'This is serious,' Pete continues, 'so serious in fact I have approached the Rugby

Union about a temporary job for a rugby coach in the USA. This will take me away for several months and give Liz a chance to back off. I will make sure she knows that I am going away to let her get on with her life without me. Luckily the job is in the summer and Edgar is happy to give me leave of absence until October.' 'A bit extreme,' I say, 'can't you just tell her outright.' 'I have tried that,' Pete says, 'but have decided that I need a clean break. My wife is quite happy with me going especially as I have said she can come out at any time to join me at the club which is in the Detroit area.' 'When would this happen?' I ask. 'If I get the job, right after the Fun Run,' he adds, 'so there will be no getting out of the Run for you.' I tell him that I am taking the Fun Run very seriously with almost daily trips pounding along the roads and into the woods.

Day to day issues command my attention for the next two weeks but I am constantly thinking about the state of the college and this is occasionally reinforced by press articles in the local paper. Someone has leaked that all is not well with our finances and that there is staff unrest. I still have no evidence of the latter. It is nearing the end of the academic year and most lecturing staff are preoccupied with exam setting and marking. There has been no unrest from the Students Union but I guess the students too are preoccupied with their end of year matters. The Director has gone very quiet with no evidence of him around the buildings and no published communiqués. Sarah has returned and told me that she has morning sickness. Her husband, it seems, is delighted at the news of her pregnancy.

Suddenly it is the night of the Mayor's Charity basketball match. The local office of the mayor has done a good job in both getting guest players and advertising the event. The hall is full and there is quite a carnival atmosphere. We have provided both sets of kit for the players. Our home kit is blue and the away one is yellow. The compere, a local DJ, asks the crowd to identify with one of the colours. For once

234

I can sit back and hopefully enjoy the occasion. However, I position myself at the end of the officials table, my usual commentary position, just in case I am needed should the situation arise. In fact, all goes well. The evening starts with the delayed presentation to Jon for the Divisional Player of the Month. The game gives the players a chance to show some of the things they cannot do in a normal match where they have to stick to a game plan.

We involve the crowd in several ways, applause level for the best slam dunk and a free throw competition for some children. Afterwards, in the bar, Dave approaches me with news that he will be seeking more sponsors over the summer. 'I have become really keen on the game and my children love it,' he says, 'If only we had bigger arenas and television coverage I am sure the game would take off and sponsors would be fighting for part of the action.' 'Dream on,' I say, 'people have been saying that for years but while the gods of football and rugby exist, there seems to be little room for anything else.' Mick then comes into the bar and Dave greets him by saying, 'I bet you are looking forward to a rest from basketball now.' 'No chance,' says Mick, 'I'm off as manager of the national team to a European competition in Hungary next week.' Dave says, 'I must remember your national connections when I try to interest sponsors. What about persuading some of the England team to play for us?' Mick is quick to retort, 'We need to be in the top division for that to happen. We have not done too well this season and now we will be losing Steen, who is going home, and our Colombian player who is also leaving the country.' 'Have you any replacements in mind?' asks Dave. 'Not at the moment,' is Mick's reply, 'although a lot can happen over the summer.'

I am told when I meet Don in the college corridor at the beginning of the week that the Audit Report is out. 'No one has seen it yet, other than the Director and his close team,' Don says. 'Perhaps we will be able to read it in the press,' I say. 'I don't think so,' replies Don, 'The Director has already started legal proceedings against the local paper for what it has printed so far.'

Meeting George-Henry later on, I repeat what Don has said about the legal proceedings, 'Yes, he has done that on his own, although college money will have to be used to pay for the solicitors, I believe,' says George-Henry, 'I foresee several problems with that, especially if some of what the paper printed rings true. However, set against any of the accusations we must acknowledge that in the past six years we have produced a financial surplus well in excess of three percent of turnover demanded by the Government and this has given us a good financial rating, despite what the doomsayers would have you believe.'

This must be the dilemma for the authorities, I consider. Although there are considerations of staff unrest, quality issues with overseas franchises and accusations of poor governance and management problems, the college seems to be doing quite well financially. Because of my visit to Cartegena and knowledge of the Greek liaison, I feel there might be more to our financial health than meets the eye. And what about these frequent overseas trips by the Director? Surely the auditors have picked up on that?

The worst case scenario that I can imagine is the college being used for money-laundering purposes. I know virtually nothing about how this process works. However, as most of our franchises are with small, local business schools or their like I can see an opportunity. Why was I given a box full of money to bring back? What about the other members of staff who have travelled overseas? They have been sent usually to supposedly check on course arrangement matters and are part of our quality control arrangements. Most of the courses are at sub-degree level and the hope is that overseas students will then come to our college to continue with their studies. On the surface this must seem a noble aim. One problem with the whole situation is that it is government money that is allocated by home-based student numbers. Any overseas courses must be self-financing. But there is a grey area. For the overseas courses who pays for the quality control? All those members of staff who have travelled and been accommodated, I think. The Director himself, plus his entourage, has been absent on overseas trips many times. Our own Management Training courses have been postponed, because of his absence, a lot of times. My mind goes into overdrive as I consider the options. Is drug money being used to pay student fees whilst the genuine student fees are paid to the Business Schools? That could be why I was given a box of money to bring home whilst the genuine student fees were pocketed by the Business School owners or their bosses.

Of course, I could be way off the mark and the process of payments could by legitimate, if somewhat unorthodox. I will be interested to read the Auditors Report if and when it is published. In the meantime I will go to George-Henry to get the latest information. I am sure during one of our regular meetings in the evening at a pub that I will be able to prime him for further information. As far as I can tell he is as concerned as I am that due process should be observed. He has used that expression to me on many occasions. He would often compare it to my rather laissez-faire attitude towards college matters. 'I cannot afford your rather cavalier approach to administrative matters, in case things come back to haunt me,' he says on occasion.

CHAPTER TWENTY SEVEN

I am beginning to take my Fun Run responsibility seriously and try to get a run in on most days. With basketball out of the way for a while, there is more opportunity for me to use my free time for myself instead of organising others. In the run I guess I will have to run at least ten miles and so I map out a few runs of that distance locally. The weather is good and the temperature is rising so most runs are done in just shorts and a T-Shirt. I also use the runs I do in the early evening as an excuse to wind down with a few beers at a local pub. Occasionally, I go for a drink with George-Henry.

'It is with envy I hear of your running activity,' he says when we meet. 'I had a bad accident playing football some years ago which buggered my knee. Running is out of the question, now, for me. I have to satisfy myself with tennis and golf, instead.' 'There you have the advantage over me,' I reply, 'my golf is poor, I even lost to Pete once when he decided to play left-handed saying he couldn't remember whether he was right or left-handed.'

Soon we are back to college business. George-Henry seems to throw caution to the wind when he begins to tell me some of the details of the Auditors' Report. 'The worst feature,' George-Henry began, 'is, as expected the overseas franchises. The Director, it seems, undertook a large amount of international travel, as we know. Not all of that, in fact very little, appears to the Auditors to have been justified. They give an example of his trips to Malaysia which over the last few years numbered ten occasions. All those trips ate into any financial gain and produced a very limited income. If the press get hold of that, they will have a field day. A further fly in the ointment is that the Governors have only recently issued the Director with a new contract. Should he have to go, under the new terms in his contract he would have to be paid the equivalent of three years' salary. Once again it comes back to the problem of the blurring between governance and management. The Director seems to have done a good job keeping the Governors out of the picture whilst he went gaily on with the support of most of the management team who could see opportunities of expanding their courses and hence their income.'

'What do you think will happen?' I ask George-Henry. 'It has gone too far to be brushed under the carpet,' he replies. 'This will give ammunition to the staff, some of whom are baying for his blood. The Union will put pressure on the Director to resign.' 'What about the money laundering that I suspect may have taken place?' I question. 'Not an issue in the Auditors' Report, as far as I can see,' George Henry replies. 'Well, I never,' is all I can say.

In the following two weeks the pressure intensifies for the Director to resign. The Union's main line of attack is the unpopularity of the franchise programme which is seen as counter-productive to expanding the number of home students. However, added to this must be the undercurrent of unrest caused by continual management changes and interference that it has led to. A couple of examples of mismanagement are brought to the fore and each is laid directly at the door of the Director. He, in turn, has gone very quiet even when the press finally breaks the news of his frequent overseas trips and the criticism given by the Auditors.

Nothing is resolved when the day for our part in the Great British Fun Run arrives. Pete and I have planned well ahead for the event. We realise that it will require an early start to get to Weymouth for the 7.00am first leg of the ten. Pete and I have hired the Student Union minibus for the day. The official run has two coaches available for the runners to use if necessary. There are seven teams of ultra-marathon runners who are running every day over the 1,000 mile route. Every region has been encouraged by the local health authorities to provide teams. In our case there are seven local teams making fourteen runners in all for each leg.

As is typical when dealing with academic staff, nothing is straightforward. Two members of staff have an Exam Board to attend in the afternoon and so will be running the first two sections. Another has wanted to make his own arrangements and our crack runner, Steve the Paris Marathon man will be chaperoned by Lee from the bar, making his own way to the start of his particular leg in Southampton. This leaves just six of us for the minibus.

The arrangements mean that I have taken the minibus home the night before and will need to start out at 4.30am to get to Weymouth by 7.00am. My first stop is to pick up Pete from his home, just ten minutes away from me. This I do. Five minutes later Pete exclaims, 'The running vests, I have left them at home.' Since we had purchased the vests to advertise the college, we cannot afford to leave them at his house. And so, we turn the minibus around and retrace our journey to Pete's house. This means we are ten minutes late to pick up the four waiting for us in the college car park. Two other runners are also in the car park, but they will be travelling separately in a car so that they can make their own way back for them to attend their respective exam board meetings in the afternoon. There is still one more to join us. He lives on our route to Weymouth and we have his pick-up point arranged. Only, he is not there. I look at my notes and see we are at the wrong junction, which he said was in a certain place. Luckily, there is a bus driver having a cigarette alongside his bus. We ask him if he knows the location of the address I have and he points down the road and says, 'You need to go two roundabouts more.' Sure enough, John is there and rather than engage in a long conversation about what directions he had given me and the actual directions we had to use, I decide to not mention it at all.

Just over an hour later, with the other two still in the car behind us, we are looking for a place called Holton Heath which is the second takeover point. Pete has two maps, one the official map for the day from the organisers and also a road map atlas. After much confusion, which includes retracing our route at various times, we eventually settle on a place where the race changeover must take place and leave the car so that it can be used for the return journey for Mike and Geoff, both of whom have to be back at college in the afternoon.

We make it to the start point in Weymouth, the clock on the esplanade, with five minute to spare before the 7.00am start. The area is desolate apart from a couple of dog walkers. 'Always a worry of mine,' Geoff says, 'I go running in the local woods usually early in the day and wonder if ever I will suffer the same fate as dog walkers always seem to by finding a dead body.' 'It would be nice to find anyone connected with our event,' I counter.

Over the next quarter of an hour several runners begin to collect and at 7.20, without any apology or explanation, the runners are lined up, the teams checked and the first leg begins at 7.25am. Maps are distributed for the day's run which seem to differ from the one that Pete has, but we have no time to study it. We leave Geoff to his fate and drive to the first changeover point where we will peruse the new maps more carefully.

Although it is billed as a relay race, the format is as soon as the first runner arrives the next group, fourteen in today's case, sets off. Geoff is the eighth runner to arrive blaming some of his performance on the need to stop at two garages to perform ablutions. The official coach is waiting for the last of the runners to arrive before leapfrogging the next takeover point with the runners who are running the third leg. Once Geoff is aboard the minibus we take off for the next takeover point where Mike, our second runner, will finish. Strangely, we can see no official coach and so are not surprised when the first runner appears and goes straight by. We start the minibus and follow our new map till we see a coach and a group of runners some mile or so further on.

Our next runner is the student, who must, so far, not have been impressed at our confusion at various points, not knowing that it had started with Pete forgetting the vests. Just after he leaves, the organisers approach us and say that it would be a good idea to get to the next changeover quickly because the front runners are making good time. Mike still has not arrived, so Geoff collects Mike's clothing from the minibus and says he will wait by the car which is nearby.

Some twenty minutes later, as we approach the next changeover point, Pete, who is running the next leg, discovers Mike's car keys on the floor of the minibus. They must have fallen out when Geoff picked up the clothes. We carry on and drop Pete at the Bournemouth waterfront, which is the next starting place. Then we drive back to where Geoff and Mike should be. On arrival we find Geoff sitting disconsolately by Mike's car but there is no sign of Mike. 'He has this very important exam board this afternoon, so he has decided to try and hitchhike back to the college,' Geoff says. 'Now I have his keys I will drive his car and see if I can find him,' Geoff adds. 'Well he is not walking anywhere between here and Bournemouth,' I tell Geoff, 'because we have just come back from there.'

We then have to drive to New Milton to drop our fifth runner, John. He has been imperiously reading a copy of the Guardian newspaper during all of our travails so far. Pete had earlier complained of a sore leg from a recent rugby match and so we backtrack to Christchurch, using the map of the Run provided. Sure enough we find him at the back of the runners and he is hobbling. We change positions and he drives the minibus whilst I finish his leg of the run, probably two miles more.

When we arrive in New Milton for the second time it is to find that John has left, but Geoff is there with Mike's car.

Geoff tells us that Mike had hitchhiked to Bournemouth. Geoff had enquired about Mike at the event the local Health Centre was putting on and a policeman had been able to help. 'He gave him directions to the train station and even lent him a £5 note for a ticket,' says Geoff. 'I will drive his car to the college. He must look a sight in his running shorts and vest. Lucky it is a warm day,' Geoff adds before driving off.

We manage to get to Brockenhurst in time to check our next runner, Ron, who has made his own arrangements, is there and wait to pick up John who finishes in tenth position after running the shortest leg of seven and a half miles.

Southampton we find has put on the largest Health Fair of all. The finishing line is at the Town Quay and the next starting point is arranged for later in the afternoon on Southampton Common. All the runners are invited to run from Town Quay to the Bargate, a short distance of about half a mile. Once there the Health Fair is to be officially opened by the Mayor after he has abseiled down from the top of the Bargate, a building which in the Middle Ages marked the entrance to the then walled town. I have left Pete to park the minibus and I join the rest of the runners in jogging up to the Bargate.

Half an hour later, we assemble for one of the coaches to take the runners to the next starting point. The other coach heads for Winchester which will be the next handover. We are in high spirits for this is to be our ace runner the Paris Marathon man and we have high hopes of having a winner of this leg. We wait for a while after the coach has departed to give the runners a chance to head off on this leg. Eventually we leave and after a couple of miles come across the stragglers of runners for this section. Among them is Steve, our ace runner. As we pass, I slide back the door of the minibus and yell to Steve, 'Come on, Steve, don't hang about at the back. It is only a short distance to Winchester, not like a whole marathon.' We then travel on. After a few miles we still have misgivings. 'I'm going to go back,' says

Pete, 'we need to make sure he has speeded up.' We retrace our route and find that Steve has fallen even further behind and is now in last position. Pete and I look at one another. We recognise that Steve is no runner. He has no ease of movement and looks out of place doing what he is doing. We have to cut our losses and get our next runner, another Geoff, to his starting point in Winchester.

Once there, I approach the officials. 'How long does the coach wait for the last runner?' I question. 'We wait until everyone has arrived,' he answers. 'I think we may be testing your arrangements,' I say, knowing that the coach has to leave in time for the next changeover. We find a telephone and call the college, explaining the situation and asking them to get a message to Lee to tell him he had better get to Winchester to pick up his runner.

In fact the winner arrives in only one hour and six minutes, and it is not our man. Our second Geoff, the head groundsman at the college, heads out of Winchester on the punishing hilly route to Swanmore. We do the same but in the minibus and I am deposited for my leg of the journey. I line up with the thirteen other runners and watch as the first runner of the previous leg arrives. It is now nearly twelve hours after I left home and a lot has happened. Immediately, six runners hare off into the distance not to be seen by me again. I pick up my regular pace and find myself completely alone meaning there are seven runners behind me. All goes well as I run along a fairly busy road towards a village called Titchfield where my leg of the run ends. As I approach the village centre, exhausted, I pull myself up to look fresh as I turn the corner towards the village square. I turn the corner, but there is no coach visible. This cannot be the end of my leg, which on the map clearly stated Swanmore to Titchfield. There is an uphill stretch to leave the village and it takes a huge toll on my reserves. Once I am on the level again and heading away from the village I hear the sound of another runner catching me up. Slowly he overhauls me. I look at him and recognise he must be one of the ultra-marathon runners. There is nothing to him. He is not tall and is all skin and bone. In turn, as he passes, he looks at me and says, 'Keep going, lad.' Just after that I spot the coach which is in the car park of a Garden Centre. I have finished eighth in a time of one hour ten minutes and thirteen seconds, having run a distance of ten miles. The minibus has left after depositing Paul our last runner and I get on the coach to meet up with the team in Portsmouth. I happen to sit near the man who had overtaken me at the finish. He is in conversation with another of his team of ultra marathon runners who have been running every day for a week. 'A bit tired today,' he says, 'that was my third leg since leaving Weymouth.' I calculate that on this day alone he had run over thirty miles when he passed me at the finish.

The end of the day's Run is quite bizarre. It finishes in Gosport and the runners have to cross the harbour entrance to Portsmouth on the regular ferry. I join the minibus which is waiting with a coach to take last runners to the Health Fair which is being held on Southsea Common. A ferry arrives with most of the runners on it and there are TV interviews and local radio spots for others. Eventually, the coach departs for the Health Fair. We wait and finally our last runner joins us. 'I had to talk my way onto the ferry,' he exclaims, 'I obviously had no money and I think they had doubts about my belonging to the Fun Run.' We laugh his predicament off and go to join the others. There is short ceremony in the Queens Hotel where all the seven teams that have joined for the day are given a medal each. To our consternation, Lee has brought Steve for his medal. We notice from the race print out for the day, that he has been given the slowest time for his leg plus ten minutes. However, just as much a surprise is that one of our runners actually won a leg of the race. It was Ron, who had made his own arrangements for the day and is not there to pick up his medal. Turning back to John, Pete says, 'You certainly fooled us there.' Lee responds by saying, 'You shouldn't be so cheeky when you order your drinks at the bar. I only repeat the order to make sure I have got it right.' 'Ouch,' I say to Pete when the others have gone, 'that is a lesson for me'.

CHAPTER TWENTY EIGHT

The college is rife with rumours. 'The Director has been asked to resign,' Don says with authority. 'I got that from someone on the Governors although it has not been broadcast yet.' We are in the college Refectory and Don is holding forth, as usual. 'Some of the reasons go back to the Communications Report. It seems that in response to questions asked about why decisions made by the Director were not challenged most of those asked said it was fear of any consequence resulting from a challenge. Some even quoted the senior member of staff who did take redundancy. Word had it that he was virtually forced to resign after leading a deputation to the Director describing the unrest of the staff about what was happening at the college.'

Don then goes on to talk about a national report that has been issued by the Higher Education Quality Committee. 'It speaks about concerns over the standard of governance in institutions of Higher Education, not just ours. It says training of Governors is required and that Governors should issue an annual report which would be available to all. In our case any report would make interesting reading since most Governors have not been involved in decisions made. Very few, for instance, have any idea of the scale of our overseas franchises and most probably don't know that the Director and his friends spend so much money and time visiting the overseas campuses.'

'That is the national report,' Don continues, 'in our own case there have been problems with a lack of internal audit and failure to take legal advice on the potential liability before the Director issued writs against certain newspapers. There is more, but I don't want to bore you with the details. Suffice it to say, we've got him now. The staff want him to go and now the Governors are catching up with the overall mess that the Director has caused.' Don does not mention the new contract that the Director has, which George-Henry told me about, and I wonder if Don knows about it. I feel I cannot ask a question about it without betraying my source of information, so I hold my tongue.

Pete telephones me and says he is off to Detroit to coach rugby. His wife, he says, will be joining him over the summer holidays. 'I hope it all works out for you, especially the Liz problem.' 'She won't follow me this time, I am quite confident, and hopefully it will have all blown over by the time I return.'

It is with relief that I prepare in the following week for my trip to New York and the First Year Conference. In that time there have been meetings involving the Director, the Governors, the Union and other staff representatives. The senior management team are also involved but at the time of my departure for New York nothing seems to have been resolved.

I think I will be able to get an update on developments if I meet with George-Henry, so I telephone him at home to suggest a meeting. 'It will be a chance for you to wish me bon voyage on my trip to America,' I tell him, not wishing to suggest I want the inside story of what is happening. However, I am in for a disappointment. 'Sorry,' George-Henry replies. 'A distant cousin of mine needs my help. It is a sad story. He is currently in a mental hospital and his wife, who lives in their home, has just died. The staff from the hospital has me listed as the next-of-kin and 'phoned me with the news this morning. I have to go to Hertfordshire tomorrow to help sort things out, including informing him of the demise of his wife. I also will have to make the funeral arrangements and take care of any other business. I have squared it with the Director to get a few days leave.' 'Sorry to hear your news,' I reply. 'I will find out how you got on when I return. I hope all goes well.' I realise now that I will not have any chance for an insiders update before I go away.

There are no developments in the next few days and I brief my staff about duties to be performed whilst I am away. The story of our phantom runner in the Fun Run is now widespread in the college and I have to admit to my colleagues that I have been taken in by the planning and execution of the practical joke.

So it is with some relief that I pack my things and take my prepared presentation with me to the airport. I have am early flight and so decide to stay at a hotel near Gatwick airport. Next morning I rise early after my early morning call from Reception and go through the tedious process checking in before boarding the 'plane. The flight itself is without incident and as we fly down the eastern seaboard I am able to pick out several landmarks that I have visited in the past. In particular, Boston I can see and even pick out Fenway Park where I once attended a baseball game. That occasion taught me that nothing much happens in a baseball match other than an opportunity to buy endless amounts of junk food and fizzy drinks.

If it was a tedious process in getting on the plane, it is a mega-tedious process going through Immigration. I am probably helped in the procedure by explaining to the official that I once taught in the locality close to the airport. 'I was in District 24,' I tell the officer. 'My boy goes to a school in that District,' he observes. All at once my progress seems to accelerate and soon I am boarding the AirTrain to Jamaica. Once there, I have a choice of the E-Train on the subway or the Long Island Railroad. Both go to the destination I need which is a hotel on Eighth Avenue called the New Yorker. I decide to go by Long Island Railroad and enjoy the ride as I see the skyscrapers of Manhattan appear before we plunge under the East River and stay underground until we arrive at Penn Station.

It is still the afternoon as I find my room in the hotel. Already I have seen a couple of people I recognise from previous conferences. I wonder if Beverley has arrived but

I decide that it might be better to get to my room and relax a bit, bearing in mind I rose so early today and, because of the five hour time difference, this could be a long day. I unpack and decide to have a lie down. No sooner have I done that than the 'phone goes and it is Beverley asking if I am settling in. 'My room is just down the hall from you,' she says, 'and I have a wonderful view including being able to see the Empire State Building.' 'You must be on the other side from me,' I reply. 'Why don't you come along and have a look?' she intones, giving me her room number. 'I might be a bit jaded,' I tell her, 'bearing in mind a bit of jet lag.' 'Nonsense,' she replies, 'I can help you get over that. We are not going to be here very long and I want to see you as much as possible. I barely got to know you when we met in Dallas. Although I cannot forget the night we had together.' I begin to wonder what kind of experiences I am going to have at this conference as I make my way to Beverley's room.

Once I am in, Beverley makes straight for the minibar. 'That is something I never do,' I comment. 'The prices are horrendous and I prefer to find a bar even if it is the hotel bar.' 'You can be seen in a bar,' Beverley comments, 'and what we will be doing is not for human consumption.' I guess this answers my earlier thoughts about the way things are going to go. It is confirmed when she places the drinks on the bedside tables and begins to undress. 'You said you were tired, something about jet lag. So bed is the best place for you.' I cannot fight her suggestion, nor, I must admit, do I want to. I only hope I can meet her expectations and not fall asleep.

All is well, eventually. I manage to raise my game and Beverley is finally satisfied and lets me drift off to sleep. I wake up alongside her and check the bedside clock to see that it is only 4.00am. She is fast asleep and so I gently get out of the bed, dress as quietly as possible and go back to my room. Once there I watch an old black and white Marx Brothers film on TV before finally drifting off to sleep again.

   The next day is the first day of the three day conference where delegates have to register before attending the opening session in the Grand Ballroom of the hotel at 2.00pm. I have been woken by a telephone call from Beverley and we arrange to meet for breakfast. I know of a small diner quite close to the hotel and give her directions. 'We need to register for the Conference,' I say, 'but we can do that in the early afternoon. That gives us a morning to explore New York City.' 'Great,' Beverley replies, 'I don't know the city at all other than what I've seen in films or on TV.' 'June is a great time to be in New York,' I tell Beverley, 'there are lots of music and cultural events and many of them are free. Central Park is a good place to see and hear a lot of the things going on. However, I have an idea for this morning and the four hours we have before we need to register.'

   Finishing a quick breakfast I lead Beverley a short distance from the diner to 32nd Street close to Seventh Avenue. Once there we get on the M4 bus that starts from this location. 'This is a good way to get a feel for Manhattan,' I tell her, 'plus it has the advantage of being cheap. You will see a lot of sights, this way and it won't cost you what it would if you took a Tour Bus. The first place we pass is Grand Central Terminal and I explain that it is often called Grand Central Station but, in fact Terminal is the correct way it should be described. 'I've seen that in so many films,' Beverley says. As we progress up Madison Avenue people get on and off and it gives us a sense of belonging to the area that one doesn't get on a subway train. We pick up snatches of conversations as people who must be regular travellers in their own locality acknowledge one another. I explain to Beverley that we are going parallel to Fifth Avenue which the bus uses on its return journey. 'There are an unbelievable number of familiar landmarks on that Avenue,' I tell

Beverley. 'Perhaps we will have a chance to see some of them later.' The bus then turns left and crosses the top of Central Park. As we approach a church building, I suggest we get off. 'By my standards this is a very young cathedral which only started being built about one hundred years ago. However, it has a huge interior. Work is still in progress to finish the building which, they say will take another fifty years.' Beverley is duly impressed, 'I've never seen anything like this before,' she says.

We return to the bus stop and only have to wait a few minutes before the next M4 arrives. We see the campus of Columbia University as we travel towards the end of our ride. Beverley is surprised when the bus enters a park and comes to a halt at its destination. 'This is criminal,' I say as we get off the bus. 'We will only have time to walk around the park. There will be no time to go into the buildings which are known as the Cloisters. They are an uptown unit of the Metropolitan Museum of Art and contain many artefacts.' I lead her to the crest of a hill banked by woodlands and meadows where she can see parts of several European monasteries and chapels which have been blended as a unified edifice. As we walk further there is a view of the Hudson River and the George Washington Bridge. Because it is a clear day we can see quite a long way down the isle of Manhattan to skyscrapers in the distance. 'This is wonderful,' Beverley says, 'but it is getting near Registration time'. 'That is why we will be returning by subway,' I say. 'We will be back in no time at all.' With that we leave the park and I show her the way to the subway station, a trip I have made several times before.'

CHAPTER TWENTY NINE

It seems that there are many delegates to register as Beverley and I make our way through the throng of people in the hotel lobby. We follow the signs to Registration and find ourselves in the Grand Ballroom complete with its chandeliers. I am given a booklet containing all the details of the three day event and as well as a name badge I receive a ribbon which states that I am a Speaker. I look for my time slot and find it is the next day at 10.00am and the venue is the Sky Lounge, which is on the 39th floor. My first reaction is that anyone attending will have plenty to look at should they lose interest in what I am saying. When I express this to Beverley she says, 'Don't be such a pessimist, I am sure that a lot of people will want to know what you are up to in England.'

The Registration Desk is being moved out of the Ballroom even as we speak. Latecomers will have to register in the hotel lobby area and join the Welcoming speeches which take place in the Ballroom. I am told over 200 delegates will be attending. I do a quick calculation that as there are nine other presentations when I do mine, then I will be lucky to get twenty or so to hear me. I realise that my input will probably be of little interest to mainstream attendees who will be keen to hear what their competitors are doing to keep students from leaving courses. My only hope is to appeal as a novelty item to break up the serious business. The rubric describing my session, which I wrote some time ago, is exactly as I wrote it. I show it to Beverley and she says, 'Well, I would have come to your talk based on that, even if I did not have another motive.' This is heartening, but I still feel apprehensive.

Beverley sits next to me as we attend the opening session of the conference. I look in vain for Kerry from Teesside who had been my British contact originally when I first found out about the organisation. Perhaps, I think, he will be joining us later. The first session is brief and consists mainly of domestic arrangements and locations for the various events that are going to take place, including my Sky Lounge one. We are all reminded of the Welcoming Dinner which will be held in the Crystal Ballroom and begin at 6.00pm. Until then, we are advised, we should make sure we are settled in.

I recognise a few people but am disappointed not to see any from the George Washington University. It may be that they are not staying at the conference venue but will appear at the dinner. In the meantime, Beverley approaches me and asks, 'Have you anything lined up for this afternoon? We have several hours before we need to get ready for the dinner.'

'Well, we went uptown this morning, so what if we go downtown this afternoon?' I say. Shortly after, we are getting the subway to South Ferry. We walk through Battery Park and look at the Statue of Liberty. I also point out the Castle Clinton National Monument. 'It was built as a fortress in the early 1900s,' I explain to Beverley, 'but it never fired on an enemy ship, although it was put to good use as an immigration processing centre for a while before Ellis Island became the main point of entry for immigrants. We then stroll along the promenade before joining the hordes of people getting on the Staten Island Ferry. 'There are a lot of visitors here,' I tell Beverley. 'This is one of the best value ferry crossings anywhere. It costs nothing and you get a wonderful view of the Statue of Liberty and downtown Manhattan.' I join the short queue on board and buy us a hot dog each and a fizzy drink. 'Now you are a local,' I tell Beverley. We arrive at Staten Island where we must get off, but quickly walk around the terminal to join the passengers waiting for the return trip. 'Staten Island deserves a longer visit,' I say.' For instance you can get a bus that takes you down to the beach near the Verrazano

Narrows Bridge but we don't have time for that. I want to try and squeeze in a quick walk in downtown Manhattan before we go back to the hotel.'

As we leave the ferry terminal I tell Beverley that she is in for a surprise. 'Most tourists know about the Battery Park and the Staten Island Ferry but not so many venture beyond the buildings of downtown Manhattan in this area. I point out the Georgian-Federal mansion with its columned porch which is the last of the row of such houses that bordered its avenue. Then we go into Pearl Street. There are glass towers all around but in a short time we come to Frances Tavern Museum, a recreation of a colonial Georgian residence. 'We don't have time to go into any of the places we pass,' I say, 'but you might want to come back one day. In my year on Long Island I spent a lot of time exploring areas like this and Greenwich Village.' We next come to Coenties Slip, so named because it was once a docking bay for merchant ships. It was long ago filled in, I inform Beverley. I can see that she is now becoming a bit anxious about getting back for dinner. We are at that moment standing on a small plaza with herringbone brick paving. I point out India House built in Italian Renaissance style to serve the merchant men who were its first inhabitants. 'Do you think we should be getting back?' Beverley asks. 'I will need some time to prepare for the dinner.' 'Of course,' I say, 'I was forgetting that my preparation time is probably much shorter than yours. That's what comes of being a man.' We make our way to the nearest subway station where to my horror I realise that it is the beginning of rush hour and the workers from the financial district are leaving their offices in great numbers. We suffer an unpleasant hot and sticky ride on the subway before emerging at Penn Station and finding our way back to the hotel.

I make my way into the Ballroom for the dinner having remembered to attach my Speaker ribbon to my jacket. Places are not assigned and I find Beverley so that we can sit together. 'You look lovely,' I say and I mean it. She has transformed herself from the street gear she has been wearing all day for the sightseeing. No wonder, I think, she had wanted to get back to the hotel earlier. We find a table suitably away from the long table which is to be occupied by the officials of the organisation. There are eight others on the table eventually and we introduce ourselves. 'There can't be many Brits here,' says a lady from Oklahoma. 'I haven't come across any yet,' I reply, 'although I expected to see the First Year Representative from England. I haven't come across him yet.' It turns out that I will not come across him because in the Welcoming Address, all the overseas delegates are introduced and asked to stand to make themselves known and receive some generous applause. Kerry is not mentioned amongst the twenty or so foreigners.

The meal passes pleasantly and we listen politely to the main speaker at the end whose main message is that we are here to help our students during their transition from high school to college. Beverley and I make our way to the bar after the event and chat with several groups of people. Several ask me about my Speaker's ribbon and I tell them where and when I will be leading a session. Some of those I speak to promise to attend.

Beverley invites me back to her room and before long we are in bed. She surprises me by saying, 'What does your wife think of you going to all these conferences in far off places?' I realise that we have exchanged virtually no personal information about each other. Our time in Dallas had been limited, although we had got to know each other intimately and our discussions had centred around me justifying my attendance at the conference to allay her suspicions that I saw it as a hunting ground for lonely females.

'There is no wife,' I respond, 'and there never has been.' Beverley looks surprised. 'You obviously like women,' she continues, 'do you mean to say that no one has appealed to you enough for you to settle down with one?' 'There was one,' I declare, 'but she left me suddenly. I was so shaken, I decided to apply for the Teacher Exchange programme to get away from my home area. That is how I know New York so well, having spent a year here. What about you? Looking as gorgeous as you did this evening, I can't believe no red-blooded American male would not have made overtures to you.' 'I have to admit that is the case,' Beverley confesses. 'It took me a long time to settle down, but five years ago I married a fellow teacher at my college. We are happy but there are no children involved although I am seriously considering trying. I am 35 years old and time is running out.' I explain about my sister Sharon and her family. 'They are children enough for me,' I say, 'although I do not see them as often as I would like. I will, of course, be taking some American stuff back as presents for them to keep in their good books.' Still, I am intrigued that her husband has not accompanied her to the Conference as so many other spouses have. 'He is at a meeting of his own in Florida,' Beverley explains. 'He teaches science subjects and has gone to Jacksonville about some research project or other.'

The rest of the night passes with displays of unbridled passion at times. It is nearly 6.00am when I walk up the corridor to my room still wearing my jacket from the dinner. I pass someone who is dressed for jogging. He looks at me and says, 'Long night, eh?' In four hours' time I am to make my presentation.

I decide to have a shower and forsake any idea of going to bed thinking I will be able to come back to my room straight after my presentation and rest then. After showering and an early bite to eat at the same diner I had used yesterday, I return to my room to pick up my notes for the session I am about to lead. Also I have thirty leaflets that Sarah has given me about the college. She uses them at her general presentations, she says. So armed I go to the Sky Lounge ten minutes before my session. The previous speaker is just finishing and I hear a round of applause for her efforts. The room has wonderful views of the Hudson River and parts of Manhattan. Good, I think, as I suspected, if people get bored they will have plenty to look at. I notice the previous speaker has used a PowerPoint presentation, whilst I will resort to the trusted and tried Overhead Projector which I am relieved to see is also in the room.

The room soon fills up and I guess that my novelty value is coming good. Beverley arrives just before I begin and she looks as fresh as a daisy. I have rehearsed my talk well and am confident that I can get across the various strategies we are employing at the college. Now is not the time to mention the current troubles we are undergoing. The audience asks some questions at the end, but I guess that my situation is far removed from theirs, but nonetheless they appreciate the notion of helping the students through my methods. I get the applause that I have become used to although no one comes up to me and says that it is the most wonderful thing they have ever heard as the lady did in Scotland. Most comments are from staff who have spent time at a British college and their impressions of that time.

Now I really need to go back to my room to rest. Beverley is talking about more sightseeing and I ask her if she can wait to the end of the day. I intimate, but I don't say, that there are other contributors I would like to hear. In truth, having looked through the programme there is nothing that strikes me as relevant to my own situation. We are already implementing many innovations and it would be foolish to return home armed with yet more before we have embedded our current ones. Beverley admits she is not too enamoured about the programme. 'Remember, I came to see you,' she says' 'and we only have such a little time.' 'OK,' I reply, 'how about we meet at 4.00pm for a drink in your room before we go out on the town.' 'Lovely,' she says. At 4.00pm I am rested and ready to go and make my way to

Beverley's room. She has raided the mini-bar again and this helps me relax as we undress and slip between the sheets. 'I want to find out everything about you,' she begins, 'to add to the news that you are not married. Your bedside manner tells me that you are not a virgin. Come on, give,' she continues.

'I will tell you about my American connections,' I say, 'but other things will have to remain private. I notice from the Conference Handbook that you work in Bakersfield. Believe it or not, I have connections quite close to you. Some of my foster parents' family moved to California a few years after the end of World War One in the 1920s. One was a bride of a GI and he funded the money for the parents and sisters of the family to go to California. Luckily for me two of the family did not want to go. One of them married a local man and eventually fostered me. My English foster parents then moved south and I lost touch with my sister who had been fostered elsewhere. It was a few years later before I was told where my sister had gone and eventually we got in touch again.' 'Poor you,' interjects Beverley, 'it must have been horrible being split up like that.'

'Don't get me wrong,' I say, 'I was actually spoiled rotten and didn't spend much time thinking about my sister. The Californian family kept in touch with the two who had remained. An airmail letter would arrive almost weekly detailing the way of life in California, although I think now the family members were putting a brave face on where they had gone. The place is called Taft.' 'I know it,' interjects Beverley, 'we have an outreach programme at the college there.' 'You are a rare Californian, then,' I say. 'Whenever I meet someone from California I ask if they have heard of Taft and they usually say no. My foster parents died in a car accident a few months after I returned from my teaching exchange. In the short time I was near them when I got back I was able to convince the two who had remained that they had chosen well when they decided to stay. I had visited

Taft at the end of my exchange year, when I did the Grand Tour. I remember being met in Bakersfield when I got off the Greyhound bus. I was taken for a meal in what seemed a plush restaurant, but as we left I noticed it was part of a Ten Pin Bowling Alley complex. The next day I was horrified to find out that Taft was an oil town, full of nodding donkeys. It was also in the desert and I was told to be on the lookout for rattlesnakes. The family could not have been more welcoming, but I still could not help but compare it to the verdant greenery of home.'

Luckily it is a lovely day and not too hot for strolling around. 'Have you anywhere you would like to see?' I ask Beverley as we take the elevator to the hotel lobby. 'I am entirely in your hands,' she responds, 'take me anywhere you like.' 'In that case we should return to your room,' I joke. 'Later, later, 'Beverley laughs. With that agreed, we set out on 34th Street to go cross town. I imagine that she wouldn't want to spend time in Macy's, which is nearby, on such a good day. We pass the Empire State Building. 'Aren't we going in there?' Beverley asks, 'it has so many romantic associations in films.' 'I thought we could go higher than that in the early evening so that you can see New York at night,' I respond. We turn up Park Avenue and eventually come to Grand Central Terminal. 'We passed this in the bus and now we need to go in,' I say. Beverley, like so many other people, is taken aback by the grandeur of the main concourse. She has time to study it when I suggest a drink at the open bar that overlooks the concourse. 'Those paintings depicting the celestial constellations against the blue ceiling are fabulous as are the high arched windows that let in so much light,' Beverley murmurs. 'Where next?' she enquires.

We walk past the Chrysler Building, which I have always admired and find ourselves entering the United Nations Headquarters. We pass an hour or so in the building which will become more interesting when the General Assembly meets later in the year. 'Enough walking,' I say as we cross to 2nd Avenue and pick up a bus that takes us to South Street Seaport. 'This is just to remind you that we are on an island. Work on this museum only began about eight years ago. It was not here when I used to come to Manhattan on my year's exchange. Unfortunately the museum is closed now but this area will give us a chance to see Fulton Market with its many eating places. Bearing in mind the time, we can find one that will suit us.'

Maybe it is the wine, but Beverley starts to become more expansive about her own situation. 'I am very satisfied with my domestic life,' she says. 'Bakersfield is interesting enough and the college provides some good cultural events, too. LA is not far away down Interstate 5 and the coast is easily accessible.' 'From what I recall,' I say, 'the Pacific Ocean water is rather on the cool side.' 'Correct,' she agrees, 'but the climate is very agreeable. But perhaps it is time I settled down to a family life as my husband suggests.' 'No more conferences, then,' I say, 'so we had better make hay while the sun shines'.

I tell her I have planned one more visit for us as we walk through the Financial District along Wall Street, passing Federal Hall and the Stock Exchange, and then along Broadway. When we reach Liberty Street I turn left and we arrive at the World Trade Centre. 'I know you think the Empire State Building is romantic, but the top of the Trade Centre has a lot to offer now that it is getting dark. Mind you, if others had had their way we would not be able to visit. In February there was an attempt to blow the building up when a group of terrorists drove some lorries, or trucks as you call them, into the underground car park and detonated the bombs that were in them. Six people were killed and over one thousand injured. The Observation Deck only reopened in April after a lot of money had been spent repairing the basement damage.

Unsurprisingly, there is a security check before we arrive at the Observation Deck. After going through the security check Beverley is duly impressed. We first visit the enclosed deck on the 107th floor and then after checking that Beverley is quite comfortable with heights we progress to the open rooftop promenade on the 110th floor for the stunning vista that greets us. Luckily for us it is a calm, clear evening otherwise the open deck would be closed. We are told we can see over seventy miles. 'Thank you for bringing me here,' Beverley exclaims, 'I would never have thought of doing it myself.' The time passes quickly and although it is possible to stay until past eleven o'clock we are down at ground level one hour after we had entered. We catch the 8th Avenue subway train and in no time at all are back at Penn Station and making our way to the hotel.

Our plans for the evening are shattered when Beverley suddenly gasps, 'My husband is here.' I look at the man approaching us and think that I would probably type him as a scientist with his unruly dress and untidy hair. 'Bev,' he says, 'I have been waiting for you to appear.' 'How long have you been here?' Beverley questions. 'Just over an hour,' is the reply. 'I couldn't find anyone who knew you or where you were,' he continues, 'I kept trying the 'phone in your room in case you came back and I missed you.' 'Why didn't you tell me you were coming?' Beverley asks. 'I tried to call you just before I got on the plane this morning, but I guess you must have been at one of the talks.' 'Very probably,' Beverley comments. All this time I have been standing near them and finally Beverley introduces me and explains how I had knowledge of New York, despite being an Englishman, and had suggested a quick visit to the Trade Centre after the day's programme of talks had finished. 'We must have left just before you arrived,' she concludes. Her husband goes to pick up his case which he has left with the concierge and I say to Beverley, 'You had better not mention all the places we have seen, otherwise he will realise we have spent a lot of time together.' 'And I wanted to spend more,' Beverley remarks.

A little while later, my telephone rings in the room, it is Beverley. 'He is having a shower at the moment, so I just wanted to say what a wonderful time I have had an am sorry that it has ended so suddenly.' 'Thank you for being you,' I say in reply, 'it has been a great time for me too. Good luck with your family plans, perhaps we will see each other again sometime. I may even visit my family in Taft one day.' 'I hope so,' are Beverley's final words as she ends the call.

The next day is the second day of the Conference and there is a full morning's programme and I select several sessions I want to attend. There is free time in the afternoon and a main speaker in the early evening. I go to the nearby diner for breakfast and find Beverley and her husband already there. I join them in their booth. 'Have you any suggestions where I might go for the morning?' her husband enquires, 'whilst Bev is at the conference talks.' 'I see Madison Square Garden is nearby. It is a pity the Knicks did not make the Play-Offs or I might have had a chance to see a game.' I tell him about my involvement with the English National Basketball League and he is impressed. 'Don't be too impressed,' I say, 'if you asked members of the general public in England about the National Basketball League most would not have heard of it. When I taught over here for a year, any High School game would have far more spectators than at one of our matches. We have no facilities for large indoor sporting events. I also coach my college team and we play our games in front of a handful of watchers.' 'You do that as well as lecture?' he enquires, 'you must make a fair amount of money doing two jobs.' 'I make exactly nothing as a coach,' I inform him. 'Our system is not like yours.' 'What about basketball scholarships?' he asks. 'Forget it,' I reply. We could go on, but both Beverley and myself have conference sessions to attend. I suggest Times Square, Rockefeller Plaza, Central Park and St.

Patrick's Cathedral as worth seeing and conclude by saying, 'I think Beverley would like to visit the Empire State Building which she can see from your room, I believe she told me.' I sense a knowing look from Beverley as I leave them.

Now my plans have changed, I decide on a trip down memory lane. I have two locations I could visit in the free time in the afternoon. The first is in Bay Ridge in Brooklyn where I played for a Norwegian football team in the New York National League. I know the clubhouse is on 62nd Street. I had learned on my stay there that many Norwegians came to the USA to work for a few years, mainly in the construction industry with the many wooden buildings around, made enough money to go home after a few years and buy their own places. In my time playing in the national league I had come across indigenously named teams like Brooklyn Celtic, Yonkers Scots and others from Sweden, Denmark and so on. Even the UK had a team, which I found out was comprised mainly of workers at Kennedy airport. My association with a Norwegian team came through a contact who lived in the same apartment block as me and was a caretaker at the school. We had a few conversations when I was settling in and he was very helpful. He was originally from Norway and a member of the social club where the team was based. One thing had led to another and one day he told me about a trial game at is club. He gave me a lift to Brooklyn where I met another Englishman called John and his wife, Sylvia. They lived not far from me and had been in the States for quite a few years. Subsequently we became good friends and I usually travelled to the games in their car.

I have two memories that I like to quote to friends when talking about my soccer experiences in America. In one, the opponents are Brooklyn Celtic and I, as a centre forward, am being marked by a ginger centre half. He spends eighty minutes of the game assuming I am Norwegian and hurls insults at me about eating fish and lots of other misinformation that he can drum up about Norwegian people. I score the only goal of the game with ten minutes remaining and comment to him as I made my way back for the restart of the game. He realises I am English and spends the next ten minutes repeating all his unpleasant epithets but this time directing them at the English. My story, however, does not compare to another told to me by a fellow exchange teacher. He had been placed further out on Long Island at a place called Patchogue, an Indian named town to which a lot of Germans had emigrated. Like me he joined his local team, and played in the Long Island League. His opponents in this case had been Lindenhurst, a mainly ex-British colony. Shortly after the start of the game he was unceremoniously upended by a cruel tackle. As he hit the ground he let out a string of swear words aimed at his attacker. To his surprise, the same player immediately held out an arm to help him get up, 'Sorry, mate,' he said, 'I thought you were a Kraut.' 'Thirty years on after the cease fire,' my colleague said, 'and the War still rages here.' In the end I decide that perhaps fifteen years is a long time and there will probably be no members of my old team around so I think a better bet will be to travel out to Valley Stream and visit my old School District.

Immediately after the last session I attend I make my way to Penn Station and buy a ticket on the Long Island Railroad. The journey does not take long and soon I am in familiar surroundings. I leave the station and cross the six lane Sunrise Highway knowing the South High School is only a ten-minute walk away. The pupils have left by the time I arrive. I am pleased to see that little has changed. The Reception area looks exactly the same with its open plan layout. I approach the desk and am ready to say that I just want a look round and that I once worked here. However, to my surprise the lady at the desk who comes to talk to me says, 'Everyone is in the Faculty Office just down the corridor on the left.' I thank her and walk to the Faculty Office. On opening the door I become aware of much animated talking. Much more to my amazement I recognise so many people. Ed, Karl, Walter, Kathy, Larry, Virginia, Joe, Gertrude, Bob, Stella, John, Gerry I see immediately. Suddenly, I am noticed. First to react is Larry, my old drinking partner in my time at the school. 'What on earth are you doing here?' he enquires. 'You've come a long way for this Reunion.' It turns out that this is the 40th Anniversary of the school and a reunion has been arranged for ex-members of staff. 'Well, I couldn't let the occasion go by without making an effort to attend,' I say.

Eventually I have to admit that it is just co-incidental that I have appeared but nonetheless cannot believe my luck. 'I was hoping that perhaps one or two of the old staff would be here,' I say. 'Not so much of the old,' I hear someone comment. The next hour is spent catching up with the last fifteen years. Some are still at the school but many have moved on or retired. Larry and I finally repair to a local bar near the station. 'Do you still live out in Massapequa?' I ask him. 'Yes,' he replies, 'I still have the sixty-two sets of traffic lights on Sunrise Highway to contend with every day out and back.' This had been a standing joke of ours when I had been at the school. Larry fills me in on some of my ex-colleagues who have not been present today. 'How about a trip to England,' I ask. 'Britt and yourself can stay with me and I can show you around.' 'I'll think about it, for sure,' says Larry. He accompanies me to the railroad station and amongst other things tells me he is taking flying lessons. 'Well, that settles it,' I say, 'you can fly over in your own plane.' We part as if time has stood still and I am still working at the school. I wonder if I will ever see him or the others again.

There is no sign of Beverley or her husband when I return and after a quick drink at the bar I retire to my room having missed the evening talk that had taken place at the Conference.

The next day is the last day of the Conference. Beverley and her husband are not in the diner where I go for my final breakfast. I attend a few sessions in the morning's programme and also go to the final meeting which is no more or less than a rallying call for the next Conference which is to be held in Chicago. I do not see Beverley there either and guess that she and her husband are using the time to visit as many New York sights as possible. I just hope that she doesn't let slip that she has been to some of them before. In the evening I make my way to Kennedy airport to fly home.

CHAPTER THIRTY

I seem to recover quickly from any jet lag. This is aided by the fact that the return flight had, for some unaccountable reason, fairly few passengers and I was able to commandeer four centre seats and lie down thus getting a fair night's sleep before being gently shaken by a stewardess who had brought my breakfast. As I exit the Gatwick Terminal, I pick up the bus to the Long Stay Car Park and am soon on the road home.

After all the excitement and hustle and bustle of New York the college seems very quiet, especially now that the students have left, when I go into work on the following Monday. However, it is not long before I am made aware that, despite outward appearances, all is not tranquil.

In my first visit to the Refectory I come across Don. He seems in an exuberant mood. 'We've done it,' he says, 'he is on his way.' 'What are you referring to?' I ask. 'I have been at a Conference in New York all of last week,' I explain to Don. 'The Director has resigned,' Don informs me. 'It came directly as a result of the National Audit Office Report on overseas operations, governance and management of the college. He might have got away with it if only one of the three was an issue of concern, but in his case he was held culpable on all three.'

Don then explains that in the case of the overseas operations the audit people quoted an example of the Director's visits to the Far East. There had been a large amount of international travel in connection with the unapproved strategy of an overseas franchise which did not seem to appear to have been justified. It did not help that his wife often accompanied him. 'The figures were damming,' Don continues, 'just in this one case seventeen visits were made over a two-year period. It brought the college an income that was only a few thousand pounds over the Director's expenses. That was just one example. The auditors said that greater care should have gone into the planning and management of the overseas operations. Thought should have been given too about the effect on the overall college strategy. A lot of effort was being put into the overseas courses at the expense of home-grown ones.'

Another member of staff arrives who, like Don, is a union member. Apparently, Don is due at a meeting and he has been sent to fetch him. I guess I will have to go the George-Henry to find out further details. I can get no sense of upheaval as I walk around the building. Since it is the beginning of the vacation I guess a lot of the staff are unaware of the developments at the top of the management structure. Before I went to New York I had arranged to have a day's meeting with my staff. I have booked a room at a local hotel so that we will not be disturbed by college business. I have just come in today to pick up some information that I want to share with the group and get Vanessa to photocopy a programme I have arranged for the day.

Now I need to get George-Henry to give me chapter and verse on what happened. He is not in his office but his secretary says that he is in the building somewhere. I decide to leave a note on his desk suggesting we meet in our usual pub in the evening. Shortly after, he calls me, agreeing to the arrangement and suggesting a time of 7.30pm. I go home to work on the programme for my staff's 'awayday' which is in two days' time.

'You chose a good time to be away from the college at your Conference,' is George-Henry greeting. 'All hell broke loose on Monday with the issuing of the latest Report. The Director had been given a copy on the previous Friday morning and then had a meeting with the auditing team in the afternoon. He had obviously seen the writing on the wall and chose to take the easy way out. Mind you, he has walked away with a good severance, so don't pity him too much.' 'What got him in the end,' I query, 'up to now he has seemed quite impervious to any accusation?'

'The list is long,' George-Henry continues, 'and goes back a long while, certainly before I arrived. But just looking at the things even I know about, it is a wonder that he has lasted as long as he has. The Governors were called to a special meeting on Wednesday and there was a full turnout. Obviously the seriousness of the situation had been relayed to them and I think some were there to defend themselves in case of any blame being put their way.' 'What were the main charges?' I persist.

'The main charges were against the franchise programme especially to the overseas colleges. The auditors thought that many were a misuse of public funds. They were aware of the poor press coverage that we have been receiving about overseas travel and poor staff relations. You may remember one of the directors resigning because of that issue. Then there were the two audits of internal controls which found no evidence of malpractice but the complaints to the Funding Council harmed the reputation of the college in their eyes. The business with *The Truth* and *The Lies* and the Director's hiring of a police detective to try and find out the authors of the latter was also mentioned. If you add to that the frequent restructuring of the college management system you get a picture of a college in chaos, according to the auditors. Apparently, the Director must have seen that the game was up and submitted his resignation almost at once. That way he can walk away with his compensation whereas if he fought for his position, he could be in danger of being fired and losing everything.' 'The press will have a field day,' I counter.

'What about your position?' George-Henry asks. 'God knows,' I reply. 'I have always got on well with him but that may be because I usually acted as he requested. My only issue was once he tried to move me into Administration and

I rejected his suggestion and was able to stay in the teaching area. Someone new may not wish to follow the same path with lecturer training but the notion of student retention must be high on anyone's agenda. My contacts with the various bodies concerned with student issues should hold me in good stead. Still we will have quite a storm before the calm,' I suggest.

The next day I meet Sarah as she is walking through the college. She asks, 'Did you have a good time in New York?' 'Yes,' I reply, 'it was a very useful conference.' 'You mean you actually went to it, I thought there may be too many distractions for you.' 'Yes, I did go and thank you for the leaflets, by the way, there was a lot of interest in them. My session went well and I think those present were impressed by what we are doing,' I say, anxious to keep the conversation about conference matters. 'Presumably, they don't know about our Director's decision to leave. Your talk was about keeping students, perhaps it should have been about keeping staff,' Sarah continues. 'That is no joking matter,'I counter, 'what about your own boss? He used to go on a lot of those trips too.' 'That was before his dalliance with Amy, his secretary,' Sarah replies. 'That seems to have got more serious, and he has now moved out of his home. He has told us that he has no intention of resigning.'

'And, you,' I enquire, 'how are you? I must say you look well in these early days.' 'Apart from the early morning sickness, everything is going fine,' Sarah tells me. 'I've even stopped drinking wine and I don't miss it at all.' 'Good for you, long may it continue,' is all I can think of saying. I don't want to raise the matter of perhaps taking another day's outing. Fortunately, she is on her way to a meeting with some of the course leaders and is late already, so we go our separate ways.

I have no further contact with her before I take my staff to the local hotel for our team bonding day. This proves successful, at least from my point of view, but I guess the opportunity for an occasion away from the college is welcomed by all. No one refers to the current situation other than in general terms about what the future might hold. What becomes clear as my Chief Technician leads one of the sessions is how much is changing on the technology front. I give a small input on the PowerPoint presentation I had witnessed. However this, it seems, is just the tip if the iceberg of current events. A future scenario is painted where a lot of teaching will be done using electronic means. The Open University is quoted as one organisation that uses TV and Radio and Computer Marked Assignments. 'They have been doing that for quite a few years now,' the Technician says. 'That is why I am pleased we have started the Teaching and Learning Project Scheme,' I remark, 'and, what's more, we are encouraging those staff who come with ideas about the use of technology.' I take heart from the fact that everyone agrees the day has been worthwhile.

Having bitten the bullet about seeing how the basketball club might be getting on, I finally contact Mick. 'At the moment, it does not look good,' Mick exclaims to my query about players for next season. 'There seems to be a mass exodus that will leave us in a weak state for the start of next season. I obviously knew about Steen, but not about Joe who will be away for at least half of the season. However, I did not expect to lose our Colombian player who has decided to return home. I had just persuaded Dave to pay for his Registration, too. One of our young stars is going to college in America having won a scholarship, Jon looks to be out with a long-term injury and we know that Toby has become disillusioned. Set against that we do have some positives with other players returning to the area, but it is going to be hard work.'

I think that the future looks to be one of constant change. My work life is obviously going to be different with a change of leadership at the top. The basketball situation is looking grim and it will probably need more of an input from me, especially if we lose a lot of early matches in the forthcoming season. And what is happening in my personal life? Sarah is now pregnant, Beverley has spoken of a similar intention and Rachel seems to have left my life forever.

There is news of Pete when I telephone his wife. 'He is really enjoying his time there,' she says. 'We speak every week on the telephone. I can't wait to go and join him in next month.'

Some things never change, I realise, when I go into the Refectory. Don is there and, on seeing me, he comes across. 'Frying pan and fire does not begin to describe it,' he wails. 'The Fat Controller', whose nickname has to do with his stature, 'has begun to throw his weight around and is aiming shots at the Union. His first edict is to stop the teaching hours allowance for Union Officials. At least the Director never thought about that one.' I tell him about the time the same man had supported a very antagonistic outsider who had tried to halt the progress when I was attempting to validate the Teaching and Learning course. 'He only backed down when that person died and was replaced by a far more temperate colleague. 'Right, that is what we intend to make him do now, back down,' Don continues.

As I arrive home in the evening the thoughts of the previous few days are still with me. I pour myself a drink and sit down to contemplate my future. Is it time to move on, perhaps? Should I stay and see what the new regime will bring? I know I will miss my colleagues, my recreation with staff members, the contact with the teaching staff and coaching students in the basketball team. And what of the Hampshire Hoops? I am not the provider of funds to keep the club going, but I am one of the many who willingly give up their time and energy to keep the show on the road. I really would miss that if any move took me out of the area.

With so much on my mind, I don't realise immediately that the telephone is ringing. It is Brian. 'The lads have decided to have one more go at the outdoor league which begins next week. Are you up for it?'

ACKNOWLEDGEMENTS

This novel brings to a conclusion the trilogy of stories for the twentieth century. The first, *Divided Families*, was concerned with events in the early part of the century, including the First World War, the emigration of children to another part of the world and the inter war period. This was followed by *Allure of the Sea* in which the same family is featured, in particular one son who for part of his life was a merchant seaman. That novel covers the timespan from 1917 to the 1980s. Now we are concerned with a shorter period of the last decade of the century and events in its time. I have made no attempt in this novel to follow my family's fortunes as I did in the previous two stories. This time I have let my mind run freely and devised plot lines unconstrained by the necessity of following events that happened in real life. John Mortimer, the prolific author and playwright, once wrote that all writing is self-portraiture as all fiction is based on one's own experience. I leave it to others to try and work out where fact and fiction divide.

Another major change is that I have used the present tense as events unfold. This, I read recently, is not a good way to present a novel. I again leave it to you, the reader, to make your own judgement.

As usual, there are many to thank. Jonathan, my son, has taken care of the many technical issues, Nicky, my daughter, has helped proof read the book and come up with plot suggestions. She is an avid reader and has much to draw on. Anne, my wife, has patiently had to listen to me rehearse plot lines.

The ideas for the cover of the book came from Julian Puckett as a result of several meetings and sharing of ideas. I know Julian to be a very talented artist and realise how fortunate I am to know him for his skill. He has also proved a talented footballer over the years we have played together!

Whenever I am describing events in the book to family and friends I have to say that it is a novel. The narrator, I insist, is not me. The events are a product of my imagination, based, sometimes, on events in real life. Where that is the case, names have usually been changed and the person given different characteristics.